# The Last Saturday

Michael Gunton

Order this book online at www.trafford.com/06-2293
or email orders@trafford.com

Most Trafford titles are also available at major online book retailers.



Note for Librarians: A cataloguing record for this book is available from Library and Archives Canada at www.collectionscanada.ca/amicus/index-e.html

ISBN: 978-1-4251-0535-8

*We at Trafford believe that it is the responsibility of us all, as both individuals and corporations, to make choices that are environmentally and socially sound. You, in turn, are supporting this responsible conduct each time you purchase a Trafford book, or make use of our publishing services. To find out how you are helping, please visit www.trafford.com/responsiblepublishing.html*

*Our mission is to efficiently provide the world's finest, most comprehensive book publishing service, enabling every author to experience success. To find out how to publish your book, your way, and have it available worldwide, visit us online at www.trafford.com/10510*

www.trafford.com

**North America & international**
toll-free: 1 888 232 4444 (USA & Canada)
phone: 250 383 6864 • fax: 250 383 6804 • email: info@trafford.com

**The United Kingdom & Europe**
phone: +44 (0)1865 722 113 • local rate: 0845 230 9601
facsimile: +44 (0)1865 722 868 • email: info.uk@trafford.com

10 9 8 7 6 5 4

# Dedication

To my exceptional wife Judith and the family
Robert and Sue, Joanna, Charlie and Caroline.

# Introduction

It was not simply a question of what you believed, it was more a decision of what you wanted to believe.

First reaction was that it was the figment of the imagination fuelled by gossip. Then, as the incidents followed each other, it was an interesting series of coincidences, no more than that.

But after the third example speculation began. Was this man a genuine healer or a charlatan at work trying to satisfy his own ego for some unknown reason? Or was it, after all, a series of incidents with no connection?

The fourth incident, a very public manifestation, imposed the question which could not be avoided. Was this the work of a genuine miracle worker or, as some enthusiasts proposed, the realization of the much hoped for Second Coming?

It had all begun, as far as journalists Martin Armstrong was concerned, when he stopped overnight in Hereford where he had trained as a reporter, on his way back to London from an assignment in North Wales. He had seized the opportunity to stay overnight and meet up with his former colleagues. He was not to know that this was the overture to a momentous story.

# Part One

## Exordium

THE LOUD CRACKLING OF HUNGRY flames, the shot-like snapping of glass, the persistent hiss of the firemen's hoses and their urgent shouts as they struggled to stem the blaze produced a cacophony of sound that stunned the senses The relentless progress of the fire which was slowly reducing what had been a thriving school into a pile of rubble was horrifying to watch.

Although he had been a newspaper reporter for many years Martin Armstrong had never before seen a really big fire and the insistent progress of the flames hypnotized him. Safe as he was, a hundred yards from the burning building, his feet firmly on the ground, his nerves still tingled with fear. He had an almost overwhelming desire to run away.

His mind went back to the days when he was a small boy when November 5th was one of the most exciting days of the year, Christmas being predominant, when Guy Fawkes inspired the person with the largest back garden to hold Bonfire Night. Children from miles around would spend the preceding weeks gathering firewood. The night itself would see the lighting of the bonfire upon which was an effigy of Guy Fawkes and a firework display, the fireworks being contributed by each family. There was little consideration given to safety rules and one of the biggest jokes, as far as the boys were concerned, was to throw jumping jack firecrackers into a group of serious adults.

The school was, for the most part, a large Georgian mansion. It had two modern annexes, one on either side, both red brick and glass with steel framed windows which completely destroyed the original illusion of grandeur. The once elegant front garden had been completely concreted over to make a spacious playground neatly marked in the geometric patterns of a netball court and hopscotch grids.

But this monument to modern education was now battle scarred and shattered. The house, the only continually inhabited part of which was the caretaker's flat on the third floor, was almost completely gutted, the windows shattered and blackened to give the hollow-eyed look of an insomniac. One of the wings was still burning briskly, its interior a white hot furnace; the other, although still standing, was belching black smoke.

Martin looked around and saw one the fire officers watching his men at work. He walked over to him and as he approached the fireman, his face blackened by a mixture of smoke and sweat, pushed his helmet back and sighed deeply.

'Under control yet?' Martin asked.

'Not really, it's a bugger,' the officer replied, 'it was going like a bloody furnace when we got here,' he added looking at the doomed building again.

'Any idea how it started?'

'Too early to say, said the fireman, pushing his helmet back from his sweating brow and looking at Martin as though he was stupid to ask such a question. Martin realized he had been.

'Was anyone inside?' he asked, trying to ask a more sensible question.

'No, thank God.' The caretaker's family was at home when it started but he got them all out himself. The idiot then went back to get the dog and almost got himself trapped. He managed to jump clear.'

'Was he hurt?' The fireman looked questioningly at Martin.

'I'm sorry. I'm a newspaper reporter by profession, not working at the moment but the questioning is a matter of habit.' The officer nodded understandingly.

'Must've done some damage, he fell about 30 feet,' the firemen looked around at a small group of people gathered on the other side of the playground. 'He's over there,' he pointed to where a dozen or so people were clustered in a silent circle staring at something on the ground.

As he approached the group it shifted slightly and through the gap created he could see a body lying on a pile of coats his head lying on a rolled up woollen jersey. He joined the circle and stared, like all the others, overcome by the fascination of another's misfortune.

'Looks like he's broke both his legs,' volunteered a little man in a paint stained overall standing at Martin's side. Martin said nothing.

'Poor sod. Got 'is wife out and then went in to get the bloody dog. Silly bugger,' the informant continued. 'The dog's over there,' he volunteered, nodding towards a small inoffensive looking black mongrel. Its dirty white face was resting on its paws, eyes darting nervously in all directions looking for further danger.

'What's his name?' Martin asked his new friend.

'Spot.' the man replied.

'Not the dog's, the caretakers.'

'It's Fred Salmons, the man replied as if everyone knew who Fred Salmons was. 'Nice bloke, see 'im down the pub every night. Always buys a round,' confirming unimpeachable evidence of the man's generous character.

But Martin had forgotten the question, he was watching the man kneeling by the side of the prostrate body, examining with swift confident movements. His hands seemed to flow as he examined the legs rather than simply moving speculatively. He looked tall and slim with well groomed fair hair. It seemed incongruous to see what appeared to be an elegant man on his knees alongside someone who could best be described as scruffy.

'That's doc Porter. He's new, only been here about a month,' Martin's informant told him. 'Don't know much about 'im.'

The doctor had an air of confidence which assured observers that he knew what he was doing, suddenly stood up and turned to a sad faced woman by his side. She wore a plastic green pinafore over a stained floral dress and had been standing watching the doctor worriedly.

'Oh, dear, will he be all right?' she asked plaintively, anxious for any reassurance that things were not as bad as they looked.

'Yes, I'm sure he will be okay, try not to worry,' the doctor said as he took her hand. She looked lovingly at the injured man who, though fully conscious, had not said a word. The doctor took bandages out of his black bag and bound the legs together so movement would not be too painful.

'The ambulance will be here in a minute, they will bring a stretcher to move him,' he explained, pushing his hand through his greying hair. He looked at her sympathetically

The woman stood by his side for a moment. Then bent down and said something to her prostrate husband and then, quickly, as if suddenly making up her mind, got up and hurried to a nearby house where several women, like clucking hens, were mothering five small children. She picked up the smallest and went inside. Already, it seemed, the neighbors living in the nearby two-up, two down, terraced houses built some time in the Victorian era, had gathered round to provide temporary accommodation for the now homeless family.

Martin's attention returned to the fire which now lacked the frantic urgency it had when he arrived. The fire brigade was obviously winning the battle with the flames but the school, run by a nearby Catholic convent, was totally destroyed.

★ ★ ★

A heavy pall of black smoke replaced the bright glow that had originally fascinated Martin but the watching crowd seemed loathe to leave the scene until the final death throes had been completed. Their attention was now centred on the front wall of the house which looked ready to fall at any minute. Firemen were busy clearing away unwanted hoses while two policemen, more used to patrolling the city centre dealing with youths who were the worse for drink, were concentrating on moving the crowd well back because they too, like Martin, were hypnotized by the scene and seemed unaware of the danger.

Even the urgent wail of the ambulance siren failed to compete for the attention with the teetering brickwork and few people saw it draw up outside the school gates.

It was a sharp cry of alarm from a watcher perched in a nearby window that finally drew attention from the wall.

'Look at 'im,' the voice ordered. It was high pitched and came from a woman in a window close to the house into which the Salmons family had disappeared.

Obediently the crowd looked at him. It was the injured Salmons who had been steadily releasing the binding from his legs, risen from his makeshift bed and was trying to walk slowly towards the house into which the woman had disappeared with the children. He was a small man, little more than five feet tall, in his late 40s. His greying hair was cut on the old-fashioned short back and side principle, his round face was clean shaven but weather-beaten and lined. He looked a kind, good natured man, Martin thought.

Two ambulance men jumped briskly out of the cab and with precise, efficient movements opened the rear door and removed a stretcher with a gleaming white pillow and red blanket and prepared to collect their patient.

Salmons, still walking slowly but with no sign of pain, turned to look at them, he seemed ignorant of the fact that their efforts were on his behalf and that he was the patient. The ambulance men, their yellow uniforms giving the somber scene some colour, were equally unaware that the man walking steadily away from them was the cause of their traffic stopping dash through the city. The only person completely unperturbed by the turn of events was Salmons himself.

'For Christ's sake lie down,' cried an alert bystander, anxious about further damage the caretaker could be doing to his legs.

'What's up?' Salmons asked innocently of no-one in particular.

The sound of his voice broke the spell that had held the onlookers. Suddenly a dozen willing helpers rushed towards him, hands outstretched to catch him when he fell. People crowded around him certain that he was in a state of shock.

Martin's reaction was instinctive and faster than the others. He darted across the yard and had the man by the arm in seconds before the others had gathered round him. Protecting him from the over enthusiastic well-wishers as best he could, he slowly steered him towards the first aid men waiting for him.

It took several minutes but eventually Salmons was sitting on the rear step of the ambulance, elbows on knees and head forward, breathing deeply as if making a conscious effort to pull himself together. The doctor was quickly by his side.

'What are you doing?' he asked Salmons like a father chiding his son. Salmons looked up, still mystified by the events.

'You shouldn't be walking about,' he added, trying to explain the situation. 'You jumped out of the window and badly hurt your legs, walking on them like will do a lot more damage to them. They must hurt your terribly.'

Salmons looked up with unseeing eyes, deep in thought. He shook his head.

'They don't hurt me at all,' he said simply.

'Can you feel your legs?' the doctor asked. There were further moments of thought.

'Yes,' said Salmons. The doctor took hold of each leg in turn and felt them thoughtfully.

'Some of the swelling seems to have gone,' he said slowly. His face took on a worried look. It was his turn to be mystified.

The crowd continued staring stolidly at the injured man, intrigued by the drama of the situation. The silence was punctuated spasmodically as some coughed nervously.

'Just stand up very slowly,' the doctor instructed Salmons. The caretaker stood obediently while the doctor knelt in front of him and reminded him quietly: 'Your home was on fire, you rescued your wife and children and then you went back into the burning house to get your dog and you were trapped by the flames. You managed to escape by jumping out of a third floor window on to concrete. Not surprisingly you broke both your legs. Don't you remember?'

Salmons nodded thoughtfully, not looking at the doctor, and suddenly stood up again: 'The children?' he asked.

'They are all okay, your wife and children are quite safe.' the doctor assured him.

Salmons, satisfied, sat down again and resumed his former pose, elbows on knees, eyes on the ground.

The doctor put his hand on Salmons shoulder, 'You will be all right,' he told him.

Salmons jumped to his feet again: 'I want to see the children,' he said, taking an uncertain step forward.

'They really are quite safe,' the doctor emphasized impatiently. 'You really must let the ambulance take you to hospital for examination.'

'My legs will be okay, I don't want to go to a hospital' declared Salmons with conviction, 'He said they would be,' he added. It seemed to Martin that Salmons was near to tears.

'Who said that?' snapped the doctor.

'The man.'

'What man?'

'The man who spoke to me,' Salmons replied impatiently. 'He spoke to me when I was lying over there,' he went on, pointing to where the pile of coats still lay. 'My legs giving me gip. I was half conscious when this chap leaned over me and said I was not to worry, that my legs was okay and I was to get up as if nothing had happened.' Salmons stood up again. 'There you are,' he said triumphantly.

The doctor, now convinced that Salmons was in a deep state of shock, took his arm and beckoned the ambulance men who had been waiting patiently for someone to tell them what was happening.

'Let them take you to hospital for a check up,' he urged.

Salmons was tired and suddenly seemed to give up trying to persuade the doctor that there was nothing wrong with him. Unaided, but with a firm grip on the stretcher rail, he climbed into the ambulance and sat down. The doctor followed him.

Relieved that their patient had at last agreed to be a patient the ambulance men almost ran round to their cab and climbed in. With another plaintive wail on the siren to announce their immediate departure, the vehicle started slowly and then, its blue light flashing, glided off into the night.

★ ★ ★

Deprived of the main actors in the drama the crowd turned inwards, buzzing with excitement at the turn of events, anxious to talk over what had happened and to speculate and gossip.

A deafening crash cut short the public debate before it got started. The front of the house buckled slowly and then, like a pole-axed boxer, it crashed to the ground. Flames, encouraged and agitated by the renewed influx of air, suddenly reared into life again illuminating the scene in a flickering glow. Bricks, torn from each other by the impetus, hurled themselves angrily to the ground in a welter of dust, smoke and sparks, some shattering to pieces by the force of the impact, other colliding with the already fallen rubble rolled drunkenly until their energy was spent. Ash and dust, impelled by the heat, billowed over the watching crowd engulfing them momentarily in a cloud of filth. Coughing and spluttering frantically in search of clear air the crowd shuffled back quickly from the danger.

The noise died as suddenly as it had started to be replaced once more by the hiss of water as the firemen, startled by the suddenness of the collapse, returned their hoses to the dying inferno.

★ ★ ★

Peace returned to the scene while the crowd, still staring like Bonfire Night celebrators, gathered their wits.

'Typical,' pronounced a tall thin man with spectacles, speaking to the assembly in general. 'Typical of the bloody health service. Doctor can't tell a broken leg from a ruptured boil.'

'His legs was definitely broken when they carried 'im away,' declared an elderly woman clutching an old handbag to her bosom as though it contained her entire fortune. It probable did. 'You could tell by the way they was 'anging,' she added nodding knowingly around her.

'Well, you can't get up and walk with two busted legs,' a young man laughed nervously.

'They was broke,' the old woman repeated.

'They weren't,' a sarcastic voice from the middle of the crowd declared. 'Stands to reason,' it added lamely.

The woman looked defiantly into the flickering ruins. 'You can't tell me,' she said to the dying fire,' that a bloke of 'is age can jump from a third floor onto concrete and not break something.'

'And you can't tell me,' an authoritative voice replied,' that a bloke of his age can prance around like a bleeding 'orse if 'is legs is broke.'

A snigger from the crowd temporarily silenced the adamant woman. Several people nodded, seeing the reasoning behind the argument.

'All right then' said another, the male voice of British compromise. 'Granted you can't jump from that height without breaking something. Granted you can't prance around if your legs is broken ' his logic was accompanied by a wave of his arms. 'What happened then?' he added lamely.

'Ere, who's this bloke he reckoned spoke to him?' another woman asked.

'There weren't no-one,' said the woman with the handbag desperately anxious to regain the floor of the debate.

'If there had been anyone I'd a seen him,' offered another female contributor. 'I was up at that window,' she pointed to where the first warning of Salmons' perambulatory activities had come from. 'And I'd have seen him if he was talking to anyone.'

'But he seemed quite sure,' said a man in baggy cord trousers held up by red braces.

'I seen 'im' said a small voice.

The man in baggy trousers clearly saw that the post of neutral chairman was his for the asking, opened his mouth to speak again but was interrupted.

'I seen 'im' the small voice repeated. It was a boy with a dirty check shirt and torn short trousers.

No-one was listening to him.

'Well I say I was watching from the window and I didn't see anyone go anywhere near him, 'cept his wife.'

'You was watching the fire,' sneered a big man in a black sweater, nudging her playfully.

He could be the woman's husband, Martin thought.

'You shut up,' she snapped. He was the woman's husband, Martin decided.

'I seen 'im,' the small voice persisted..

A fireman, drawn into the crowd by the need to remove unwanted equipment, looked up.

'You mean the fellow in the white sweater?' he asked. 'I saw him when we were helping the caretaker towards the gate. Big chap he was, I thought he was going to offer to help but he just stood there.'

That's 'im.' the boy shouted excitedly. 'I seen 'im too.'

Pleased at the prospect of being recognized as being right for the first time in his life by adults the boy turned to the nearest adult who happened to be Martin.

'He's got a white sweater with a round neck. It frightened me when I saw 'im 'cos I thought he was me Dad and I'm not supposed to be out. He's got a sweater like that.'

Several people in the crowd now admitted that they had seen the man, they suddenly remembered.

Martin smiled to himself. Two minutes before everyone, with the exception of the small boy, had sworn no such person existed but now, because his presence had been confirmed by someone as important as a fireman, they had known about the man all the time.

Martin stood and listened for a while as the discussion about the man in the white sweater continued with the boy enjoying his moment in the limelight. Several of those present had relatives with similar sweaters. He looked about him. The fire, though not completely extinguished, had lost its interest and there was nothing to be gained by hanging around.

★ ★ ★

Dr John Porter, closed the door behind him his brow was creased in deep thought as he put his coat on the Victorian hat stand and went into the kitchen. He was surprised to see his wife sitting at the table drinking Ovaltine and reading a book.

'What on earth are you doing up?'

'Couldn't sleep. How was it?' She knew he had been called out to the fire because someone was hurt.

How was it, he thought. He couldn't say it was all right because it wasn't. How could he have made such a mistake with his diagnosis? He was convinced that the caretaker's legs were broken despite what the man said and did but when they got to the hospital the x-rays showed no fracture. Although there was some heavy bruising all the bones were intact. It was impossible.

'All right,' he eventually answered. 'But odd.'

'Odd, why?'

'Well Salmons, caretaker at the school jumped out of a third floor window at the school and dropped some thirty feet to avoid the flames. When I examined him I found he had, not surprisingly, broken both his legs. Then he said he felt fine, stood up and walked away. At the hospital they confirm that there were no broken bones. Bloody funny,.'

Candice shrugged, only marginally interested in what her husband had said, 'Never mind darling, come to bed.'

'I'll have a drink first,' he replied. He was not surprised by his wife's lack of interest as he often thought she did not listen to what he was saying. 'You go up I won't be long.'

He looked at his wife. She was, he thought beautiful beyond belief. Even after ten years of marriage he was as deeply in love with her as when they first met. Just over five feet tall, petite with jet black hair which fell to her shoulders. Her pale blue eyes had a sparkle which indicated a lively personality. Her hour-glass figure was neat with small breasts and tiny waist. She was French and exuded sex in the way that most French women seemed to. They just looked as though bed was their natural habitat. On the other hand most attractive English women looked good but gave no perceptible invitation.

He had met her at a medical conference in Paris. She was with one of the French doctors to whom, he thought, she was attached. He was surprised when, later, she accepted an invitation to dinner. The invitation had been repeated and several exchange visits followed until Porter's eventual proposal was accepted with alacrity. She had settled down in Hereford without any of the expected problems. She had such an outgoing, pleasant personality that she had been welcomed by his friends . It was a good marriage.

He drank his scotch and glanced through the evening paper distractedly without taking in what he was reading, stood up, put the lights out and went to bed.

He turned on his side snuggled down and put his arm round Candice, his hand on her right breast. She murmured pleasantly.

'Funny about those legs,' he thought drowsily,' I'm sure they were broken.' He fell asleep.

* * *

It was mid-morning on a Saturday when Martin rang Tubby.

'That you Tubby?' he asked when the phone was eventually answered. Tubby did not like answering the phone on a Saturday as there was always a chance that it meant work so he often pretended to be out.

'Who is that?'

'Martin'

'Martin who?'

'Martin Armstrong you twit. Are you getting old?

'Good God, what the hell are you ringing me for, on a Saturday. Where are you?'

'In the Green Dragon. I'm passing through and thought it might be a good idea to call and see if we can meet.'

'Sure. How long are you here for? I could come in about and hour. How's Barbara?'

'No idea,' said Martin. 'We separated about two years ago.'

'I'm sorry, I had no idea. What happened? No, tell me about it later'

They arranged to meet for lunch. It was a meeting Martin really looked forward to.

Tubby had been responsible for him becoming a good journalist. Martin had become a newspaper reporter fairly late in life but had started on the Hereford Journal as a junior reporter. His only relevant knowledge, which made life easier for him, was that he knew about politics, particularly the politics of local government. The fact that none of the other reporters had the slightest interest in the subject gave him the opportunity to make a good impression. But Tubby had taken him in hand, taught him the finer points of newspaper practice, what not to do and, most importantly, a few valuable tricks. He had been a sort of one-man training school for which Martin had always been grateful.

When Tubby arrived and they had sorted out who was drinking what, and had a desultory argument about who was paying, they sat and looked at each other.

'Good to see you again,' said Tubby. 'You've done reasonable well since you left us.' Martin was pleased, the term 'reasonably well,' from Tubby was a compliment of the highest order. What are you doing here?'

Martin was relieved by the inquiry because it enabled him avoid what he knew would be Tubby's most searching question.

It was the question Martin did not want but knew he would get. He tried to even further delay it by mentioning in detail the fire at the school and the mistake the doctor had made over the caretaker's legs.

'It was interesting because the caretaker had been told both his legs were broken. But he got up and walked away after being told to do so by a man dressed in black trousers and a white polo-necked sweater. I saw the man but he looked fairly normal and simply walked away.'

Tubby refused to be diverted.

'I'll send some to talk to Porter on Monday,' he said offhandedly. Tell me about Barbara.'

'I had to be in North Wales at the aerospace factory on an Airbus story and I was in no hurry to get back to London I thought I'd pop down here and relive some old memories. You're an old memory.'

'So what happened with Barbara?

He could not delay the answer any more. He had been married to Barbara when he was working on the Journal and Tubby had 'adopted' the couple as his surrogate son and daughter. He had grown very fond of Barbara and Martin knew he would strongly disapprove of the break up.

'My fault, I'm afraid,' Martin admitted, 'I put the job first.

'You bloody idiot, She is a lovely girl.'

Martin reflected, true, she was a lovely girl and very patient. Unfortunately he tested her patience to its breaking point. Anxious to make a name in journalism he always found something more important to do, a story to follow up, an interview to carry out. She understood at first but when he forgot to visit the hospital when their son was born, because he had the opportunity to interview an hitherto difficult person to contact, it proved too much for Barbara..

It had been a friendly parting and Martin had to admit to himself that he found it was easier to work without the responsibility of a wife and child. Almost the worst part of the break was the rift it caused with his Mother who was a deeply religious person and was strongly against the divorce, and greatly regretted the fact that she would be separated from her grandson.

She knew about the horrors of divorce. His father had been both a womaniser and a heavy drinker and after being found too many times in the brothels of Birmingham by his police inspector father. He was forced to divorce his wife and was consigned to the colonies. The main outcome for Martin was that he was brought up with an antipathy towards both sex and drinking. They were antipathies which had faded with time.

The two men chatted for a while about the Journal, what the reporting staff were like now and what had happened to some of Martin's former colleagues, what Martin had been doing and when Tubby thought he might retire.

'I'll check with Porter about the caretaker,' he said standing up. 'I have to take the wife shopping, sends her love by the way.' They shook hands and parted.

★ ★ ★

Martin returned to London the following morning and went straight to his Earls Court flat to bathe and put on a complete change of clothing. He did not enjoy living out of a suitcase, preferring to be reasonably fastidious in his dress, fresh shirt and socks every day, different suit, matching tie and change of shoes. For the past six days he'd been shuffling around with the few clothes he had taken with him, using the hotel laundry whenever he remembered to get his dirty clothes ready in time for the chambermaid.

He made himself a cup of coffee and scanned through the post. A few bills, boring circulars, offers of millions of pounds if he returned his 'lucky numbers' within the next seven days. Nothing else. He didn't really expect anything of importance. All his friends were too idle to write, the telephone was ample communication for making arrangements or finding out whether you were still alive or not.

★ ★ ★

It was three days later and Martin had just returned to his flat after a lone meal at his favourite Indian restaurant when the telephone rang.

'Hello, Martin' said a firm male voice. It was Charlie James, the night Editor from the Examiner. 'Get in here as soon as you can,' he ordered without preamble. 'And bring an overnight bag with you.'

'Why, what's up?' Martin asked, a tinge of excitement flowing through him.

'You're off to Norfolk, or somewhere like that. Just get in as soon as you can.'

Martin knew better than to ask any questions. He just said 'okay' and replaced the receiver. It took him no time at all to put a few clothes and essentials, which always had ready in case of emergencies into his suitcase and only twenty minutes to drive to the office near Fleet Street.. He went straight to the news room where he received an ironic cheer from his colleagues. It was always fun when someone else was being sent out late at night. Charlie James was waiting for him. A wadge of papers in his hand. He smiled a greeting to Martin and thrust them into his hand.

'Read this,' he instructed.

'What is it?'

'It's copy of a piece which appeared in the Norwich Weekly. I want you to go and investigate.'

Martin flopped in a chair and started reading. The story was written by a woman, Miriam Cartwright, one of the Weekly's district correspondents. It was headed 'Miracle in Harwood.'

*'A nine-year-old boy who has been a cripple since a motor car accidents five years ago is now walking and running, thanks to a mysterious visitor to his home village of Harwood,' the story began.*

Martin felt a twinge of disappointment. It was not the sort of story he thought he was going on, it was not his sort of story, it was a gossipy bit more likely to be seen in a tabloid scandal sheet. He had come across this sort of thing before, the miracle healing. But when it was investigated it was usually found that the person who claimed to have been cured had not been as sick or damaged as reported and was not now as perfect as the writer claimed.

The Cartwright piece explained how the boy had been watching his friends play football but could not join in because he had been crippled for five years. Then he suddenly put his crutches aside and ran to join his friends. Frightened that they would be blamed for taking his crutches off him and making fun of him they had taken him straight home to his Mother who, at first, was very cross but calmed down when she saw the boy was all right.

Martin skipped through the rest of the badly typed pages and put them down on Charlie's desk giving him a scornful look.

'This is a load of crap,' he said. 'This sort of thing doesn't happen.'

'Well it looks as though it has,' Charlie replied, 'anyway the old man wants you to go and have a look at it. Get down there as soon as you can.'

'What ! Tonight !' Martin looked at his watch. 'It's gone eleven !'

'Yep. Now. There's no such thing as time on this newspaper,' Charlie grinned broadly.

'Oh Christ, this is worse than bloody Italy,' Martin moaned, 'I've got a mate in Rome, works for the Sun, spends his bloody time tearing round the country on weeping Madonna stories. Seems like statues are bursting into tears every ten minutes. This is worse than that. He can't be serious.'

'Well he is old son. I suggest you get your arse to this village as soon as poss. We will want a story early tomorrow so we can plan the page, at the moment it looks like the only thing we can lead. on. We're sending a photographer, Frank Spedding. He'll meet you down there.'

Well that was something., He didn't have to take Spedding with him. Martin couldn't stand the man, he never stopped talking about his sexual conquests and you knew damn well he was lying.

'Supposing it's not true?.'Martin tried.

'We'll run a story about misleading reports and charlatans pretending to be healers. We'll think of something.'

'I thought this was supposed to be a serious newspaper.'

'Desperately serious,' said Charlie. 'Go and write a serious story.'

* * *

The first thing he had to do was to find out where the bloody hell Harwood was. He went to his car and got out the map. Good God ! The bloody place was near Norwich, the worst place possible with no motorways going anywhere near. What a waste of bloody time, he thought.

Martin sat in his small Ford, bad tempered and impatient, and considered. There was absolutely no point driving there straight away and arriving in the middle of the night. Better to go home, have a few hours sleep, start early before the traffic built up and arrive at about breakfast time. He would still have time to make enquiries, write his story and, hopefully, file it before lunch.

The drive up the M11 and A11 was quick and trouble free, as predicted, as it was only six thirty in the morning. Almost the first thing he saw as he approached Norwich was a signpost to Harwood. With a sigh of relief he followed it down a series of roads each gradually deteriorating in breadth and quality until he found himself driving down a single track punctuated every now and then by passing places carved out of the bank on either side.

Hidden down this narrow road, nestling in one of the few wooded hills of Norfolk he felt as though he was driving into some sort of twentieth century Shangri La, a place that had remained undiscovered by the modern world.

That this was untrue became painfully obvious as he turned a sharp corner to see the first signs of civilisation, neat black and white, half timbered thatched cottages - all genuine - but with tall, inelegant steel television aerials or disks, impinging on the medieval architecture by sprouting from their stubby chimneys Martin slowed down to walking pace as he drove over a dirt splattered patch of road and past a disinterested group of Friesian cattle whose big brown eyes stared blankly out of kind black and white faces and seeming to asking who was interrupting their normal peace and quiet. Passing them he dropped slowly down a short hill and into the village itself.

The tranquility of Harwood was immediately overpowering. The village itself stood in a basin formed by the junction of three narrow low valleys, two of which carried bubbling streams into a third which bounced gaily from boulder to boulder for another five miles before it ended up exhausted, merging with the majestic salmon rich waters of the River Yare.

For no reason whatsoever as he looked at the silent deserted scene he expect a space ship to suddenly land and a Martian step out and demand 'Take me to your leader.' It was totally irrelevant but then, he thought, so was this bloody story.

Standing in the silent village it was easy to hear the hypnotic gurgling of the streams to but to find them a stranger had to search the hillsides among trees growing from soft. yielding banks of yellow wort, weld, heather, hilberry, thale, cress and broom.

In this soft bosom of nature lived a population of seven hundred souls, many of them retired farmers, some businessmen who commuted daily into Norwich, Lowestoft or even further away, and farm workers some of whom had rarely ventured into the hard world beyond Norwich itself.

Their homes, placed carefully around the village or on the low hillsides, were all thatched by expert hands. Some were very old, built traditionally using timber, wattle and daub, a few more modern, were constructed with bricks straight from the local brickworks.

The village green, an emerald base to the imaginary basin, was irregular in shape and boasted an ancient oak tree slightly off centre. It was, boasted the villagers, the only oak tree in England in which King Charles II had not hidden during the Civil War, mainly because he had never been that way. But it served many purposes. It was shelter in a rain storm or a haven of shade on a hot day. To the children it was a storm tossed pirate ship searching for Spanish treasure, a fortress against the invading Vikings, a space ship encircling some unknown planet or just a climbing frame to be to be conquered in as many ways as possible. The traditional way for the boys of the village to show their bravery was to see which was the highest branch they had the nerve to jump from. The most viable branch was 21 feet from the ground. Some had done it. There had been no broken legs, so far.

The major adversaries in the battle for the attention of the village folk, the inn and the church, stood on either side of the green, glaring at each other. Every Saturday night the Happy Ploughman fired a broadside at the church. disgorging drunken, rowdy customers in a torrent of cheerful noise. Every Sunday morning the church of St. Athelstan replied with an organized salvo of bell-ringing which reverberated throughout the village attracting the neatly dressed inhabitants, some with hangovers, as a magnet attracts pins.

But the inn always won the final skirmish. On the stroke of twelve noon each Sunday the congregation spilled out of the church and. like released elastic bands, returned to the warmth and conviviality of the Happy Ploughman's bars, public and private.

As Martin drove past the church and through the deserted village he could not help but think that the village was an ideal setting for the sort of cock and bull story he was on.

He stopped the car opposite the only tiled building in the village, a large grey house of indistinguishable architecture which had been built at the turn of the century to house its vicar. Judging by its size the parishioners had expected a man of single mindedness and many children. These qualities may have been fulfilled in the past but now half the rooms were unused for the Reverend Charles and Miriam Cartwright were childless devoting their energies, emotions and instincts entirely to the benefit of their congregation.

Tall, angular and with a shrill voice which could be carefully modulated to a pious level if and when the need arose, Miriam Cartwright welcomed Martin with surprise. Strangers visiting the vicarage before breakfast were not an every day occurrence. Her cool greeting melted into enthusiastic warmth when she realized that Martin was a reporter from one of the great national newspapers who wanted to know more about her story. She was flattered. She would, she made clear, advise Mr Armstrong as best she could.

A cup of milky, sweet coffee from a flowery, wafer thin china cup fortified them while they sat at the breakfast table discussing the story. The reverend gentleman, it was explained, was still asleep as he had been very busy lately. Martin however, was anxious to get out of the house as soon as possible, preferably with Mrs Cartwright. He had her exclusively at the moment and he didn't want any reporters from other papers knocking on her door and exciting her. She would become unbearable, and he would not get his exclusive story.

Martin soon made it clear that he would like to meet the little boy concerned as soon as possible. Mrs Cartwright was only too happy to take him, but it still took half an hour of gossip and pottering to prise her out of the house and into the village.

They went straight to a small cottage bounded by trees and with a small front garden littered with toys, coloured balls and a brand new bicycle.

'This where dear Philip lives,' announced Mrs Cartwright, waving her arms like an illusionist revealing the truth. 'His parents went to Norwich yesterday and bought him his very first bicycle. I don't know whether he can ride it yet but he was very excited when he got it.'

She had hardly finished her explanation when a small boy in grey trousers and an old multi-coloured pullover with frayed cuffs and holes in both elbows, came running out of the front doorway. Grey socks hung untidily round his legs, which were very thin, and concertinaed around his ankles. His shoes were dirty and down at heel.

'Hello Philip darling,' she simpered. 'This is Philip,' she said to Martin unnecessarily.

'Good morning Mrs Cartwright,' Philip answered politely. Martin had the impression she was not exactly a welcome visitor.

'This gentlemen is a newspaper reporter,' she drooled. 'He has come all the way from London to talk to you about how your legs got better.'

She might as well have introduced Martin as a prize cabbage for all the impression she made on Philip.

'Hello,' he said shyly.

At that moment his mother, a harassed woman with a thin, pointed face and rimless glasses came to the door. She was not overjoyed to see visitors so early in the day but smiled when Martin was introduced.

He stood looking at her while Mrs Cartwright went through her introductory speech again. Beryl Green had little obvious to boast about. Her thin summer dress in orange and brown stripes could be seen in their dozens on the racks of British Home Stores. It did nothing for her figure which had obviously been abandoned years ago. She was flat chested, her stomach flabby and the flesh around her hips and thighs was plentiful and uncontrolled. No stockings hid the varicose veins on her legs and her slippers had seen better days. But she looked kind and gentle, wrapping a protective arm around Philip when Martin's mission was explained, as if fearful that he would remove the magic spell that had made her son walk.

Martin's friendly, encouraging smile must have warmed her because she invited them into the house and looked shyly at him as they moved into the living room. It was small with a battered three piece suite and scratched sideboard standing on a frayed carpet. The room did have the luxury of a television. A pile of clean washing stood on the gate-legged dining room table awaiting ironing. Newspapers and several copies of a farmer's magazine were quickly pushed into a rack standing by one of the two old arm chairs while Mr Green's slippers lay in front of a fireless grate.

They all sat down at Mrs Green's bidding, she on a dining room chair next to Martin, her arm still around the boy standing by her knee. Mrs Cartwright sat in one of the easy chairs.

'This gentleman wants to talk to you about the man you met on the Green,' his mother told Philip.

'But I've told you all about him,' he boy said impatiently. 'I've told everybody.'

'You're quite right Philip,' said Martin. 'But you know grown ups sometimes get things wrong,' he added confidentially, The boy nodded understandingly. Mrs Cartwright shifted uncomfortably in her seat, bristling at the implication. Martin looked at her knowingly to put her mind at rest.

'You tell me if I am wrong,' Martin continued to the boy. 'Last Sunday you were standing on the Green by the big tree watching the other children playing.'

'Yes,' the boy interrupted shuffling from one leg to the other. 'They were playing tag and I couldn't play because I couldn't run and they said I would always be 'it' and I wouldn't be able to catch anyone,' he added quickly.

'And while you were watching a man came up to you and asked you if you would like to play with the other children.....'

'And I said yes but it wouldn't do any good because they would always catch me and I couldn't catch them,' Philip offered.

'What happened then?'

The boy put his hand on his mother's knee and twisted his legs self consciously. Mrs Green was about the speak to him but after a warning glance from Martin, said nothing.

'Well'...he said that if I really wanted to play,' the boy look at his mother nervously.' I should put my crutches by the big tree and go and join the others, he said I would be all right and that it wouldn't hurt.' The boy stopped to think.

'Did you do as he said?' Martin asked.

'Well.... I was frightened. I said that my Mummy and Daddy had said I must always use my crutches else I would fall down and hurt myself.'

'What did he say?'

'He said my Mummy and Daddy were quite right but they did not know my legs were better. They would be very happy when they found out.'

'Then what did you do?'

'Well.... he was very nice and kind so I thought that if it would make Mummy and Daddy happy I would do it. So I walked with my crutches to the tree and put them up against it.

It didn't hurt me so I walked a few steps. I didn't fall down. So I went to the others, but not very quickly.'

'What did the other children do?'

'They thought it was funny and said I would get into trouble if I didn't use my crutches.. The man had gone away so we all went to my house and told Mummy. She was very cross at first but when she saw I was all right she was happy like the man said she would be.' His mother, who was listening as though it was the first time she had heard the story, gave him an affectionate squeeze.

'Philip, would you be very clever and tell me exactly what the man looked like? 'Martin said to him.

'He was big,' the boy replied.

'Bigger than me?'

'A little bit. But he was darker.'

'You mean his hair was dark?'

'Yes, and his skin was brown too, like Daddy's when he's been out in the sun all day.'

'What was he wearing?

'He had dark trousers and a white pullover like Daddy's.'

'What sort of pullover?

'A white one with a round high neck, like Daddy's.'

'What did he speak like? Did he have a funny accent?'

Philip shook his head rapidly: 'He had a deep voice. He didn't shout at me.'

'Is there anything else you can tell me?' The boy shook his head.

'Have you seen him before?' The boy shook his head again and began twisting his legs impatiently as if he wanted to go away.

'Thank you very much Philip. You have been very very helpful. Your legs really are all right now, they don't hurt you at all, and you can walk?'

'Yes,' said Philip. 'And I can ride my bike,' he added proudly.

'He's been quite normal since,' said Mrs Green, 'but we have to take him to the specialist next week to have some tests.'

'What does the doctor say?'

Dr Blackburn, who has looked after him since he hurt himself, says Philip should use his crutches until he sees the specialist. But it seems a bit silly when he can walk without them He says he may have been hypnotized or given a pain killer. He wasn't very nice about it.'

Martin, who had now been joined by his photographer, was anxious to get out to try and meet some of the other children. But he had to wait while photographs of Philip and his mother and, of course, Miriam Cartwright were taken. He stood up as a sign of imminent departure and encouraged by this there was a general embarrassed shuffling around and they were allowed to say their goodbyes and leave.

News of his presence had obviously spread quickly for a posse of small children had gathered outside. They were all anxious to tell Martin what had happened but they all confirmed what Philip had said. And when they saw the photographer at work they were anxious to talk. They all agreed that the man was tall and sun tanned. He wore a white polo neck sweater and dark grey trousers with sandals. Some said that he wore socks but others disagreed, suggesting that he had brown feet. That was all they knew. They had not seen him before or since. They had all been worried when Philip walked towards them without his crutches. They thought his parents would be angry and that this would rebound on them so they took him straight home.

Martin spoke to a number of other locals none of whom could recall seeing the man.

They all had their theories. He was a hypnotist, he was a gypsy, he was a faith healer, a spiritualist with a message from above, the boy had got better naturally but no-one had realised it before. Nothing that was of any use to Martin.

Dr Blackburn, a short man with a big ego and a permanent frown, would have none of it.

The boy's legs are still useless, he said defiantly. He should be using his crutches, some sort of numbness had set in. He could have been given pain killers so he could not feel any pain. He did not want the gutter press invading the village looking for a sensational story. Anyway he had work to do so kindly get out of his surgery. Throughout his tirade the doctor glared at the cringing Mrs Cartwright who he clearly held responsible for this outrage.

After thanking Mrs Cartwright for her help Martin went back to his car and drove away.

As he drove back up the narrow lane he passed two cars, both of which looked as though they contained reporters he recoognized from other papers. Tough luck men, he thought. I've got my story.

⋆ ⋆ ⋆

Martin filed his story after persuading the landlord at the Happy Ploughman to let him use the empty bar to sort out his notes and dictate his story to the newspaper on his mobile. He then drove into Norwich. He was not entirely happy with his story. When he had finished dictating it he felt that it was incomplete, that he had missed something. He checked his notes carefully but all that did was to confirm that he had used every relevant detail. But he felt that there was still something wrong.

He had waited on the phone while the Editor looked at the story and much to Martin's surprise had been enthusiastic about it. But like all newspaper editors he had wanted more. Who was this man? What was he doing? What did the police say? Where had he gone? 'Find out all you can, in fact, find the man and interview him. If you think he's genuine take him off to some hotel, offer him money, anything, but keep him away from the other bloody newspapers,' Martin was instructed..

Easier said than done, thought Martin. How the hell am I going to find him? Anxious to get away from the village before any of the other journalists, if indeed they were news men, found him and started asking questions, he drove towards Norwich, hoping against hope, that he would pass a man wearing dark trousers, a white sweater and sandals. It was close on lunch time so he stopped at the first pub he came to which advertised food.

Martin sat at his table, his mind wandering as he looked around the restaurant. Most of the tables were occupied by couples chatting intensely or families trying to make the children behave. At the next table sat a young couple deep in conversation. The girl, an attractive, well groomed brunette, gazed intently at her companion. The man, of average build, about 30, was gesturing gently obviously trying to explain something. He was neatly dressed in dark grey slacks, sweater and blazer. Nice to see someone not in jeans, thought Martin, he hated the classless, boring garment which, in his view, had long become a sort of uniform.

He sat back. He could not get out of his mind that something odd was going on. He felt he ought to be doing something, seeing something but he could not think what it was. He had a premonition that something was going to happen but he could not work out whether it was good or bad. There was something he should have done, or could do, that he hadn't. It was a most uncomfortable feeling.

Martin tried to enjoy his meal and to read his newspaper but both were spoiled by the thoughts as yet unrecognized which were at the back of his mind.

He continued looking round the room but each time his eyes returned to the intense young couple. There was something about them that he should notice. He now felt what was akin to anticipation as he looked at the couple closely. They were getting ready to go. The man paid the bill, stood up and walked round the table to hold his partner's chair as she rose.

Its that bloody white sweater, Martin suddenly thought. The young man was wearing a white roll-neck, or polo-neck sweater. What was it the little boy had said? 'A white pullover with a round neck.' It could have been a turtle- neck sweater of course, but one of the other children had given a description more in keeping with the one this man was wearing. But he wasn't tall, he wasn't dark and he was probably too young. He certainly wasn't the mystery man.

Martin's mind started working overtime. It was the second time he had heard that phrase.

There was something else. Martin's mind was now thrashing around, digging in his memory bank like a frantic schoolgirl looking through her drawers for a missing garment. He'd seen someone in a sweater like that himself recently. But where?

He looked up again as the couple went out of the door, the girl first followed by the man.

That was it! On reflection he himself had seen a man wearing a similar sweater at the Hereford fire. He'd simply walked away when they took the caretaker to hospital. And there was a mystery there too. The mystery of whether the legs were really broken. Well, it was very unlikely that it was the same man. The other one had been some 200 miles away on the other side of England.

* * *

Harry Gregg was not happy. True, his patrol car was comfortable particularly in bad weather but, after twenty years in foot on the beat in Northampton, driving in a car seemed the wrong way to work. A policeman's job, he felt, was to patrol his neighbourhood on foot, getting to know people, the good and the bad, to help where possible and, of course, keep the peace. Harry was an affable man who enjoyed talking to people and establishing long term friendships. Chatting up potential villains was one of his more enjoyable hobbies.

His role now, as what he called a 'tinned copper' seemed unrealistic. Cocooned as he was in his mobile 'can' all he could do was observe at comparatively high speed what was happening on the surface of the community of Northampton, he had no idea what the local gossip was, who was doing what to whom and he had few opportunities to catch evil doers before they evil did.

Although only 46, he had given some thought to early retirement and spending his time putting his garden straight, but his pension was not yet high enough to maintain his wife Mabel in the standard which she thought was her right

Now, driving along a quiet suburban road towards the town centre it seemed strange to be thinking about his retirement at his age and having nothing to do all day. He began reflecting on his life. It had not been without its moments but on the whole was pretty standard and boring. A trouble free youth was followed by army service, the police force, marriage and children. He had achieved little at school apart from learning to read and write, which he thought was something of an achievement. He could work out the odds on a bet and calculate the winnings, if any. He never bothered with the mathematics of loosing, nor did he waste time regretting it He had left school at 16 and after two years learning to become a butcher had decided to join the army, the two activities seemed to have some relevance.

Thanks to his time in the army he had a different approach to his police work than his colleagues, most of whom had joined the force straight from school. His belief was that they had been programme during training so that any individuality or imagination had been squeezed out of them consequently they all responded to the same problems in the way they had been instructed. Their questions to suspects and their response had been fully programmed so that whatever the answer there was a programmed response. Any attempt by a suspect for a reasonable approach, or reasonable explanation or discussion were totally ignored as if an instructor had ordered 'they all say that, pay no attention.' He did not agree with the standard guilty until proved innocent approach, adopting the opposing view whenever he could. He did, he thought, listen to what was being said then used his commonsense. As a consequence of this independent view promotion was a long way off.

The highlight of his army service was his translation to manhood thanks to the professional attentions of a German barmaid called Helge. He looked good in his uniform which showed off his six feet one inches, curly blonde hair and blue eyes. He had attracted many admiring glances from young maidens since he was a teenager but he had been passionate about football and had neither the inclination or the opportunity to exploit his good looks.

Harry drove on over the Nene river bridge his mind still reviewing the past when he was suddenly brought back to reality. Ahead of him, in the middle of the road was a man waving frantically for him to stop. Almost immediately Harry saw a tangled wreckage by the roadside.

Excited eyewitnesses quickly described what had happened. A sports car driven by a young man at high speed along the Andrews Road which ran parallel to the river, had collided with a saloon driven by a woman who had already crossed the bridge and was on the way home with her small daughter. The saloon had ricocheted off a milk float parked at the roadside and this had sprayed the road with a mixture of broken glass and milk. The saloon had rolled over, ending upside down against a lamp post spilling out petrol which had streamed into a rapidly forming pool in a leaf-blocked gutter. The sports car had come a stop against a brick wall. Its driver badly shaken but seemingly unhurt.

The saloon was almost crushed and it seemed unlikely to those who had run to the wreckage that anyone could have survived. Frantic efforts were being made to release the occupants before the petrol exploded. Two men were trying to pull open the twisted passenger door while others on the driver's side were trying to talk through the window to a woman who seemed alive but unconscious. There was, however, no hope of releasing her on that side as the door was jammed against the lamp post. The little girl was lying in a heap inside the upturned roof of the car. She looked either unconscious or dead.

Within minutes of Harry's arrival, just as he was about to take charge of the rescue operation, a fire engine and an ambulance quickly called by another witness arrived. The firemen leapt from their machine as it stopped and ran to the crashed vehicle while the officer in charge ordered two men to lay foam over the petrol and oil still streaming out of the car. Another police car arrived and the crew, after a quick word with Harry, started talking to the sports car driver and witnesses.

The civilian rescuers fell back as the experts took over with axes, wrenches and crowbars. 'Need cutting equipment,' said the leading fireman to Harry, 'but daren't risk it with all this fuel lying around.' Harry agreed and moved away to organize control of the growing crowd.

It took almost twenty minutes for the firemen to wrench off the passenger door and gently lift out the little girl who by now had regained consciousness but was tearful and crying for her Mother. They handed her to the waiting ambulance men who laid her gently on a stretcher.

Releasing the woman was more difficult, not wearing a seat belt, she had been thrown forward into the windscreen and then sideways as the car rolled over. She was hanging upside down, trapped between the seat and held up by a bridge created by the buckled gear lever. The firemen found it difficult to work in the confined space and at such an awkward angle. Finally, they had to drag the car away from the lamp post and, now that the fuel spill had been made safe, cut away the driver's door completely.

As they pulled the door away and the woman was helped out, unharmed except for some severe lacerations She suddenly saw her daughter Amanda lying on the stretcher by the ambulance. Giving a low cry of horror she moved quickly towards her, giving a smile of relief when she saw the girl was alive. She spoke to her and then stood up, looking around as if seeking someone. She then quickly walked to where Harry was standing but instead she looked a man standing by his side. Harry had not noticed him before.

'Thank you,' she said to him.

The man, tall and dark and wearing a white polo-necked sweater, smiled.

* * *

To Ruth Morton the accident was just another instalment in what seemed like a plot to destroy her completely. Once she had ensured that Amanda was unharmed she fell into the depths of self-pity. The fact that she had miraculously escaped from an accident which could have killed them both, with only cuts and bruises which looked worse than they actually were was of little solace to her.

Her life had started well as the only daughter of two well-respected teachers and all had gone to their well laid plans, school and university. They were happy when she decided to follow them into the teaching profession. Then she had met Tim. At 27 years he was literally the tall, dark and handsome man of gypsy prophesies. He was entranced by her genuine smile under a cluster of bubbles of black curly hair which framed her unlined pale face with its happy brown eyes. He was a dealer in the City making lots of money and could take her on luxurious holidays, buy her expensive gifts and take her to the best places. He was incredibly impressive.

Within a year of their meeting he had proposed and they were married. Then the curtain came down on the great romance.

Even on their honeymoon he was eyeing, and sleeping with a young woman in the same hotel. When they arrived home he began a series of affairs which he took little trouble to hide. When she objected he hit her and this continued throughout pregnancy.

When Amanda arrived, a beautiful baby with a happy face, he took no further interest in her and even less in their daughter. Life became unbearable until she could stand it no longer. When he was away for the weekend with one of his mistresses, she packed, gathered up her daughter and drove purposefully to her parents in Northampton. A week later her father died after a heart attack. It was only two days after the funeral that she discovered she no longer had access to their joint bank account which she had thought still existed. While she was contemplating this Amanda caught meningitis and for a time it was touch and go whether she lived.

The child recovered and regained her health and, financed by her mother, Ruth began a new life living with her, got a new teaching job, and began to make new friends. It was after a visit to one of these that she was involved in the car crash.

She was still half conscious lying trapped in the car, worrying about her daughter and awaiting her release that she was startled to see a face at the window. It was a man, he said nothing but just looked at her with his gentle dark brown eyes. She immediately felt a sense of release: she knew that she would be rescued and that all would be well

* * *

The confusion in Martin's mind over the identity of the man in the white sweater was intensified while he was still in Norwich, ostensibly searching for him so he could satisfy Charlie's demand for more information and an exclusive interview.

It was, of course, hopeless for no-one had any idea what had happened to the man after he left Harwood. With a feeling of despair he sat in his hotel room and turned on the television. It was a boring chat show with guests talking about problems specific to East Anglia where, it was alleged, an influx of illegal immigrants was having a detrimental effect.

Martin was only half interested until the programme gave way to the local news. The third item was about a dramatic escape where a woman and her daughter had escaped unharmed after an horrific car accident near Northampton which had caused far reaching traffic congestion.. Cameras showed the scene as firemen struggled to free the victims from the car. Fortunately there was a happy ending and viewers saw the woman and her daughter being released while the commentator described what a miracle it was that they had not been killed.

Martin, relaxing in his chair, suddenly sat upright, stunned by what he was seeing. As the cameras drew back from close-ups of the scene it began to show the crowd that had gathered to watch. He saw, or thought he saw, the slightly blurred figure of a tall man on the edge of a group of people. He was tall, he was dark, and he wore dark trousers and a white polo-neck sweater. The scene had changed within seconds.

Unable to believe his eyes Martin thought for a minute then grabbed the telephone and called reception.

'Do you by any chance video what is being shown on television?' he asked. Without introduction.

'No, sir, we don't video anything.'

'Can you find me the telephone number of the East Anglia TV office in Norwich?'

'Yes sir,' there was a short pause before she gave him the number.

He rang it immediately and, after he had explained who he was, arranged to call in and look at a copy of the current news.

Forgetting everything else he drove to the office and told them he was trying to find someone urgently and thought he had seen the person on the news item about the Northampton car crash. Obligingly they showed him the item and there, very clearly as the video was paused at the precise spot requested, he could clearly see the man. But it proved nothing. The man was tall, dark, and had dark grey slacks on and a white sweater. But man's face meant nothing as not a single witness at Harwood had described what it was like. It all meant nothing but an amazing coincidence.

★ ★ ★

Arnold Grimshaw settled down in his seat in the corner of the railway carriage with a sigh of satisfaction. It made a change to get a seat never mind one in the corner. He looked at his fellow commuters and a warm glow came over him. They all looked at him with the same glare of jealousy that he gave them when he had failed to get a seat.

Sighing smugly again he opened his Daily Examiner and quickly scanned the front page. Nothing very exciting, the usual reports of tragedy in another part of the world and disaster round the corner. His eye caught a heading 'Boy in Miracle Healing' and he scanned it quickly. He was half way down the column when he realized that the story was quite interesting so he went back and started again.

When he had finished he dropped the paper down on his knees and stared out of the carriage watching the countryside flash by. It was a nice story, he thought, made a change from the bad news and rubbish one read every morning. He began to wonder whether the boy really had been healed or whether it was simply some sort of hoax. He hoped it wasn't, not only for the boy's sake, but because it would be splendid if something like this really did happen, it would help to balance all the other stories of man's inhumanity to man.

Arnold sank into the depths of day dreaming, oblivious to the houses and factories that now raced past the window. There have always been people, he mused, who claimed to be able to heal others but you never knew the truth of it. Most of them proved to be charlatans. The last real healer got short shrift when he was here and he would probably get the same if he came back. Blimey ! What a bloody mess he'd find if he came back now. He'd have his work cut out in the Middle East again…wonder if he could do the feeding of the five thousand trick in Africa? God, he'd never cope.

A sudden jerk as the train drew to a standstill at Waterloo station brought him back to reality He stood up and gathered himself together and, for a change. was first out the carriage establishing a good lead in the race for the underground.

By the time he had reached the 'Drain' underground for the City Arnold's luck had run out and he was once more jammed into an upright position as other city folk in various shapes, sizes and aromas crushed into the carriage behind him.

Grimly holding on to a post near the door he looked at the sea of blank faces around him.

All expressionless and dull, hypnotized already by the daily routine, conditioned to discomfort. Good God ! We all look alike, he thought. He looked at his reflection in the carriage window and saw a man of medium height, white shirt and conservative blue and white spotted tie and dark grey three piece suit. Neat haircut, his was slightly shorter than the others and they all had black rolled umbrellas. I bet they've all got black socks on with highly polished black shoes he told himself. And science fiction writers thought clones were an idea for the future ! What the hell was he doing here anyway? Was it so important to be a banker and join this human floodtide every morning? What would a second Messiah think of the daily rat race....couldn't imagine him catching a tube train....if he had any sense at all he would stay out of London.

He reached the Bank tube station and began to walk down Queen's Street to his office musing about what his first task would be and thinking about the day ahead, little different, he thought, than the days that had gone before.

He was deep in thought when he was smashed in the face and hurled backwards into the group of people that were following him, all ending up in an untidy and baffled heap.

Grimshaw, totally disoriented, tried to get to his feet but was continually unbalanced by those around him also trying to sort themselves out. Gradually he came to his senses, first trying to work out what had happened, then examining himself to see if he was damaged He felt numb but could not identify any pain and his hearing was still unaffected. He was struck by the strange silence around him. No-one was shouting or screaming, there was only the semi-silence of struggling bodies and the over powering smell of explosives, rather like Bonfire Night.

'Bloody bomb,' he heard someone say. He looked up and saw the cause of the blast: the wreckage of a London bus, its roof torn off and a big hole in its side on the upper deck.

Suddenly, as if it was part of a film script, there was a burst of activity as those around regained their senses and moved to see if they could help the injured. Then those who were regaining consciousness began groaning or calling for help. Several people had been badly cut by flying glass, other were holding damaged limbs and more were bleeding from wounds. The immediate reaction was that it seemed only one person had been killed. A mutilated corpse dangled from the hole in the bus. The driver was badly hurt but was alive and being tended by some of those who professed medical knowledge.

As Grimshaw was taking all this in ambulances arrived and paramedics professionally set about their work sorting out the scene.

'A suicide bomber' commented a man standing next to Grimshaw. 'We're bloody lucky.'

Grimshaw nodded agreement, still not able to speak after the shock.

'How many killed?' he eventually asked.

'Only one as far as I can see. Several hurt but only that bugger seems dead' he nodded towards the corpse. 'The bomber himself. That's what I call justice.'

'Difficult to believe it after that explosion,' Grimshaw finally said.

The police had arrived in numbers and were questioning those around. Grimshaw told them he saw nothing but gave his business and homes addresses in case they wanted to talk to him again.

He walked slowly towards his office, all thoughts about his first task out of his head. He doubted whether he would do anything that day.

⋆ ⋆ ⋆

Like every other journalist in London Martin was assigned to cover what had become known as 'the London bomb.' Most were given the task of seeking out those who had escaped the explosion and other witnesses and getting their personal stories. Martin was given the job of making contact with the police and covering their efforts to identify the bomber and find any associates.

The bomb and its implications, that there may be other bombers waiting to strike, put all thoughts of the man in the white sweater out of Martin's mind. What had happened in the recent past faded into insignificance compared to the terrorist's activities.

Newspaper and television coverage continued unabated for the next few days with Martin carrying out his journalistic role of commentating on police activities and their success in identifying the dead bomber and some of his known associates.

It was when he was watching a television review of what had happened that his mind was suddenly dragged back to what had been occupying it before the explosion. The programme reviewed what was known of the bomber's activities before the explosion, where he had been seen and his probable route into London. It showed where he had boarded the bus and then the scene immediately afterwards when the victims were staggering away from the wreckage. Martin watched as a young woman, covered in blood, was help staggering towards a nearby ambulance. As they did so the commentator remarked that it was incredible that no-one, apart from the bomber himself, had been killed by the explosion.

As if on cue, recalling his memory of the mystery of the events of the past few weeks, that Martin suddenly noticed a figure standing by the ambulance. There was no doubt about it. He was incredulous. It was a man, he was tall, he was dark and he was wearing dark trousers and a white polo-neck sweater.

'God Almighty,' Martin shouted to himself. It could not be true. It was impossible. It was too much of a coincidence. This was the fourth occasion that this figure had been connected with a dramatic incident involving human beings. Martin's nerves tingled with anticipation, his mind a confused tangle, as he mentally reviewed the past events and perceived coincidences and tried to decide what to do. It was a very tenuous link and he doubted very much whether the Editor or anyone else would think much of it. But it was a link, a link that could not be denied.

Sitting at his desk in his flat watching the television news to see if the police had made any progress in their search for the bomber's associates, he was convinced. that there was more to it than just coincidence. But if that were true what was it all about?

He'd got an interesting story about an identical figure being seen at four incidents in different parts of the country. If you thought about it sensibly there was probably a man in a grey suit or a woman in a blue dress also at the same scenes. But he knew in his heart that there was more to it.

Having come to that conclusion he had to establish exactly what he could write. He would look a fool if he just wrote a story about four instances when a man in a white sweater was involved in mysterious events But no-one knew who he was and he could not be found. People would laugh their bloody heads off. There must be thousands of white sweaters being worn every day.

And if he could convince anyone that there was a link what could he say that link was?

Was there really such a person as a miracle healer? For a faith healer to be successful he always thought that it was the patient who had to have the faith. These 'patients' didn't even know the man, never mind whatever powers he might have. So what then?

Then he became less convinced. What had he got? A story about a man who jumped from the third floor. A doctor who thought his patient had broken both his legs but later x-rays proved him wrong. Well, that sort of thing had happened before. A terrorist bomb in a London bus which had killed only one person, the bomber himself He'd got a woman in a car crash who should have been killed but wasn't. There were many car accidents, he knew, when people clambered out from smashed up wrecks with only scratches and bruises. A chap in a sweater was probably watching.

So what. The only real evidence of a miracle was at Harwood when someone no-one had even seen before or since, told a small boy his legs were stronger than he thought, and this proved to be true.

Not a soul could actually identify this man, only two small children and a fireman remembered actually seeing him, and there was no incontravertible evidence of a spectacular healing.

The drawback was that this man, if he was one person, had said nothing, claimed nothing and had just vanished.

Or was he just a figment of his own imagination? Should he, in fact, even bother to write a story. He could ignore the fact that he had seen him on television at the London bombing and simply report that he could not be found, nor anyone who had actually seen him in the flesh. He wouldn't have much of a problem with his Editor because no other newspaperman, as far as he knew, had any knowledge of the coincidences.

No sooner had he come to this conclusion than he remembered that he was a professional journalist and he had what could be a major exclusive story or made into one. If the newspaper used it the others would try and follow it up and if they could find anything to support it they would either ignore it or attack the Examiner for giving publicity to charlatans. He would never forgive himself if it turned out to be a major story he had not written. Neither would his Editor.

He decided to write a story as he saw it and leave it to the Editor to decide. He made up his mind that he would throw all caution to the wind. Now, he felt, he was really justified in putting all the 'coincidences' together.

It did not take long for him to produce a story for he had been preparing it in his mind since the Philip Green episode. He had convinced himself that there was more to what had happened recently than immediately became obvious. He was by now absolutely sure that there was a link between the various episodes. There simply had to be.

Developing the story he described how a man wearing a similar garment had been seen at the fire at the Hereford school, the car crash and the terrorist bombing. He avoided the use of the words 'miracle' and 'healing' as being too emotive.

He described all the speculation that the people at these events were making about the man, although he had no reason to believe that there had been any speculation, he had heard none, but he knew there would be once his story appeared.

'This is a bit bloody much,' said Charlie who came on the phone after scanning the story.

'Are you sure about all this. It'll cause a hell of a fuss if we use it as it is.' Charlie was always difficult on a Sunday. He did not like interrupting his weekend even though he had been doing it for years.

'Charlie, I'm absolutely sure. I was at the fire and thanks to you. I was in Harwood. I have met the boy and seen the results. I've seen the photograph of the car accident where you can clearly see him and I saw him on telly at the London bomb. I know it is the same man'

'There's not much detail about him. Who is he?'

'I've no idea. But I know I'm right Charlie. Its an exclusive story, you'll leave the rest of them standing if you use it, believe me.'

'Well I'll see what the old man says,' said Charlie dubiously. 'Stay at home tonight we may want a word with you after he has seen it.'

Martin replaced the receiver . He heaved a sigh of relief as if a load had been lifted from him now that he had put his thoughts in print and told someone what he had been worried about for days. The die was cast - if the paper decided to use the story.

★ ★ ★

Martin awoke early the following morning, leapt out of bed, dressed quickly and went to the local newsagent and bought all the newspapers. He took them home, put on the kettle and made a cup of tea before settling down to read them.

The Editor of the Examiner had obviously been persuaded by Martin's arguments for the story had been used but he was disappointed by the headline which appeared half way down the front page. It read ' Miracle Healing Astounds Medical Profession' and only briefly covered the other events without Martin's speculation about the man in a white sweater.

But Martin had been a newspaper reporter for a long time and was used to such disappointments.

The other newspapers, particularly the tabloids. Banner headlines exploded from front pages. The Daily Sun, using the whole of it's front page, announced to its readers: 'Miracle Worker Restores Crippled Boys Ability to Walk"; while the Morning Mirror's ' Miracle Man Saves Woman from Certain Death' sent a shudder through Martin as he read it. The serious papers were more circumspect in their treatment of the story, the Telegraph Today's 'Crippled Boy Cured' being typical of all of them.

Martin sat back with a feeling of satisfaction. He had got the exclusive story of the four events which he was sure were related, he had written it first and clearly the other papers had read his in the first edition of the Examiner and reproduced, only slightly altered, his story in their second editions. It had happened before.

There was much speculation about who the man could be, they all assumed it was the 'same man' and it was clear that a major effort had been launched by the other papers to find out who he was.

His reflections were interrupted by a telephone call from Charlie: 'You've seen what the other buggers have done with your story.' It wasn't a question 'You better find him before they do and get an exclusive interview. No excuses, find him and talk to him. Let's get to the bottom of this quickly, it's our story.'

'Do I get any help?'

'You've got this far on your own and I can't spare anyone to help you. Prove how good you are.' He rang off. Not a word of thanks for the exclusive.

★ ★ ★

# Part Two

# ADVENT

GRACE GOLDER EASED HERSELF MORE comfortably in her seat. God ! She was tired of sitting, tired of listening to the radio, tired of looking into blank space, even tired of listening to Alice reading to her. She felt tired and fed up about every damn thing But none of this was obvious to anyone around her.

Grace, an orbicular little woman, blind as she had been for fifteen years, she presented a picture of unblemished happiness. Crowned with a mass of closely-packed grey curls which framed her head from ear to ear, her open face always carried a cheerful smile. Her favourite dress was light blue reflecting optimism, which fell just below the knee and was adorned with a small brooch but no belt. She abhorred belts because she believed that all they did was accentuate the amount of body she carried unnecessarily about her middle.

The only indication she allowed of her disability which she described as her 'sight restriction' was the white stick she carried when outside. She did not use this with the hesitant tapping of the insecure blind person but swung it from side to side in a confidant sweeping motion, oncoming people were quick to move aside.

Normally the last person in the world to feel sorry for herself, she was getting increasingly frustrated by the fact that she could not see. But there was nothing she could do except make the best of what as very definitely a bad job. A carelessly laid carpet, a turned up edge and preoccupation with household problems had caused her to trip at the top of the stairs and fall full length to the bottom. Several bones were broken, her skull fractured and she seemed near to death for several weeks. She was convinced, however, that it was far too early to meet her maker so this was avoided by a fighting spirit that over the years had helped her to overcome her blindness. It was the same spirit that carried her through a further major crisis two years after the accident when her husband Harold had died suddenly following a heart attack which left her alone in the world.

Always optimistic, cheerful and lively in the company of others there were times, when she was alone, that the future seemed bleak and pointless. What was life when you couldn't see it, when you missed the changing seasons, could not see your friends, could not pick up a book and read a few pages to while away the time, could not look at and admire the pictures of the great artists? She did not care much for television although she sometimes switched it on to listen to the dialogue and imagine what the picture might be. It usually had nothing to do with what was actually appearing on the screen.

Grace was the first to admit that she owed everything to her friend and companion Alice Pettiman. Alice, a spinster whose great love had been killed in the Second World War, had devoted her life to her ailing mother and, on her death, had transferred her devotion to Grace.

It was Alice who walked into the room and broke Grace's current spell of temporary self pity. They were a perfect couple. Grace, who was always neatly dressed and well groomed had all the appearance of a successful woman. Despite her affliction she was always smiling and treated almost every crisis as a source of amusement. Alice was shorter, had thin brown hair which was 'never right' and a thin sharp face which always looked concerned. She rarely smiled or laughed but this was not an indication of inherent sourness it was a reflection of her constant worry that Grace would be all right and that nothing should upset her. Although she had known her for a number of years she did not understand that it took a catastrophe of monumental proportions to disturb her friend.

'Are you all right dear?' she asked. She had an unfailing ability to sense when Grace was feeling low and having one of her blacker moods.

'Yes, thank you,' Grace replied 'I'm just having one of my 'why did it happen to me' periods. Don't worry, I'll get over it'

Alice smiled and began tidying up the room. It did not need her attention but she always liked to make sure that everything was in its usual place so that Grace could find it and not fall over items of furniture or anything lying around.

'Did you hear the news on the radio?' Grace asked her after a time.

'Yes, I was listening in the kitchen,' said Alice, looking across at Grace, her face full of anxiety.

'That was interesting about the man who helped that little boy.'

'Yes, it was, said Alice warily. 'And I know what you are thinking. Do please be careful dear.'

'What do you mean?'

'Well I know you. I bet you're thinking that if he is a faith healer he may be able to do something for you.'

Grace sighed deeply. 'Yes, you're right. I couldn't help thinking about it for a while. If he can cure a crippled boy he could probably do something for me. But I suppose there is no point.'

'Let's wait and see what happens shall we. Let's see if we hear anything more about him. There may be absolutely nothing to it. You know what those newspaper people are like,' Alice replied, busily dusting the spotlessly clean table. 'Anyway, no-one knows where he is,' she added hopefully.

* * *.

John Porter sat at his surgery desk deep in thought. He was intrigued by what he had just read in the paper about what happened at Harwood. His wrong diagnosis of the caretaker at the school fire still mystified him. He was a good doctor and he knew it. He had never made a wrong diagnosis in the twenty four years since medical college. It was highly unlikely he would do so in such a simple case as a pair of broken legs.

The events of that night were firmly engraved on his memory and he'd been told later that the man Salmons said spoke to him had been wearing, among other things, a white sweater with a roll neck. Now, in the newspapers. was a report of a crippled boy being able to walk and ride a bicycle after being spoken to by a man in a white sweater with a polo neck. It was too much of a coincidence to ignore.

John Porter had never been one to take seriously faith healing, miracle workers or Christian Scientists - anyone who believed that the mind could dominate matter to the extent of repairing physical damage or curing disease.

The human body was like a car and it broke down. Parts of it sometimes failed to function. When a car broke down no amount of faith would make it work, you had to do a repair job - a doctor's job was to repair the human body. You couldn't always repair a car, particularly an old one. You couldn't always repair a body or perhaps find replacement parts for it that were broken beyond repair.

Porter was firm in this belief. Too often he had been called to a patient too late because they had been influenced by some misinformed 'healer' who thought they could do the job.

He was snapped out of his thoughts by a persistent buzz on his telephone.

'Your wife,' his receptionist announced.

'Have you seen the paper?' Candice asked without waiting for him to speak.

'Yes, I suppose you mean that bit about the boy in Harwood?'

'Yes, funny isn't it?'

'Well, interesting.'

'I mean this boy spoke to a man wearing a white sweater. That's how they described the man at the school when your diagnosis went wrong.'

'That's what they said.'

'It's too much of a coincidence isn't it?'

Porter did want to commit himself, not even to his wife.

'It's worth thinking about.'

'Well, if it is the same man that means your original diagnosis was right. You can stop worrying about it.'

'Yes, the trouble is that if you accept that, a whole new avenue of questions opens up.'

'Such as?'

'Who is this man?'

'If it is the same person,' said Candice.

'Two or three occasions could be a coincidence, four is asking a lot.'

'Well, whatever it is, I still say it puts your alleged wrong diagnosis into perspective. It was not wrong,' Candice replied with emphasis.

Porter looked out of the window. 'It is more important than that,' he said thoughtfully.' I need to know whether there is such a man, who he is, why he keeps appearing in different parts of the country and what he is doing. After all, we only know about four incidents because a reporter happened to be at the fire, happened to be told to follow up another story, happened to see a report in a newspaper and happened to see this man on the television. There may be other instances where he's done something similar and no-one has noticed. I have to find out more.'

Candice said nothing for a moment and then, in a resigned way, said: 'I'll see you when you come home,' and put the phone down.

The question facing Porter now was how to find the man, last heard of in London at the time of the terrorist bomb. Who would know where he might be now? The answer came quickly, obviously, the police. He recalled that Jack Hedley, one of his golfing friends was in the traffic division of New Scotland Yard He had a weekend home just outside the town and was a keen member of the golf club.. He would know where the man was because there were bound to be large crowds and large crowds caused traffic chaos.

He rang Hedley using his direct line number.

'Hedley here,' said a sharp voice.

'Porter here,' said the doctor in the same manner.

'Oh John, what the hell do you want. Can't you play on Saturday?'

'Nothing to do with golf,' said Porter, going on to explain the information he needed.

'You're not kidding,' Hedley replied quickly, 'The man is a bloody nuisance whoever he is. Causes chaos everywhere. We've just been discussing it. All I know is that the Cambridge police have asked for help for traffic control at the weekend. Nothing to do with me but it may be a good clue.'

'Thanks a lot,' said a grateful Porter, 'That's all I needed.'

* * *

'It's a load of bloody rubbish. The chaps at the factory were talking about it. Christ, its bloody marvelous what some people will believe.'

Joyce Thomas looked up from her ironing. She was what her friends described as a 'homely woman' with a comfortable figure and a cherubic face in direct contrast to her husband. He was slightly taller and dressed comfortably rather than smartly and had a pasty complexion which gave him a permanent unhealthy look. She loved her husband dearly but there were times, quite often in fact, when she thought it was him who was talking the rubbish and not the multitude of people he accused.

'Oh ! Fred, must you swear so much?'

'It's enough to make any bugger swear,' he replied. 'I don't know. Just because some bloke tells some little sod that he's been buggering about on crutches when he should have been tearing about like a blue-arsed fly, you and a lot of other silly sods start talking about a miracle healing. It makes you want to vomit.'

Fred Thomas sat back in his chair and turned to the sports pages of the newspaper. His grimy hands gripped the pages as though he thought someone was about to snatch it from him. He had not shaved and the thick blue growth on his chin , bushy black eyebrows unkempt black hair made him look even angrier than he was. He was angry because he had read the story in the paper and heard it on the news, and had thought it quite interesting. But the scorn poured on it by the lads at the factory had made him change his mind. He was not happy about it but he didn't want to appear to be a bloody fool.

'Well it is interesting dear,' his wife went on. 'After all, there's no doubt he made the little boy walk.'

'Bloody nonsense if you ask me. It's probably a bloody capitalist scheme for making the workers pay.'

Joyce found the logic of this very hard to follow.

'In what way dear?'

'Well, stands to reason. They'll build this bloke up to be something special and then he'll start saying that it's wrong to go on strike and demand more money because that's only bloody greed and we should all look after our fellowmen. Load of cock.'

Joyce returned to her ironing. Momentarily her mind was wrested from thoughts of the little boy and his legs by the fact that Jimmy's trousers had a split up the back and the school term started soon. It would take more than a miracle for her to get the money to buy a new pair.

She looked back at her husband who was now deeply engrossed in the sports reports. She did wish he would not turn every argument into a war between the bosses and the workers. She had never been really happy since he had joined the Birmingham branch of the Communist Party. They seemed so angry about everything. But he was her husband and as long as he was happy that was all that mattered and she would not interfere.

Trouble was that Communism didn't seem to make him very happy. That's why there were not so many of them left.

It was just as well that she decided not to interfere. While Fred was all for equality among the workers when it came to the domestic scene he quickly reverted to the Victorian idea that a woman's place was in the home doing exactly what her husband, the breadwinner, demanded. He was boss in the home, she was one of the workers, and she had no trade union to help her.

There were times when his lectures on the way workers were being exploited really got her down. She wanted to say that she was one of the exploited workers but had never had the courage. She felt sure that that the 'other side' must be right sometimes but she did not know enough about it to argue.

'Looks like we'll be out again next month,' Fred said enthusiastically.

'Not again?.' she snapped, making a quick calculation about how she was going to manage on the measly strike pay his union usually managed to scrape together,

'No bloody strike pay either,' said Fred.

'Oh! No !,' said Joyce, shocked.

'Well its not us that's striking. Delivery drivers are striking over a wage claim and we're coming out in support. If we didn't they would lay us off anyway. Sure to. We'll have to go on the dole. We've got to show solidarity. Once the buggers think we won't stand together we're beaten.'

As the phrases that Joyce knew so well rolled off his tongue there was a moment when she nearly screamed.

'I don't see how you can say that all that business about the boy is a load of rubbish,' she said, trying to change the subject. 'There seems no doubt that the little boy can walk now when the doctors said he wouldn't be able to.'

'Balls,' said Fred

★ ★ ★

Harry Gregg was a tired man as he walked slowly up the road towards his neat little semi-detached house.

It had been one of those days.

Traffic on his route had been heavier than usual and he had to spend more than an hour sorting it out and getting it moving. Then his patrol car had developed engine trouble when he was as far away from the police garage he could get. Then when he got back to the station the Inspector had admonished him for failing to fill in a load of forms to do with a case he was on. He was enjoying his life as a policeman but could not accept some of the meaningless procedures, such as form filling, which he thought had nothing to do with crime fighting.

He opened the garden gate and meticulously closed it behind him, making absolutely certain that the latch dropped home. If he didn't make sure that the gate was closed all the bloody dogs in the neighbourhood would be in the front garden crapping and piddling over his roses.

He had already got the key in his hand when he reached the front door, opening it with an air of eager anticipation. To Harry one of the joys of arriving home was the smell of his supper cooking. It was a homely smell, it meant that he was back in the haven of his own world. His slippers would be waiting for him by his chair, the evening paper would be neatly folded and waiting on the side table with a bottle of Guiness and a glass alongside.. After a drink and a glance through the paper his meal would be ready and then he could settle down and watch the telly. His wife would sit opposite sewing or knitting and occasionally she would look across towards him to make sure all was well. That, to Harry, was what living was all about.

It did not take him long to realize that something was wrong. The evening paper was still stuffed in the letter box, there was no smell of cooking. He walked into the kitchen and saw that the oven wasn't even on and the table wasn't laid. There were none of the usual signs of a meal being prepared. In the living room his slippers were missing and so were the bottle and the glass. It was painfully obvious that Mabel was out.

What the hell was going on, he asked himself angrily. He did not like his routine being altered and it was not known for Mabel to be out when he got home.

Disappointed and annoyed Harry took off his jacket and hung it carefully over the back of his chair. He went into the pantry and got out his Guiness, took a glass from the shelf and was just about to return to the living room when he saw something that made his stomach writhe. The dirty dishes from breakfast, the plates, egg cups, spoons, knives, cups and saucers, were still lying in the sink untouched.

Harry was a man of routine. A military background, recognizable by his 6' ram-rod straight frame, had taught him that a disciplined routine was essential to a successful life. Rise at 0530hrs, breakfast 0600hrs, leave home 0645hrs, arrive work 0730hrs, carry out instructions, leave 1730hrs, home 1815hrs, relaxing drink 1900hrs, supper 2000hrs bed by 2300hrs. This plan had to be shuffled sometimes when he was on a different shift but that was the standard. Now it had all fallen apart.

A feeling of apprehension swept over him. In eight years of marriage he had never known Mabel to leave the washing up. She must be ill.

Hurriedly he put down the bottle and glass and, taking them two at a time, ran upstairs expecting to find his wife lying prostrate on the bed. But when he reached the bedroom there was still no sign of her and the bed was unmade, just as he had left it in the morning with his pyjamas lying untidily across his pillow.

The feeling of urgent concern that had replaced the original anger now gave way to frustration. What had happened? Where was Mabel for God's sake?

Had she been taken to hospital? The idea made his heart miss a beat. Now he became frightened. But surely someone would have phoned the station and told them. They would have sent for him. It had happened before when one of his mate's wife fell ill.

Harry stood on the landing lonely and concerned wondering what to do next. Criminals in the town would have been fascinated to see the man they thought as a tough copper standing there like a lost boy.

Then he had an idea. If anyone knew what had happened it would be Doris Pocock next door. She knew everything about everyone in the road, a devout curtain twitcher with a fertile imagination and a ready tongue. Much as he hated asking her she would be the one to know.

Worriedly Harry ran back downstairs and into the living room to get his coat. He was just putting it on when he heard a noise at the back door. He rushed into the kitchen and saw his wife unconcernedly walking in. A big woman with a middle age spread that went in every direction. She was dressed for visiting in her best clothes. She was in a smart Marks and Spencer dress with a high collar. She wore sensible shoes and a hat shaped like a turban. Harry noticed, she was wearing a hat. He had always thought it odd that even in these days of hatless women Mabel felt it was an essential part of dress when out visiting.

'Where the hell have you been?' he asked angrily without thinking.

'Oh dear ! Are you home already?' Mabel replied nervously.

'Of course I'm bloody home. It's gone six. I was worried to death. Where've you been?' Harry's anger was rising again now that he knew his wife was unhurt

'I'm sorry dear,' said Mabel, putting the kettle on and hurriedly lighting the grill. She had not even stopped to take off her coat. 'Go and sit down and have your drink. The meal won't be long I'm sorry I'm late but I've been talking.

You've what !'

'I've been next door talking to Doris.'

'All bloody day!

'No, silly, I went shopping early and I met Mrs Gilbert and we had a cup of coffee. Then Doris invited me to lunch and then we went out again. I don't know where the day has gone.'

'Bloody hell,' Harry fulminated.' I've been working all bloody day and I come home and there's no bloody meal waiting, the kitchen is filthy, the bed isn't made and you've been out...talking.'

'There's no need to swear so much. Go and sit down, the meal will be ready in a jiffy.'

Harry was not going to be pacified so easily.

'I don't want a bloody drink. I want my meal. I'm hungry. I've been working all day and I'm tired. It's bloody incredible that I have to go out to work all day and then come home and do everything myself.'

'What exactly did you do yourself?' Mabel asked.

Harry looked round angrily. 'I got my own drink and I .......was worried to death. I thought you were ill. What the hell have you been talking about all day, Mrs Gilbert's piles?'

'No dear. The man.'

'What bloody man?' said Harry, feeling pleased that he had something else to shout about.

'You know dear, the man who made that little boy walk. We heard that he was supposed to be talking to people on the Meadows so we went down there to see what he was like. But there was no-one there. It must have been a rumour.'

'Lot of bloody twaddle if you ask me. What about my meal?'

'I didn't ask you and it won't be long. And I don't think it can be twaddle because the little boy couldn't walk at all without crutches and now he is able to walk, play and ride his bicycle. It is a miracle.'

'Who do you think this bloke is? Jesus f...... Christ?' shouted an exasperated Harry

* * *

Ruth Morton was not a woman who scanned the newspapers on a daily basis or who watched television avidly so she was unaware of the publicity the man was getting. But she could not get him out of her mind. She had known many men in her time and had experienced various reactions but never had there been one like him.

When he looked at her through the car window it was a calm, steady gaze that gave her the feeling that he knew her innermost thoughts, that all was well and there was no cause for concern.

She was a sporadic church goer but recently her enthusiasm, such as it was, had waned. Stories of what was happening in the world, the storms, the famines and civil wars that killed millions of people and, more importantly, the sufferings of children at the hands of their parents and others filled her mind. So where was He when all this was happening? God loves us all and is protecting us, the vicar intoned regularly at church services. These phrases, like many others, meaningless, she thought, God could be very choosy. But on what did he base his decisions?

Occasionally, very occasionally there was a sermon that made you think. She wanted to believe in God, in fact there were many times when she felt close, in sadness or joy, when she prayed asking for help in times of trouble or thanks in times of happiness.

She did not have a difficult life. After the divorce she had returned to teaching . She lived comfortably with her mother and Amanda. She had no great worries but felt her life had no real purpose. Teaching young children was all very well but she needed more.

She had thought many times of seeking another religion, one more relevant to what she was thinking, one with a bit of life about it, one that enthused members on a regular basis. She had always envied people like the West Indians whenever she saw them at worship on television They always looked happy and smiling, singing with great unashamed gusto and thoroughly enjoying their worship.

She did not for one moment believe that the man who had looked at her in the car was some great spiritual leader but there was something about him which made her feel she could talk to him. It might be enough if she could just look at him again and listen to what he was saying.

* * *

Tears rolled down the cheeks of Miriam Cartwright as she busily prepared lunch. She was not peeling onions, she was trying to get over the latest row with her husband.

Writing that story about Philip Green for the Citizen was turning out to be the worst thing she had ever done in her life.

Dr Blackburn, who saw himself as the leader of the community as he knew almost everyone thanks to his profession, had been incensed and had let his feelings be known in very certain terms to the Reverend Charles Cartwright who, Blackburn alleged, was responsible for his wife's behaviour. The story would cause nothing but trouble, the media would make fools of them and the village would attract hordes of inquisitive visitors. To the Reverend Charles, a mild-mannered man, unconsciously subscribed to Dr Blackburn's view that he was a very important member of the community.

To her horror Charles had taken Blackburn's side and had forbidden her to write any more articles for any newspapers on any subject.

To make matters worse Dr Blackburn's fears had been fully realized.

Martin Armstrong had proved to be the first of a horde of newspapers reporters who descended on the village during the day. They had spent their time questioning everyone they could find, boosting the sales of the Happy Ploughman and making an appalling nuisance of themselves with their constant search for information. As predicted Harwood was fast becoming a popular tourist site.

'I cannot understand what got into you,' her husband had admonished her. 'How could you possibly believe that a perfect stranger could do for Philip what many doctors and specialists have failed to do. Think of my position. You've made me look a complete fool. We will have to leave the village.'

Miriam was shocked. 'But I was only reporting what had happened. I don't see how it affects you and don't see why we have to leave the village,' she sobbed.

'It didn't happen and that's the truth. Someone is lying. Think of the effect on Philip. Dr Blackburn says that when the hypnosis or the drug he was given wears off the psychological effect will be devastating and the boy may never walk again, even with crutches. You've probably helped to destroy his life,' said Cartwright as he stormed out of the house.

Utterly distraught, she sat at the table for over an hour before she felt she could get on with her work.

This morning's outburst had followed the Reverend's decision that it would be better if she did not attend the Women's Institute's meeting that afternoon.

'Better you stay at home and ask God to forgive you,' he had told her.

What was there to forgive, a bewildered Miriam asked herself. Philip had been walking and playing happily for several days now. There was absolutely nothing wrong with him. Whatever had happened that day Philip Green was cured. There was no doubt about it.

She saw her husband walk past the house towards the church. 'God forgive you,' she said out loud, and with heavy emphasis on the pronoun, to the departing figure.

⋆ ⋆ ⋆

There was very little about Edward Forbes MP for Sussex North that was genuine. Even his appearance owed much to the skilful use of technology and chemicals. His black wavy hair would have been heavily streaked with grey, as would his thick black well manicured moustache, if nature had been allowed to take its course.

His piercing light blue eyes would have been slightly less blue and much less piercing with the contact lenses removed. His tight stomach which gave him a neat slim, athletic appearance would have indicated the early stages of pregnancy if it was not for a well constructed corset belt he wore each day. His height was enhanced by hand-made built up shoes cleverly constructed to hide the fact that he was lacking in stature.

Politically he leaned to the right. But this was only for expediency's sake. When, at the age of 25, he decided that a political life was less demanding than a proper job he had studied the constituencies which were strategically placed between his Sussex home and the West End of London. Then he considered which of the chosen constituencies were likely to need a new member in the foreseeable future. The Members of two of them, both Conservative, had already announced their impending retirement. Edward Forbes, BSc (Econ) from the London School of Economics, therefore decided to become a Conservative. He targeted Sussex North with its Conservative majority of 11,000 as his future seat.

Enriched by a substantial legacy from his coal merchant grandfather which had been fortified by a substantial sum when his father, a financial consultant expired, he bought a small property in the constituency and joined the local branch of the party.

Edward Forbes was not one of the world's great doers, neither was he particularly knowledgeable or experienced. But he had three valuable advantages - he had money, he could speak well without disclosing the fact that he had no real grasp of what he was talking about, and women fancied him. To complete the package and make life a lot more pleasant for him, he fancied women.

Supported by this doubtful armory he quickly made progress through the party hierarchy. When the time came a substantial donation to party funds, a carefully thought out speech in which he managed not to commit himself to anything, and with the support of the women's branch, several members of which would been embarrassed to admit exactly how well they knew him, gained him the position of prospective candidate. A year later, despite the fact that the Labour Party won a narrow three seat victory, he won his seat with a majority of just over 6,000.From then on he had it made. He had a regular income to lessen the drain on his still substantial capital, he didn't have to do anything except vote in the right lobby on the instructions of the Party Whips and probably serve on a select committee on a subject in which he had absolutely no interest. His maiden speech made little impression on either his colleagues or the opposition members so he was in absolutely no danger of promotion to a position of responsibility. He settled down as an anonymous back bencher but with the social kudos of being a Member of Parliament.

While his political activities were kept to a minimum his amorous activities were maintained at boom levels. He had, he was sure, screwed most of the fanciable females in both his own and neighbouring constituencies and was currently running three mistresses - one in Kent, one in Middlesex and a third in the Royal Borough of Berkshire. Distance not only made the heart grow fonder, it was a damn sight safer.

Edward Forbes had little stamina for long term affairs. Variety, he averred, was the spice of life and although she did not yet know it the young lady of Kent, a lissom blonde of 22 years called Pauline Knox was about to be dropped. She had translucent dark brown eyes magnified by huge gold rimmed glasses and a magnificent pair of perfectly formed breasts. It was this feature that had first attracted Forbes, her ability in bed was the second, nevertheless her replacement was already well established in Forbes' mind.

As a reward for past services he had invited her to spend the weekend with him at a discrete little inn near Cambridge where they were unlikely to be spotted. His plan was to spend the weekend with Pauline doing what he did best and then break it to her that for career reasons - a promotion to a position in the Government - he could not see her any more. The fact that the story was not true, and was unlikely ever to be so, gave him no cause for concern.

The inn he had chosen was of no great architectural interest, it lacked charming olde worlde bars so it did not attract a wide clientele. It had only four small double bedrooms so the odds on them being booked by anyone he knew were long enough to be acceptable.

Forbes picked Pauline up late on Friday afternoon at the Elephant and

Castle tube station.

He thought it was unlikely anyone around there would recognize him. He was not aware of the fact that it was very unlikely that anyone he met in the corridors of the Palace of Westminster would recognize him either.

They drove to Cambridge with constant assurances of undying love and his left hand up her skirt. He had long perfected the art of motorway driving with one hand. This entailed driving at a steady 65 mph so that the attention of the police was not attracted and in the inside lane so that one did not have to constantly take part in lane manoeuvres. Pauline was not averse to this mode of travel for she spent most of her time with her legs cooperatively apart.

After dinner Forbes ordered champagne to be sent up to their room and went upstairs with Pauline to await its arrival. In Forbes' view Pauline was one of the most athletic sexual partners he had ever had. What she could do with her body was a source of constant amazement and he was quite sure that if necessary she could do it hanging from the proverbial chandelier. First, of course, you had to find a sufficiently substantial chandelier and then you had to work out how to do it.

Forbes' great delight, after an hour or so of foreplay was oral sex almost to the point of climax and then a final threshing around in what the Kama Sutra describes as 'the congress of a cow.' Pauline threw herself into the exercises with so much enthusiasm and energy that Forbes almost regretted his decision to bring their association to an end but he rather fancied the new girl and really could not keep four of them on the go. Pauline, he felt, would accept his decision to end the affair more philosophically than the others.

The following morning, after another thrashing session and a late breakfast, Forbes went down to the bar to get some cigarettes. He was both surprised and alarmed by the number of people already drinking. It seemed an unusual number even on a warm summer morning. He had to wait ten minutes before the harassed barman came over to serve him.

'Big crowd here today,' he commented as he put his money on the counter.

'Too many and I'm the only one on duty,' the barman grumbled.

'Any reason for this or is it usual?'

'It certainly isn't usual. It's these bloody rumours.'

'What rumours?'

'This bloke who is supposed to have cured a crippled boy up near Norwich. They say he's coming here this weekend.'

'This weekend ! When? Where?'

'I've no idea, its only a rumour anyway,' said the barman as he moved away to the next customer.

Forbes stood at the bar thinking quickly. He had vaguely heard about the boy but had not paid much attention. Slowly it dawned on him that if it was true that this chap was coming and the crowd in the bar was any indication of the interest created it meant that masses of people from all over the place would be here. There was sure to be someone who would recognize him. God Almighty! It would also mean masses of pressmen crawling around looking for a story. Well, it wasn't going to be him.

Forbes rushed out of the bar, instructed a surprised receptionist to get his account ready, and ran upstairs to Pauline.

'Get dressed, pack quickly, we're going. Don't ask any questions, just do it.'

⋆ ⋆ ⋆

Martin was now following yet another rumour, that the man would be in Cambridge the following day, Sunday.

Martin had always been intrigued how rumours started. It only needed one person to hear something which could be of interest to someone else. Most people like to feel important and if they haven't done anything important to give them social status, then knowledge was their only passport to minor prominence. The information is usually introduced with the much abused phrase 'don't tell anyone else but...' imparting that importance to someone else. Lesser information could be passed on with ' you know I'm not one to gossip but I hear that....'

Human beings, being who they are, humans, it would be impossible, Martin thought, for at least one member of the man's group of followers, not tell someone, confidentially, what was planned.

On the other hand it was not unknown for an experienced journalists to tell someone associated with the man's group that they had heard where the man was going next. It was almost certain that the person being spoken to would point out that the journalist had got it wrong. 'I hear from a reliable source that the man is going to Oxford this weekend' the reporter would say. His informant, sworn to secrecy. would most likely smile knowingly and say 'I think you've got the wrong university city.' As there are really only two places naturally associated with universities the rest is easy. People with knowledge cannot help advertising the fact.

According to the rumour Martin had picked up from someone who said they were friends with Dr Porter, the man was spending the weekend, staying with friends. Martin did not hold out much hope that the story was true but he liked Cambridge, enjoyed staying at one of the local inns, and decided to spend the weekend there himself.

As he drove into the picturesque town he was surprised by the number of people around. It was a warm summer day and he thought the University was down but there were certainly many more people than he would have expected. The river was probably proving to be a welcome cool spot after shopping and sightseeing on a hot day.

But as he drove towards the town he knew that it was more than a holiday crowd. The people were more like animated football supporters leaving a stadium after a convincing win by the home team, except that the local Cambridge eleven would have been lucky to attract more than the proverbial man and his dog. It was in one of the lower leagues and it wasn't the football season anyway

The day had dawned with a clear blue sky and a temperature that rose steadily as the morning progressed. To Martin the weather was the only cheerful thing about the last few days. Rumour about the mystery man had been rampant. He was reputed to have been seen in Leominster, in Worcester, South Wales then Norwich and then he had gone west, north, east and south. Martin had chased around most of south-eastern England in search of him but without success.

The story about little Philip Green was still a live one and reporters from most of the national newspapers, and some of the local ones, still had Harwood under siege as they waited expectantly for the boy's condition to deteriorate. It hadn't yet.

Martin, for reasons he could not explain, was convinced that the little boy was permanently cured and that the main story lay elsewhere. He would never have described himself as a religious person and he had little time for organized religion. As a small boy he had been forced to Sunday School every week with an occasional visit to church in the evening. He enjoyed the hymn singing mainly because he was in love with one of the women in the choir who was at least three times his age. He admitted that this was only because she was the only female member of the choir who used make-up and thus stood out from the others.

As he had grown older and observed the way so-called Christians acted towards and spoke about each other he realized it was not for him. He quickly came to the conclusion that the best, true Christians were to be found outside the organized church. He thought he believed in God. When he was in trouble he certainly did. When all was well he rarely gave him a thought.

He found it difficult to believe the statement that 'God is everywhere.' The fact that almost everyday there was a horrible event, to an individual or a community that didn't deserve it, seemed ample proof that he wasn't. He wondered why no-one within the church ever seemed to question this. 'Oh, it's God's way' never seemed to him to be a satisfactory or acceptable answer.

He had never seen God, bearded or otherwise, as a person to whom he would confess himself to be 'a miserable sinner' He strongly objected to the phrase. He wasn't a sinner, he was a human being open to temptation and fallible. He saw God as someone within his consciousness, an imaginative friend with whom he could talk. He himself knew when he was doing something wrong and he knew there would be some sort of punishment and that he had brought it upon himself. He understood that the ups and down of life were life itself and you had to learn to handle it

* * *

Martin was lucky to park his car in a city noted for its narrow streets, taking a space which was being vacated as he arrived. He got out and walked in the direction of one of the town's most popular areas, known strangely as Jesus Green.

Despite the problems on his mind he could not help but appreciate the beauty of the area through which he was walking He had, as usual, done his homework and studied a map.. He made his way along Victoria Avenue and the River Cam opposite Jesus College. The Green itself, just north of the City centre, is divided by avenues of London Plane and Horse Chestnut trees. It had been there for hundreds of years and in 1133 was the site of a nunnery. He had read that Jesus College itself was established in the 11th century and there was a distinct historic feeling about it.

The Green boasted a toilet block with 'facilities for the disabled' and a refreshment kiosk and it was the large, animated crowd that surrounded both that surprised him. There was a strange mood about the place, something different, very different.

Martin stopped a young couple walking away deep in conversation.

'Excuse me, could you tell me what is going on? There seems to be an awful lot of people around.'

'It's incredible,' replied the young man. 'There was a woman here who was blind when she arrived and can now see after talking to some bloke who walked past her, absolutely incredible' he added as they walked away.

Martin's stomach once again did its athletic summersault.. Surely he hadn't missed him again? The sudden awareness that the man was here and had seemingly performed another of his 'miracles' was shattering news. Not only had he apparently missed seeing the man in action at last, satisfied his curiosity and confirmed his theory that this man was responsible for a number of strange events, but his news editor would kill him and then sack him, for not getting the story. He hurried further into the gardens hoping to God that he would find someone or something that would help him save the situation.

He quickly looked around at the groups of people busily discussing what had happened. It was like a scene from a Buckingham Palace garden party, the women in colourful print dresses, the men nattily dressed, mainly in lounge suits and tie..

But over on one side, near a wall, a bigger group was gathered around a small white haired woman who seemed to be explaining something to her audience. Martin walked up to the group and unceremoniously pushed his way to the front. It was no time for polite excuse me's.

'There is no other word for it,' the white haired woman was saying to those around her who were listening intently. 'It was a miracle, it just happened.' Those around her began asking questions but Martin quickly interrupted. He just had to get some facts and get them fast.

'I'm sorry,' Martin said urgently. 'I wasn't here and I didn't hear what you said. Could you explain what actually happened?' The assembled audience murmured their approval. They had heard it before but they desperately wanted to hear it again.

'Well young man,' she said smiling, displaying a row of level white teeth, 'what happened was that I was blind. I couldn't see a thing, but I can now see you. And it is not an unpleasant sight,'

'Thank you,' said the abashed Martin,' but what exactly happened?'

'I came here with my friend Alice,' she turned and looked at her smiling companion, 'who has not got as many grey hairs as I imagined and she is far more beautiful. We had heard a rumour that the man who made that little boy walk at Harwood was coming here today. I have been blind for fifteen years after an accident at home. I wanted to come and hear what he said and, if possible, to talk to him. It never occurred to me that this would happen' she said, forgiving herself a little white lie. 'I was standing listening to all the noise when Alice told me he had arrived and said it looked as though he was going to walk past us. She had just said 'here he is now' when I suddenly felt queer. Not ill or sick or anything like that, just very strange. And there he was, looking at me. And I was looking at him. I was staring into his dark brown eyes and brown smiling face. He was just' she paused dramatically, 'there. He didn't say anything. He just smiled at me. At first I dare not look away in case he was all I could see. But then I noticed all the people around me. Some were crying but others were just staring open-mouthed.'

'It was very strange,' her friend interrupted. 'Grace didn't say anything. She didn't shout 'I can see' or anything but we knew, just by looking at her face, what had happened. It was absolutely fantastic. A miracle...there is no other word for it.'

'There certainly isn't,' said Grace. 'I never thought.......'the tears were welling up in her newly sighted eyes. The emotion of the occasion overwhelmed her. Alice put a protective arm around her and with the help of some bystanders, began to move her away.

'I'll take her for a cup of tea,' she explained. 'It has all been too much.'

'What happened to the man?' Martin asked anxiously.

'He went,' Alice replied. 'He didn't say anything to Grace. He just walked away. That way,' she nodded in the direction from which Martin had come. How could he have missed him , he thought angrily.

He looked back anxiously but they was no-one in view who could possibly correspond to the image of the man he had in his mind.

'You don't know where he went I suppose,' he asked hopefully.

'No luv, 'Alice replied. 'But he might know,' she added nodding again in the direction of a tall, hawk-like man. 'He was with him.'

'Just one more question. What was the man wearing?'

Alice thought for a moment. 'Dark brown trousers and sandals and a jumper, a white one, like a fisherman's.'

⋆ ⋆ ⋆

Martin looked around in desperation. He just had to find the bloody man. The use of the expletive in his mind made him feel slightly guilty.

The next shock came when he saw someone he thought recognized, it took a moment or two to place the man. It was Dr Porter, the doctor who had misdiagnosed the caretaker's broken legs at the Hereford fire.

'Dr Porter?' he asked with surprise in his voice.

The man turned: 'Yes, do I know you?' he asked, smiling.

'I was at the school fire in Hereford when the caretaker was hurt jumping out of the window,' said Martin, not wishing to make a point about the leg diagnosis. 'I'm told you might know where he is going. Who is he?'

'Well, he calls himself an emissary with a special mission to remind, inform and explain,' the doctor explained mysteriously

'What about the so-called miracles?'

'He does not claim responsibility for those, in fact, he will not comment.'

''I'd like to meet him and possibly interview him,' Martin said hopefully.

'Not a chance of that I'm afraid. He has no wish to talk to the media he has made that quite clear.'

'How do you know that?'

'He has already turned down several requests since I joined him.'

'Who from?'

'Your journalist colleagues, they've already tried it.' His comment hit Martin like a slap in the face. The buggers had already talked to him, or at least, tried to.

'Join him, when did you join him?' Martin asked trying to pretend he had not heard that other journalists had been trying to talk to him.'

'A few days ago'

'How did you find him? I've been looking for him for weeks.'

'I was lucky, I heard a rumour about where he was.'

'Where is he now?'

'He's gone.' said the doctor with finality

'Why won't he talk to the press. I would have thought it would be a good way to get any message he's got well known.'

'He doesn't trust you. Not you personally, your profession in general He does not want words put into his mouth and he has no confidence that any of you could accurately report what he was saying. He will only talk to ordinary people in small groups.'

'He's not going to get his message very far if he only talks to small groups,' Martin suggested.

'You will be surprised how fast and how wide word of mouth can travel.' He is very much aware of the British press axiom 'never let the facts spoil a good story'

Martin smiled: 'depends what sort of journalist you're talking to.'

'And he knows, and I know, that a reporter is not necessarily responsible for everything that appears in print. Editors and sub-editors have minds and imaginations of their own. They know what story they want to appear, whether it is true or not, and most journalists do as they are told.'

'That's not true of all newspapers,' Martin declared.

'It is too big a risk for him to take. He wants people to learn the truth from him.'

'Can I ask you where he is going next? Asked Martin hopefully.

'I am sure you will hear,' turning away to signify that was all he was saying. He set off in the direction of the town.

Martin watched him depart. He felt he was losing control of the story, if he ever had it. All the newspapers were now working on it and could not help but agree with Porter that some of his colleagues, or competitors, would use their imaginations if they could not get the facts. Best find them and find out what they were thinking and saying.

* * *

The problem facing Martin was to work out where his journalistic colleagues might be. He was pretty sure that would be together so that they could keep eye on each other to avoid one of them pulling a fast one over the others. There was always a pub they all used to swap stories, try to find out what each other knew, and give misleading clues to competitors.

It wasn't a very difficult problem to solve. He only knew two pubs in Cambridge, the 16$^{th}$ century Eagle which was popular with American servicemen during World War II, just north of the city, and Fort of St George, another 16$^{th}$ century establishment with an interesting history. The Fort was the obvious answer because it stood in Midsummer Common, a stone's throw from Jesus Common and therefore the shortest walk.

'Just in time to buy a round,' was friend Frank Faulkner, of The Daily Times, greeting as he walked in. Martin looked around and recognized a half dozen other journalists round the table.

'I see the vultures have gathered,' he replied, passing his Barclaycard to the barman. ' a drink for each of them,' he told him,' but only one.'

'So what do you know?' asked Faulkner.

'Nothing more than you do,' Martin replied.

'Come off it,' said Faulkner derisively, ' you started all this with your four coincidences story, and I just saw you talking to Porter.

'The four coincidences was simply alert journalism and meeting Porter was a complete surprise, I didn't even know he had joined the man.'

'He's more than joined him,' said Faulkner, 'he's now acting as his spokesman as the Man himself won't talk to us.'

'I don't blame him,' said Martin, 'not with him around, he added nodding towards Tony Graham of the Daily Sun. 'He makes it up as he goes along. I bet he's already written his story so it doesn't matter what actually happens.'

'Come off it,' Graham laughed, 'you can't be serious about this chap. All we've got is a bloke who walked away when a doctor said his legs were broken, a woman escaped unhurt from a car crash, as lots of people do, a boy who walked when everyone thought he was crippled and a man who was unhurt in a terrorist bomb attack which only actually killed the bomber himself. There are dozens of such escapes every day and we don't call them miracles.'

'But your paper does,' Faulkner pointed out, referring to that day's headline

'That was just a crowd pulling headline, the story never mentioned a miracle,' said Graham. 'You're all taking it too seriously.'

'What do you think?' Faulkner asked Martin. Faulkner was one the most senior reporters in the newspaper world and was highly respected. He was a good friend of Martin's who admired him because of his serious attitude to his profession, his accuracy and his factual and balanced reporting. Faulkner on the other hand, realized that Martin was as serious about his work as he was and tried to be just as accurate. Both men went to great lengths to check the accuracy of their facts unlike most of the reporters in their group who would use whatever information they could get without checking. It was all, they explained, in the interests of speed. Graham, for example, was noted for thinking of the headline first and then making his story fit it

'It's just an interesting story of coincidences at the moment.' Faulkner replied, 'probably all of them will eventually have acceptable explanations. But you cannot overlook this latest incident. The woman was certainly blind, had been for years according to her friends. Now she can certainly see, since she met the man. One minute she was as blind as a bat then, without him saying a word, she can suddenly see his face and then everything else. All she said to her friend was 'I can see' there were no great histrionics. For her it just happened. Now explain that.'

'It's all very well to say that such events have and do occur without anyone saying anything. Since the story first broke we've had reports of 'miracles' from all over the country. We all know that most of them are hoaxes but you can never be sure,' said Martin, anxious to protect the veracity of his story.

'Well we can't check the bloody lot of them,' said Grant. 'We're stuck with what we've got.' The others nodded thoughtfully they we all totally mystified. There was nothing more to say.

★ ★ ★

Faulkner signalled to Martin to join him in a corner of the room.

'What do you really think?' he asked seriously.

Martin put on his thoughtful expression, looking into the distance as if seeking guidance,

'There's too much evidence. I don't know who the hell he is but this afternoon's events cannot be ignored. The woman is intelligent and certainly not an attention seeker. I really believe that she was blind. Her friend Alice has looked after her for years and has nothing to gain from lying. Everyone here who knows them agrees. The crippled boy could also be genuine and I actually saw the caretaker break both his legs. I know he was in terrible pain after he had jumped and he couldn't have put that on. The woman in the car crash and Grimshaw are different except that they did not know each other yet they gave the same description of the man they think helped them. 'I think we've got to accept the fact that we've got a story, a very important story and we'll have to go carefully with it, not like Grant and his mates,' Martin added , putting his thoughts into words for the first time.

'Couldn't agree with you more,' Faulkner replied.

★ ★ ★

'Give me the bloody paper Joyce.'

'Wait a minute. I'm reading.'

Fred Thomas scratched his stomach angrily. The bloody woman knew he liked reading the morning paper over breakfast. She was well aware that he didn't like anyone else looking at it first and getting it all creased up and out of order. Women had no bloody idea how to read a newspaper. He picked up a spoon and stirred his almost black tea irritably. What the hell was the matter with her, she never looked at a newspaper normally.

'Oh come on, give me the bloody newspaper,' Harry moaned like a frustrated child. 'You know I like to have it with my breakfast.'

'Just a minute. I'm reading.'

'You can read it later, you've got all bloody day and I've got to go to work.'

'Aren't you on strike or something?'

'Don't be bloody silly, that was last week and you know damn well we were only out for a day.'

'Well I can't tell the difference,' Joyce replied impatiently

Although talking Joyce did not take her eyes off the paper and this annoyed her husband even more. She was not even noticing that he was refusing to eat his breakfast until he got his newspaper.

'Oh, for Christ's sake come on,' he shouted, almost beside himself with frustration.

'Honestly, you're like a child. Can't you wait just a few minutes. I'm reading about this chap who's been performing miracles. Now he's made a woman see and she's been blind for fifteen years. He sounds lovely.'

'What bloke?'

'It's in the paper.'

'I haven't read the bloody paper,' Fred shouted again impatiently.

'Well you remember, he made that little boy walk. Before that he rescued a man who nearly died when he jumped out of a window, then he saved a woman in a car accident, then the little boy, now the woman.'

'What's 'is name Errol Flynn?

'Don't be so silly Fred. It doesn't say his name, but I wouldn't mind him looking at my arthritis.'

'Give me the paper and let me read it. Sounds just like the sort of bloke West Ham need next season. Maybe they'd win a bloody match.'

Joyce looked across the table at him with a gesture of hopelessness. She pushed the paper over.

'Do you good to read about something other than football. It's not the only thing in the world you know.'

'No, there's beer, fags and birds,' Fred replied, smiling with the smugness of a child that has at last got its own way.

He glanced at the story on the front page and sneered: 'He's another of these bloody do gooders. The only people they ever do good to is themselves. Come to God they say and hold out their hand for the divi.'

'It's nothing like that. He doesn't do anything of the sort. He doesn't say anything he just.....well, its just what he's done for other people.'

'Who do they say he is?'

'They don't.'

'Well then,' Fred said conclusively.

Joyce moved out of the kitchen and went upstairs to make the bed leaving Fred to get on with his breakfast. He turned to the sports pages and started looking through them quickly.

He was anxious to get to work early that morning. he wanted a quick word with Sharon before she disappeared onto the upholstery line to start work. Sharon was one of the few girls in the plant he hadn't screwed and he intended to put that right as soon as possible. She had only been in the factory for about three weeks and had grabbed the attention of all the men immediately on arrival. In her early twenties, a short, bleached blonde with big tits, tight little bottom and usually short skirted, she was one of those girls the blokes described as 'asking for it.' Well, if anyone was going to give it to her it was Fred himself.

He finished his breakfast, folded the newspaper, stood up and nearly fell as the room suddenly swirled around him. He held on to his chair and shook his head. He felt sick. He sat down again. Slowly the room slowed down and the feeling of nausea went away. He stood up again and went for his coat. Must've got up too quickly he thought.

* * *

Fred Salmons had never understood what the fuss was all about. As far as he was concerned he had got his family out of the burning school, as any husband and father would have done, and gone back to get the dog. He did not know that in a burst of inconsiderate selfishness Spot had got himself out at the first smell of smoke. He was not one to hang around.

Salmons had found himself in a smoke filled room with flames bursting through the doorway. The only other exit was the window. It did not occur to him that he was on the third floor, it was a matter of leaping out of the window or death by burning and as far as he was concerned there was no choice. He jumped but he was unable to judge where the ground was so he was unable to prepare himself. He knew he had hurt his legs when he landed, it was a long drop, and was quite prepared to accept that his legs were broken when the doctor told him. They did hurt a lot.

Then this chap came along and said he was very brave to rescue his family as he did. If he stood up he would find that although they would feel sore his legs would not hurt and he would be able to walk. The man seemed very reasonable and kind, and as his legs did not hurt as much as he thought, he took off the bandages that were holding his legs together while everyone was looking at the fire and then stood up. Then there was all this fuss with the doctor making him go to hospital, Doris being unnecessarily upset and then the x-ray people saying his legs were all right. He could have told them that in the first place.

In the following days Fred became fed up and bored with people talking about his legs. In the council offices when he went to see what was going to happen at the school he was an object of great interest, at home when visitors called they sat and looked at his legs ignoring what he was saying while in the pub with the boys every night he had to put up with torrent of poor jokes on such things as how he was going to get his leg over.. Everyone wanted to know about his bloody legs.

All he really wanted was the peace and quiet of home, when the children had gone to bed, to be alone with Doris to whom he had been married for 15 years, and his beloved stamp collection. Although he could not spell it, he always described himself as a philatelist although it was not strictly true as he was not interested in the value or history of the stamps for he could not afford those worth anything. What pre-occupied him was the number of countries his collection represented. He knew from a self-professed expert that there were 193 countries in the world, 61 of them having colonies, and therefore separate stamps, which meant his target was 251. Although he had well over 4,000 stamps it represented only 202 countries. He would buy cheap packets containing a hundred or more used stamps and spend hours searching through them for a new country. It was an occupation that made him very happy. He wanted nothing more.

He had been sitting quietly at home watching television but when two friends of Doris came visiting and started talking about his legs again. He had had enough so he apologized and made a quick escape to the Parson's Arms. It was no better there.

'Hello Fred boy, still walking around are we?' was the greeting he got from Jack Broad.

'Stuff it mate,' replied Fred politely.

'Miracle man are we?' asked Dave Thomas.

'Pack it in lads, I've had enough of all this bloody leg talk. They are both all right and they always have been,' said Fred gruffly.

'Not according to the papers,' said Jack.

'What the hell are you talking about?'

'It's in all the papers,' said Dave. 'Your legs was broke when you jumped but according to the Examiner here you were cured by this mystery man.' Dave added, showing him the paper.

'What bloody mystery man? What the hell are you talking about? And what are you doing reading the Examiner? I thought it used too many long words for you.'

'My boss showed it to me this morning. Said 'you know this Fred Salmons chap don't you?.' Its all here, how you jumped and broke your legs and then this man spoke to you. just how you described it.' Dave thrust the paper towards him.

Fred sat and read Martin's story in horror. There it was, his name, in print, in the Examiner. And all the other stories. What the bloody hell would Doris say?

'Bloody rubbish if you ask me,' he said, throwing the paper on the table.

'Well it may be,' Dave replied, 'but it's in all the papers. Not just your name but the fact this bloke gave some woman her sight back after fifteen years.'

'You can't believe a bloody thing you read in the papers,' said Fred settling down to the serious business of drinking.

To his horror when he got home Doris had already been shown the story. Her friends had brought the paper round.

'Fancy you being in the Examiner,' she greeted him.

'Lot of rubbish if you ask me.'

'Well I don't know. Mrs Graham knows a woman whose sister-in-law lives in a house near Harwood. She knows the vicar's wife who was the one who reported the little boy being made to walk and she says it is quite true. According to Mrs Graham this man is going to be in Winchester. She and Mrs Wright are going to see him. Why don't we go then you can see if it is the same man?'

'No. You go if you want.'

'I'd much rather you came with me.'

'I'll think about it.'

⋆ ⋆ ⋆

Dai Griffiths felt his life was in turmoil. He had always done his best. He had looked after Gladys, she had never gone short. And when the children were born he had worked longer hours to provide all the things they needed. They had always been well dressed, had as much pocket money as he could afford and he had made sure that they always did what the other children did. He did not want people to think that he could not do as well as other parents.

Then it all fell apart. His work in the Ebbw Vale coalmine disappeared when the coal industry in South Wales died. He managed to get a job in Barry Docks, move house down to Barry Island and found life pleasant again. He worked in the fresh air, he did not get to dirty and they could also see the sea from where they lived. It was better than a black pit face and a view of row upon row of terraced houses.

It had been hard at times, particularly during strikes at the mines and the docks when money was short but he had done it. Times may have been hard but Dai, small and sturdy, was built to handle them.

He was constructed like a miniature tank or, considering his Welsh background, an over-inflated rugby ball, might be more apt. His round head, hair closely cut, rested on a round, hard muscular body resting on two powerfully constructed legs. Apart for the military and sporting analogies he might have served better as a useful road block.

Now he felt it had all been of no use.. His son 19-year-old Huw thought he was now too good for his family. He had actually called his father working class as if that was an insult. Megan, not yet 18 years was never at home, perpetually out with friends Dai did not like, incessantly drinking and smoking and going to discos. It was no life for a seventeen year old girl. She ought to do more to help her Mother.

Now he was arguing with Gladys and he hated doing that.. She had remained silent during most of the rows he had with Huw and Megan but after his last outburst at Megan had gone out even before he got home again, Gladys accused him of being too hard on her.

'You don't even try and understand them,' she accused. 'Megan is now a young girl and they have more freedom than we did. Huw is finding his feet. Yes, he's getting too big for his boots it is only a phase he's going through, he'll get over it, but shouting at him every time you see him isn't going to help.'

'It's a question of duty,' Dai replied. ' We've given them everything they've got and the least they can do is stay in and help you. Huw has got to learn respect and Megan has got to do more to help you. When I was her age I had to be in by nine or there was trouble. And I was a boy. My sisters weren't allowed out on their own until they were over eighteen. She'll come to no good with that crowd she is always with, you mark my words.'

'Times have changed Dai, and you've got to understand that otherwise we will lose them altogether.' Gladys replied, looking at him carefully.

'Why has she gone out before I got home. She couldn't have been in the house for more than five minutes?'

'She didn't go to work this afternoon. She wasn't well.'

'If she wasn't well why has she gone out tonight?'

'She was frightened.'

'Frightened? What of?'

'You.'

'Me? What have I done to frighten her? All I do is point out the dangers of knocking about with that crowd. I haven't hit her. Some fathers would've.'

'Well she's got some news and she is frightened about how you will react,'said Doris nervously.

'What sort of news? Is she in some sort of trouble. I warned you she would be. No-one ever listens to what I say but I'm right time and time again. What news has she got?'

'Now stay calm Dai. Don't get all worked up. It'll do no good.'

'What news?'

'She's pregnant, she's going to have a baby.'

'A what !!'

'A baby. She's about three months gone but she's been too frightened to tell us.' I suspected something was wrong but I wanted to wait for her to tell me.'

'She's bloody right. She's got something to be frightened about. I'll kill her, bringing shame on this family. What will the bloody neighbours say. I'll be the laughing stock of the bloody pub..'

'That's typical,' Gladys sneered. 'All you care about is yourself and what the neighbours will say. I'm the one who has to face the neighbours every day. I'm the one who's going to be laughed at. Anyway. what are we going to do about it?'

'Do? Nothing. She can get out now as far as I'm concerned.'

'Get out You mean leave home? Where?'

'I don't bloody care this isn't her home any more. I don't want to see her again. After all I've done for the little bitch can make her own way now. That's the way she wants it. She thinks she's grown up well from now on she bloody is.'

'Dai, you don't mean that.'

'Oh yes I do. I'm going to the pub. Get her out before I come home.'

* * *

Miriam Cartwright slammed the front gate behind her angrily. Charles really was too much, she thought to herself. He's an authoritative, domineering, arrogant religious bigot, she muttered. She stomped down the road towards the village. Surprisingly tall and thin her main feature was a narrow humorless face with steel blue eyes framed by metal glasses over which she peered at the target of her attention. Her overall appearance was not enhanced by a shrill voice which she tried to modulate in normal conversation but that grew in intensity whenever emotion was involved.

The reason for Miriam's uncharacteristic anger was her husband's continuing opposition to anything to do with the man involved in the incident on the village green. He would not even rationally discuss even the faintest possibility that Philip Green had been cured.

When the story about the blind woman appeared in the national newspapers Miriam had grasped the Examiner enthusiastically and run into Charles' study with what she thought was more evidence that what had happened to Philip could be genuine. He would not even look at it never mind read it. Charles, a large and portly man with thinning brown hair and the self satisfied smugness of a typical churchman, gave the article a cursory glance.

'You know my view of newspaper reporters,' he said sternly. 'They are dissemblers.. They make up stories, tell lies and have no understanding whatsoever of the truth. It is a word that is not even in their vocabulary.'

'But it shows that other people think there is something in it. The doctor who looked after the caretaker even thinks there is something in what the man did.'

'What caretaker?'

'The caretaker of the school which burned down. He jumped out of a third floor window and broke both his legs and the man healed them,' Miriam said impatiently.

'I don't know anything about a caretaker, a fire or broken legs and I don't want to know. Now please leave me in peace. You know I'm working on my sermon and I don't like being interrupted,' The Vicar said pompously.

'Well he is supposed to be in Winchester on Saturday and I'm going to see him,' she declared.

'Oh no you are not,' said the Vicar. 'I forbid it.'

'I'm sorry Charles. I have always done what you wanted me to do, but this time I am going to do what I want.'

'You cannot go, suppose someone recognizes you. They will think you are there with my agreement. It will destroy my reputation'

'They may think, quite wrongly, that you are open minded and have asked me to go and listen to him to see what I think.'

'Rubbish. Anyway, you heard me, you cannot go and that is the end of it.'

'I'm sorry Charles. It is not the end of it. I am going.'

The vicar looked at his wife open mouthed as she stormed out of the study. There was nothing more he could say.

* * *

Could it really be true?

Arnold Grimshaw was torn between hope and disbelief. He took off his glasses and gazed into space with unseeing eyes. He had read everything available about the man but could still not make up his mind. Could such a thing really happen? Could there be such a person?

Normally a thrifty man who counted pennies and spent only what was absolutely necessary, he had bought every morning paper on his way to the station and every evening paper on the way back. All the reports were the same, the facts didn't change only the views being expressed about them.

Had the man really healed a little boy, made a woman see, and all the other things? Was it the same man?

Arnold Grimshaw desperately wanted to believe that the man was genuine, that he had some great gift and that his presence was really going to mean something. he even considered whether the man could be the much prophesied 'second coming' that many predicted would always happen. He thought to himself in lower case letters because he couldn't dare think that this could be true.

But why not? Thousands of people believed, some had even predicted, that one day another man would come to earth to do what the previous prophet had done. No-one could say he wasn't needed. Probably now more than at any time in history. What with all the violence in the world, the permissiveness, drugs, crime, drink and the utter selfishness he could not have picked a better time.

He had been fascinated by these thoughts ever since the first report was published. He was never one to discount eccentric ideas or unconventional people without first studying or listening to them in great detail. He believed that there could be no such thing as flying saucers, but he wouldn't be dogmatic about it. He did not discount ghosts and thought it quite possible that there was something in spiritualism. He did not read the daily astrological forecast in the daily papers but he thought there might be something in astrology. He had no religion, he did not attend any church, but he never denied that God could exist but he was not sure in his mind as to what form the Deity might take. A benign old gentlemen was how he usually imagined him.

Although he never joined in controversial debates at the office or at dinner parties he was deeply concerned with what was going on in the world.

He desperately wanted to believe in something. Theologians drove him to despair. he invariably knew what they were going to say even before they started speaking. They trotted out all the well known cliches and they were so desperately petty about each other.

Arnold Grimshaw believed himself to be a lucky man although there were few among his friends who would agreed with him. Brought up as an only child in a family deprived of the breadwinner by a road accident when he was very young, he had devoted himself to his widowed mother until she died. By this time he was forty years old and had resigned himself to bachelorhood when he met Liz, a divorced woman who was lonely and needed the companionship of a mature man.

She was a good looking woman with luxuriant auburn hair. Her ears were small and delicate, her hands small but plump. Her mouth was exceptionally attractive, wide, very red with the help of lipstick, with great fullness and width. She had small even teeth which she displayed to the full when she smiled. After a short courtship they had married and settled down to what Arnold thought would be a blissful life. He had not known when he married that she was an alcoholic. She had managed to control her drinking habits during their early months together.

The truth dawned on him slowly. Bottles of whisky were emptied much faster than he thought was usual. Empty glasses were discovered in surprising places, behind plants, in the bathroom, behind the pedestal in the loo. At first he thought nothing of it . And when, on one or two occasions he found Liz slightly drunk when he arrived home from work he naively thought it was because she need something more to do with her day, a little job in a shop or something.

The facts hit him between the eyes one evening when he arrived home after they had been married for six months.

He entered the house, hung up his hat and coat, shouted 'it's me, darling' and walked into the sitting room. It took him several seconds before he could understand the scene in front of him. The room was wrecked, chairs were overturned, books pulled from their shelves, the coffee table was on its side, the standard lamp lay on the floor, its shade crinkled and torn and the mantel shelf completely devoid of all the trinkets it usually displayed.

'My God !' he muttered. What the hell has happened. We've had burglars.

Where is Liz? Is she hurt? The questions flashed through his mind in a kaleidescope of pictures.

He raced upstairs to the bedroom and burst open the door. Liz was lying naked on the bed, fast asleep. She had urinated where she lay. He walked round to look at her, still fearful about what had happened. The smell of whisky was overpowering. He shook her. She grinned in her sleep. She was out to the world, drunk.

She slept through the night. Arnold tidied up the room as best he could, found an empty whisky bottle under the settee, cooked himself eggs and bacon and sat thinking about the future. There was nothing he could do at that moment so, after checking that Liz was still asleep, went to bed in the spare room.

The next morning when he awoke he smelled breakfast cooking. He slipped on his dressing gown, it was Saturday and no need to rush off to work, and went downstairs.

Liz greeted him with a smile.

'I was just going to wake you,' she said. 'Breakfast is ready.'

'How are you this morning?' he asked.

'Fine, how are you? ' she asked.

'I'm all right,' he said with emphasis. 'I thought that after last night you might not feel too good.'

'No, I'm great,' she said as she gave him his second plate of bacon and eggs in ten hours..

Nothing more was said and it became clear to Arnold that she had no memory about what had happened the night before.

It had happened several times since then and Liz's drunkenness had become more and more regular and obvious. They had talked about it several times and on each occasion she had promised to stop drinking. She never had. It had increased to such an extent that most of their friends were now aware of the problem and avoided them.

Arnold was at a loss what to do. He read all the books and articles on alcoholism and realized that a cure would only come when the sufferer admitted they were alcoholic and admitted it to themselves and truly wanted to do something about it. Liz would not admit that she was an alcoholic, just someone who drank too much.

Unfortunately for Arnold, despite her failings, he was deeply in love with Liz, and was the eternal optimist. Something would happen to stop her drinking he was convinced.

He pondered about the man he had read so much about. If he could talk to him he might received advice about how to handle his problems.

But then, could this man help if he persuaded Liz to go and see him? The idea seemed a good one until he admitted to himself, deep in his heart, that he would never be able to persuade her to go.

⋆ ⋆ ⋆

When he left Dr Porter and Candice on Saturday, Martin had been unable to get the woman out of his mind. He carried a vision of her wherever he went and whatever he was doing. She was firmly implanted in his subconscious and would not let him go. If there was such a thing as love at first sight, then this was it, he thought. The fact that she was a married woman troubled his conscience only slightly.

He had spent a leisurely morning in his room looking through the newspapers and listening to the radio before deciding to go down for a pre-lunch drink and to see if he could find out what was going on in the world outside the hotel.

His stomach churned nervously as he walked into the lounge bar. Candice was sitting in a window seat by herself. He paused momentarily and then walked straight over to her, his eyes confirming every vision he had carried with him since their first meeting. When he first saw her she was dressed in shades of blue, today it was black. A tight sweater which once again emphasized the perfect domes of her breasts. Tight black trousers encased her shapely bottom and firm thighs and clung tightly around her calves.

'Hello again' he said as she looked up and smiled at him. 'What a pleasant surprise to see you here. Is your husband with you? he asked hopefully.

'No, he's busy. I am here on my own.'

'Can I get you a drink?' It was difficult for him not to show the excitement he was feeling within him.

'Thank you, I'll have a Bloody Mary,' she replied, finishing the drink that was already in front of her.

Martin looked around, signaled a waiter, ordered the drinks and sat down.

'Is he with the man?' he asked.

'I don't think so. I think its medical business.'

'By the way, what is the man's name? It seems silly to go on referring to him as 'the man.' He must have a name?'

'I've no idea,' Candice replied. 'I've never heard my husband refer to him by name.'

'How did they meet?'

'I think it was through a friend. John was very concerned about his wrong diagnosis of broken legs and then somehow heard that a friend of his had actually met the man and spoken to him. John arranged a meeting and since then has been pretty sold on him.'

'Do you know anything about him, who he is, what he is doing?'

'No, I'm afraid I can't help you,' she said with a smile.

'Can't or won't?' Martin asked.

'I know very little and John has asked me not to talk about him, particularly to journalists. And you are one aren't you?'

Martin smiled self consciously. 'Yes I am but I wasn't asking professionally. I was making conversation,' he lied.

'Well let's converse then,' Candice grinned. 'Tell me about yourself.'

'Nothing to tell really. Newspaper reporter, 35 years old, unmarried although was once, no children, no girl friends. Nothing. I lead a lonely hard working existence.'

'What happen to Mrs Armstrong?'

'She's now Mrs Someone-else. She left me for another.' He noticed Candice's look of sympathy. 'No, it was my fault entirely. I was too involved with work to pay enough attention to her. She found someone who would give her the attention she deserves.'

'I know the feeling,' said Candice. 'I am left alone for long hours while John works at his job and a multitude of other interests - the homeless, abused children, the environment, you think of a good cause and he's involved.

'I would have thought you were a damn good cause,' said Martin chivalrously.

'Thank you kind sir,' she replied.

'Look, I'm going to have lunch here, will you join me?'

'I'd love to,' Candice replied enthusiastically.

After further idle chat they moved into the restaurant for lunch. Throughout the meal they talked animatedly around the many things they found of mutual interest. They covered a wide range but every time Martin asked a question about the man Porter was meeting, it was brushed aside and the subject changed.

Suddenly she asked him: 'Did you invite me to have lunch with you because you like me or are you just acting like a typical journalist and trying to pump information out of me?'

'Because I like you, of course,' Martin replied, embarrassed. 'But I'm afraid the man is always at the back of my mind because I am supposed to find him and interview him, sorry.'

'Alright, I forgive you. But I really cannot help you because John tells me nothing. I do know that he will be away this weekend. He is spending it with a university friend. I do know that the friend lives in Micheldever which is near Winchester. That's all I know.' replied Candice, looking straight at him. 'Let's get back to me liking you,' said Martin.

* * *

# Part Three

# REFLECTION

A BLAST OF TRUMPETS AND trombones opening Wagner's 'Ride of the Valkeries' shook the television set as Grimshaw dived frantically for the remote control to reduce the volume. He did not want his neighbours disturbed. The fact that he lived in a large detached house with considerable space at both sides and back and front was irrelevant. He cared about his neighbors peace and quiet. He was like that.

The Wagner piece introduced The Peter Potter Investigation every Wednesday at 9.30pm. It was probably not the most suitable piece of music but Wagner was the programme director's favourite composer and he used his music whenever possible.

The Peter Potter Investigation was a programme that Arnold Grimshaw refused to miss. It was the only production on television that he insisted on watching and would go to great lengths to ensure that he was near a television set at the right channel, at the right time, on the right night. Of course he did possess a video recorder but he had no confidence in his ability to set it properly. He had often had to suffer Match of the Day because of a wrong programme setting.

It was not that he liked the show, in fact he disliked it so much that that to deny him the opportunity to see it was like refusing a madman the opportunity of banging his head against a brick wall so he could be denied the feeling of pleasure when he stopped.

Peter Potter was a cynical young journalist who had cashed in on the healthy desire for vicious satire that years of domination by the Establishment had engendered in the Great British Public. He achieved, in a short space of time, doubtful national fame by being obnoxious to everyone he interviewed, particularly the target of his investigation. His particular spot became a weekly battle between the insensitive and rude Potter and some poor inarticulate person who had allegedly offended society, or Potter, in some way but who had been either brave or foolish enough to agree to appear on the programme. It was remarkable to Arnold that every week some poor sod would offer himself up for sacrifice on the altar of Potter's self esteem. But at least they could say that they had been on television.

The interviews quickly became a test of stamina for the guest to see how long he could endure the loaded questioning, innuendo and vitriolic rudeness of Potter before he or she lost their temper. Several of his targets had ripped off their microphones angrily and stormed out of the studio. All good publicity for the programme.

Eventually satire, largely through over exposure, had lost both its original appeal and its vast viewing audience dwindled and it was removed from the programme schedule.

After a short absence, too short in many people's view, Potter had returned to the screens with an hour long show devoted to discussion on a specific subject with several distinguished, so-called expert guests.

The young television personality had mellowed with experience. He was no longer rude but he was undaunted by reputation and although his sarcastic tongue was still capable of hurt it was under tighter control. Arnold still hated him heartily.

On this particular evening Arnold was at home, Liz was in bed sleeping off yet an other exhausting battle with the bottle. Arnold switched the set on to be greeted by an advertisement extolling the virtues of a well known margarine that could not be distinguished from butter. Margarine was not something that could be found in the Grimshaw larder. Shortly it faded away surrendering the screen to the title and credits of the Peter Potter Investigation, its classic signature tune faded away and eventually, the Potter face appeared.

Arnold turned the volume up slightly but not too loud not wishing to wake Liz who would otherwise come downstairs and talk throughout the programme. He flopped back in his chair, put his feet on the coffee table, not possible of Liz was around, and prepared to hate.

Just as he had settled the Potter face, smiling and toothy, leaned out at

Arnold and went into action.

'Good evening and welcome,' said Potter. He grinned at Arnold while he waited for the audience applause to die down.

'Tonight I want to be serious,' he smirked, leaning even further forward confidentially. The audience laughed uproariously. Potter being serious was usually the prelude to the crucifixion of some poor innocent.

'No, I mean it,' he went on. The audience laughed even louder and Arnold squirmed in his chair.

'Has Jesus Christ returned to save us all again?' he asked. The audience became silent. Arnold sensed trouble. 'That is the question being asked all over Britain today.'

'During the past week, 'Potter continued,' the newspapers have been full of stories about a man who as far as we know has no name and no job but is described in the press as a teacher. He has, it is reported, performed miracles of healing. He arrives in some small town or city suddenly, draws a crowd which usually causes trouble, performs some sort of magic and disappears without trace. I don't know what you think about it all but it strikes me as a load of old rubbish,' he said. The audience sniggered. This was Potter at his worst.

'Tonight I have with me Doctor John Porter, from Hereford, who was one of the first people to meet this teacher man and who has, I understand, become a close friend.' The camera flashed on to the unsmiling face of Porter looking nervous and unsure. 'Melvyn Craddock, writer, critic and self confessed agnostic.' A close up of a smugly smiling, cherub faced man in an open neck shirt. 'And the Very Reverend Barnaby Charles, Bishop of Leominster.' On the screen came the picture of a fat, self satisfied, almost bald man of about fifty, grinning broadly. 'And finally Frank Faulkner, Chief Reporter of the Daily Times and best selling author.' It was funny, Grimshaw, thought that all authors who appeared on television were 'best sellers.'

'I want to ask Doctor Porter first,' Potter went on, turning to the visibly unhappy doctor. 'You have been with this man, you have talked to him and heard him speak. Are the stories about him true?'

Doctor Porter hesitated, fiddled with his hands, straightened his tie and looked terrified as the camera zoomed in for a close- up.

'It depends which stories you listen to,' he began apprehensively. 'It is true that he describes himself as a teacher. It is true that his message is more spiritual than temporal and if you want to take a very broad view you could say that there are similarities to the message of what he says with the message two thousand years ago. But I must point out that there are many hundreds of people in many religions who do that every day.' The doctor sat back looking more relaxed and slightly more confident.

'Has he performed any miracles?' Potter asked doubtfully.

'He himself would not use that word,' Porter replied, smiling broadly. 'Certainly several people are said to have recovered from illnesses or disabilities after meeting him. I myself clearly saw a woman who had been blind for fifteen years regain her sight when she met him.'

Potter looked at the doctor quizzically and with obvious disbelief.

'You mean you actually watched him cure her?' he gasped.

'No, I saw her with her friend before the man came along. She obviously could not see, you could tell by her eyes and how she was looking in a different direction from those around her. Moments later, when she was close to him her reaction was amazing as he looked at her. You knew immediately that something important had happened. She looked him in the face. You could tell immediately that she was actually looking at him.' he added convincingly looking directly at Potter giving a first sign of confidence, but the television presenter still looked doubtful.

'What do you think Bishop?'

The Bishop smiled like a genial father surveying his family.

'I think, Mr Potter, you summed it up perfectly well in your opening when you described it as a load of old rubbish. The idea of this man claiming to be the second Jesus Christ and performing miracles is ludicrous beyond belief.'

'He has not claimed to be Jesus Christ,' Porter interrupted, 'or that he has performed miracles. If you want to criticize, and you are perfectly entitled to do so, then at least get your facts right. If you really want to find out the truth you must learn to be more conciliatory in discussion.'

'Just a minute doctor,' said Potter, 'I'll come back to you.'

'To even suggest that he might have something to do with the events of two thousand years ago is blasphemous.' the Bishop insisted, surprise by Porter's outburst. The doctor's early nervousness had conveyed the wrong impression.

'Wouldn't you claim in your profession to have something to do with the events of two thousand years ago?' asked Porter ignoring Potter's restraining hand.

'That is entirely different. I am an ordained Minister of the church.'

'In other words you're paid to do it,' snapped Porter.

'Just a minute,' said Potter holding up a restraining hand to Porter. 'We'll come to the discussion shortly. I want to hear from Mr Craddock.'

Craddock, who had been lounging in his chair, feet stretched out in front of him in a gesture of detached interest, sat up, a cynical smile on his face.

'It's a matter of total indifference to me,' he sneered, looking round at the audience for approval. 'I don't believe any of it, the events of two thousand years ago or the events of today. The idea of a supreme being of any sort leaves me totally unmoved.'

'That's very helpful,' said Potter with a hint of sarcasm.

'Well I mean,' Craddock continued. 'I'm afraid I can't believe in a God of any description. You only have to look around the world and see the state it's in to come to the conclusion that he is not doing a very good job. If God, or even this man, can heal people who are ill why are they so discriminating? If you can heal one person why not heal the lot and make the world a better place.' The audience clapped.

'That's a very valid question,' said Potter, turning towards Porter for an answer.

'I am not going to attempt to try and explain God or how he works. Each man has his beliefs. But if you will remember from your Bible Mr Craddock, if you have one or have ever even looked at it, much of Jesus' healing was done with those who really believed, those who had faith.'

'Oh I've read the Bible,' said Craddock shortly. 'I wouldn't mind betting I've studied it more carefully than you. I accept that in this book, the authenticity of which has never been proven and, after all, the New Testament which records all these miracles, is only the jottings of a select few so-called disciples who cannot really be described as independent. It does indicate a certain amount of faith by those healed. The relevant chapters are largely written from memory and memory can always be suspect. But that's not the point. Are you really trying to tell me and our audience that the people this man claims to have healed.....'

'He doesn't claim anything,' interjected Porter, '.....really had faith that he would be able to do it. Rubbish.'

'I'm interested to hear two laymen claiming expert knowledge of the Bible,' the Bishop joined in. 'I don't think I would be exaggerating if I said I had probably studied it more than either of you. The Bible is generally accepted by the Christian religion to be a true account of those historic days. There is plenty of evidence that Jesus existed and performed the acts with which he is credited......'

'I'm sorry Bishop but I don't want this programme to become an earnest theological debate. There is a time and place for that...although I can't think of either the time or the place at the moment,' The audience burst into laughter. 'What I'm interested in is this man. Who is he, where is he from and what is he doing? The man is either a confidence trickster or a rogue who is taking advantage of those in difficulties, of the simple minded....'Potter continued.

'And those fed up with the church and all its self important pomposity,' Craddock interrupted..

'He certainly isn't over impressed by the church,' Porter came in.' He is not sure that it has adapted the Christian message to this century or that it really cares about people in the way he feels was meaningful. It seems more concerned with itself, its own organization, the theological differences within its own ranks and arguments with other religions.'

'There aren't any basic theological differences,' the Bishop burst in. The audience roared with laughter and Craddock made a great exhibition of falling about with incredulity.

'There is a debate within the church about the interpretation of certain passages within the Bible,' the Bishop went on amid further bursts of laughter.

'Now come on,' said Potter, 'we're getting away from the point. Would Doctor Porter please tell us about the man. I'm interested in the fact that although he's been receiving a lot of publicity for over a week he hasn't yet been interviewed by the press, he hasn't explained himself publicly and he hasn't made his message public knowledge so that it can be studied and considered.'

'And he has no intention of doing so,' Porter confirmed. 'His message, he says, is for the ordinary people. He wants them to hear his words and come to their own conclusions. He does not want his words interpreted by a bunch of biased journalists who would not be able to resist the temptation of putting their own elucidation on his words. Who he is, where he comes from are totally irrelevant to his work,' said Porter, firmly and enthusiastically. 'Unfortunately he has had his views confirmed after being told that one News editor's view of his job is simply to sell newspapers any way he can.'

'But by expressing that view he can avoid having to answer any embarrassing questions,' interposed Craddock sneeringly..

'I think the whole thing is extremely dangerous,' said the Bishop. 'Who knows where it could lead. We could soon have hundreds of so-called miracle workers appearing all over the country.'

'As a matter of fact,' said Porter, looking directly at the Bishop,' he has made his views on religion very clear. He believes that the church is similar to a theatre. In the same way that a commercial theatre caters for those with artistic instincts who want to be entertained, and sometimes led into thinking, and is led by actors who play roles; the church is a theatre for those with religious instincts who want to be entertained, sometimes led into thinking, it is led by the clergy who play roles and use props to emphasize matters considered to be important. It has little to do with religion What are described as services are little more than meaningless rituals most of which are intoned without feeling,' Porter added.

'There is no supreme being who must be obeyed, he explains, He does not use such expressions but tries to pass on only an image created by a collocation of guidelines or basic rules which should govern the whole of humanity. We know the original set of rules as The Ten Commandments of the Bible. But these are not unequivocal instructions about what you must do and not do, they recognize the vulnerability of human beings and are therefore presented as targets to be achieved.

The rules set down by Jesus were also established by the leaders of all the other religions but each interpreted in a way which is more relevant to their culture. These religions are all based on one God and, he strongly emphasizes, they are complementary not antagonistic' declared Porter with emphasis..

'The Christian message was given to us two thousand years ago. It does not need interpretation by a man with no credentials, no religious background or education as far as we know,' the Bishop sat back almost out of breath looking genuinely disturbed.

'I must take issue with the Bishop,' said Porter after receiving a nod to continue from Potter who was being remarkably silent.

'Christianity, as Craddock says, is based on a book written two thousand years ago. It is, again as Craddock says, largely a collection of stories handed down by word of mouth. In fact the existence of Jesus has never been proved beyond reasonable doubt. There is a strong body of opinion, in fact, which credits most of the work of Jesus to an earlier Apostle.

'But that is not the point. The point is that whatever the truth of the history of those times the image of Christianity and the way it was put forward was applicable to that period..

Many of the ideas and meanings are not relevant in the twentieth century. The reason that the church, whatever its denomination, fails to attract large numbers of people is that it tries to impose archaic ideas and theories on people who have much more knowledge and understanding of the world in which they live than those two thousand years ago. With space travel and modern scientific knowledge how can you expect modern man to believe in the Creation? How can he believe in Adam and Eve when he is now taught how man has evolved?'

'That's rubbish,' snapped the Bishop. 'Very many people believe all that and have no difficulty doing so. They believe because they want to believe.'

Porter looked at the Bishop sympathetically, not wanting to make such a devoted person look an idiot.

'You have to admit that one of the greatest failures in the history of humanity is the fact that religions of all types, although they have been taught over thousands of years have failed miserably. Despite all the teachings of peace and harmony there is still war, poverty and antagonism. Most of the wars that have been fought throughout history have been fought over religion. Those professing to be religious have simply being paying lip service to the Ten Commandments without giving them any real consideration. Almost everyone fails to observe them in their entirety and use the feeble excuse that we are now living in a modern world with different rules and values. If one section of the community decides to ignore any one of the rules it is called 'the permissive society' as if this is some great achievement. They seem unaware of the fact that if you lower the standards in one area you strengthen excuses to lower standards in other sectors.

'If your knowledge of religion is as comprehensive as you claim you will be well aware of the fact that both Christianity and Islam grew out of early Judaism,' Porter concluded with authority.

'The whole thing is a load of cod's wallop,' said Craddock.' The conceit and arrogance of human beings is beyond belief. You really believe that we are something special,' he added. looking pityingly at Porter and the Bishop.

'You, you sanctimonious old fraud,' he said to the Bishop amid laughter, 'have the downright arrogance to believe you are something special, a special messenger of God. That you, whose only claim to fame is an expensive education and thirty years undetected crime and the boring ability, or lack of imagination, to stick at one thing for all those years, you think you are in a position to dictate to other people how to live, what they should and should not do,' Craddock's voice reached a high pitch of incredulity.

He went on: 'You have the damn cheek to stand in a bloody pulpit every Sunday, intone a lot of mumbo jumbo and then preach tolerance and understanding when you can't even be tolerant with the doctor here or try to understand what he is talking about. Never mind your attitude to me and people who think like I do.'

'You are just as bad,' Craddock went on, turning to Porter. 'People like you want to believe you are so damned important. That all the universe, the stars and galaxies, the sun and the planets have been put there so some piddling little human beings, almost the smallest thing in the whole universe, can prepare themselves for something greater.' Porter looked shocked by this unexpected personal attack he really did not understand.

'Why the hell can't you accept that the human race is nothing, just a bunch of cells and organisms which, like all other cells and organisms, have happened by accident and not design and will eventually die and disappear forever. You might just as well say that it is the worms who are the most important inhabitants of the Universe. Hell, for all we know they might even believe they are.' Craddock sat back in a crescendo of clapping and laughter. He knew how to rouse public support.

It took almost a minute for the laughter to subside.

'There I'm afraid we must leave it as we have other issues to discuss' said Potter, his face wreathed in smiles. ' Is this man a messenger from some greater intelligence or is he a fraud and a hoaxer? Whatever the answer I am sure we will be hearing more about him in the newspapers and on this programme.'

⋆ ⋆ ⋆

'We've just heard from Dr Porter that all the religions have the same basic aims so, we wonder, how do we contrast this with the Muslim terrorist activities, such as the London bomb, whose aim seems to be to kill as many innocent possible as possible in support of their cause.' Potter continued.

'I think you should be very careful before you generalize about the responsibility for the outrages,' said Frank Faulkner, making his first major contribution. 'We have been bombed by IRA terrorists for years but we don't describe them as 'the Irish,' as though all the people there were responsible. We understood that they were a small minority of criminal fanatics. These London bombers do not represent the majority of Muslims either here or anywhere else in the world.

'If you read Islamic texts you will see that the act of inciting terror in the hearts of defenseless civilians, the wholesale destruction of buildings and properties, the bombing and maiming of innocent men and women and children are all forbidden as detestable acts according to Islam and Muslims. Muslims follow a religion of peace, mercy and forgiveness and the vast majority have nothing to do with recent violent events. If an individual Muslim were to commit such acts of terrorism they would be guilty of violating the laws of Islam.

'I've heard the Man on this subject, if you will forgive me for re-introducing him,' Porter interrupted, giving Faulkner an understanding look 'He believes that those who equate Muslims as terrorists, including Muslims themselves, have no real understanding of the Koran. Those who persuade people to wrap bombs around themselves because they believe that striking at the enemy will ensure themselves life in Paradise are both liars and charlatans,' Faulkner explained. 'The trouble is that most young people, particularly those who live in the Western world have no knowledge of Arabic and are incapable of reading the Koran so they depend on the interpretations given to them by fanatics who have their own agenda..

'That means that it really is the responsibility of Muslims in general because their religious leaders should be making greater efforts to explain to young people, particularly those who do not speak Arabic, what the Koran actually says and what it means,' said Craddock.

'I can tell you what the Koran says,' interrupted Faulkner,' as I've studied it so I can write with more authority. The act of inciting terror in the hearts of defenseless civilians, the wholesale destruction if buildings and properties, the bombing and maiming of innocent men, women a child are all forbidden and detestable acts according to Islam and the Muslims. Muslims follow a religion of peace and mercy, and forgiveness and the vast majority have nothing to do with the violent events some have associated with Islam.

If an individual Muslim were to commit an act of terrorism, this person would be guilty of violating the laws of Islam. And that's a fact,' Faulkner declared.

Potter was shaken by the emphasis Faulkner put behind his statement.

'Well, he said, after a pause, 'unfortunately the clock has caught up with us and we have no time to pursue this problem. We may return to it next week. Our thanks to Dr Porter, the Bishop of Leominster, Melvyn Craddock and Frank Faulkner. It has been an interesting and informative programme. Goodnight to you all, see you next week.'

He looked round to thank Porter for his contribution but the doctor had moved quickly to catch Faulkner to continue their conversation privately.

★ ★ ★

Arnold Grimshaw turned off his television, his mind confused and bewildered. Much of what he had heard confirmed many of the unfocused thoughts that had occupied his mind for years.

He had always felt that church services were meaningless rituals during which congregations echoed a prepared script week and week, year after year, without any original mental activity. They never seemed to question anything, they followed the script religiously, very apt word he thought. It certainly was a theatrical performance.

He found the comments on the various religions perfectly obvious. He had always wondered why Christians should fervently believe that there was only one God when clearly roughly three-quarters of the world's population believed the same thing about their Gods. The expression 'only one true God' was arrogant and thoughtless. If there really was only one God why he should have only one son. The idea of a number of apostles or sages or whatever, interpreting the original message in a way that was appropriate to their cultures seemed totally acceptable. He had been surprised, whenever he thought about it, that all the religions seemed to have the same basic aims and set the same sort of standards but in a way that was relevant to them.

And that bit about the Muslims. All the Muslims he knew were normal human beings who wanted to be the best they could. One had only to see what happened when there was a national disaster anywhere in the world. People raced to help the suffering regardless of nationality or religious beliefs. He had come to the conclusion, along with many others, that if people were left to follow the basic Rules, or Ten Commandments, whatever they called them, the world would clearly be a better place.

He had always had very strong views about death, convinced that no-one actually died until the very last person they knew on earth died. Death took them away as if they were going on a long holiday from which they would not return. They continued living in the memory in the same way. If they had been close then you could still talk with them, relating your problems and thoughts and, more often than not, you would remember the sort of answer they would have given you. Whether you liked it or not they could still influence you as they had when they were alive. The joy of memory was that in most cases you remembered the happy events, in others you could remember and try and understand what had gone wrong at the time and, hopefully, forgive them or yourself. They were still, in almost every sense, alive.

The more he thought about it the more he convinced himself that his life needed more purpose. Although he was unavoidably diverted by the problems caused by his wife Liz he realized he needed more. For years he had convinced himself that his model making hobby, steam driven and highly complicated, fulfilled his need, but he knew it didn't..

He had started it was a boy of 12 in a home where both parents were successful in their respective professions, banker and teacher, occupied much of their time at the expense of attention to young Arnold. But he did have a happy home and got most of the things he wanted, so he wasn't complaining.

Now he needed more. If the man was someone special, and Grimshaw was almost convinced he was, then he would need help even if it was only for crowd control. He decided to find Porter and see what he could do.

⋆ ⋆ ⋆

Grace Golder watched the programme through a flood of emotions. Delighted, fascinated and intrigued that she was able to watch television, astonished at what well known people, about whom she had mental visions really looked like in the flesh, furious at the attitude of some of the speakers, infuriated by the pedantic attitude of the Bishop, and concerned at what she could do to help the man.

Grace had always been more concerned about other people than herself. She was careful that she was immaculately dressed so that she did not draw attention to herself, she was very concerned about what, as a blind person, she would look like. She wanted her eyes to look as normal as possible and it took some time for her friend Alice to convince her that that her eyes looked straight ahead steadily and did not move about wildly. The only difference, she was told, was that her light brown eyes were vacuous, without expression. As a result she refused to wear dark glasses and carried only the slimmest of white canes which could be folded away out of sight. She had also refused the use of a guide dog on the ground that other people needed one more than she did.

When the show finished she had made up her mind that she would go and look (an unusual word for her) for the man and ask him what she could do.

⋆ ⋆ ⋆

For all the eighteen years of their marriage Miriam Cartwright had been a dutiful vicar's wife. She had looked after him well, tended to all his needs, stayed silent when he was bad tempered and unreasonable each week when preparing his sermon, had played a full role in church activities, regularly visited the sick and old and tried to help those in need.

She had never criticised or argued with him even though she did not always agree with what he said or indeed, his interpretation of the Christian message.

Now, however, their marriage was nearing crisis point. The disagreement over the man, his reported actions and views, was driving a dangerous wedge between them.

It was not that Miriam thought that the man was anything special. She did not know enough about him to make a judgement. What she could not stand was Charles' uncompromising attitude towards him. Charles had no more knowledge about the man than she did but he was dogmatic in his view that he was no good, a fraud, a fake and probably a swindler. He showed no inclination towards forgiving her for being responsible for the first report about him. Charles, a vicar, a preacher of tolerance, would not even discuss the subject with her.

He was incandescent by the report that the man saw the church as a theatre and its services as a meaningless ritual. The idea of a Deity which governed all religions which, in turn, had their different but relevant interpretations was totally beyond him

'Without any doubt the man is a fraud, full of wild notions. The Church of England is the only true church, based on the words of Jesus Christ recorded in the Bible. I am quite sure of that,' he declared, brandishing his dog-eared Bible in his right hand like a trophy which he had just received.

'I wouldn't be surprised if he didn't advocate women priests as a way of winning public opinion.' he said shrewdly, knowing that such a statement would enrage his wife making his point.

'What's wrong with women priests?' asked Miriam rebelliously.

'Everything,' Charles laughed. 'If Jesus had wanted women priests he would have had women disciples to spread the word. Mind you, in one respect women disciples spreading the word wouldn't be a bad idea. Women never stop talking the message would certainly be spread especially if it was described as confidential' He laughed out loud in a self-congratulatory way. He was incredibly pleased with himself.

'Women played a very submissive role in his day. Things are different now, Miriam pointed out ' Women now play a very important roles in a number of professions. And they do it very well.'

'That's a matter of opinion,' Charles shrugged. All you've got to do is read the newspapers and see some of the damn fool conclusions they come to.'

'Well, not all in your profession agree with you. There is a strong call for women priests in the Church of England, there are already one or two. You cannot stand in the way of progress.'

''Progress!' said an astounded Charles. 'Saint Paul was right when he said women should adorn themselves modestly and sensibly in seemly apparel, not with braided hair or gold or pearls, or costly attire but by good deeds, as befits women who profess religion. Let a woman learn in silence with all submissiveness. I permit no woman to teach or to have authority over men, she is to keep silent,' Charles intoned, proud of his ability to quote the great man.

Miriam was nonplussed. 'That was two thousand years ago, she said feebly, peering over her glasses with what she hoped was a silencing glare.

'Nevertheless, it says it all,' Charles stared back, recognizing his wife's favourite way of silencing him.

They both turned away to indicate a temporary cessation of activity.

To Miriam's chagrin matters were exacerbated by newspaper reports of riots and trouble whenever the man appeared. They added fuel to Charles' fire. Charles said very little but left the newspapers open at the report pages on her place at the breakfast table each morning. She read them avidly because, unlike her husband, she really wanted to know, she wanted all the facts she could get.

As time passed it became increasingly clear that the only way she was going to find the answers she required was to go and find the man, listen to him and, if possible to speak to him.

Her remaining problem was how to achieve this. She could not reveal her plans to Charles. He had already forbidden it and she would never openly defy him. On the other hand neither could she lie to him, it was inconceivable.

The problem puzzled her all morning and it was when she was peeling the potatoes for lunch that the answer came. She looked at the potato as she peeled the skin away; potatoes are grown by farmers; her friend Mary Galloway was a farmer's wife; their farm was in Andersfordby near Cheltenham which at least was on the way to Winchester where the man last appeared. She would go and spend a few days with Mary, find out where the man was and go and see him. It was an ideal, semi-honest plan. Charles would not object if she said she was going to stay with Mary. It would be the truth. If, while she was away, she accidentally happened upon the man she could not be accused of duplicity.

Mary might even want to meet the man herself.

Miriam wiped her hands and went to the telephone and tapped out the number, her hands trembling because she was, in a way, defying Charles.. Mary was delighted to hear from her. After exchanging news headlines such as how so-and-so was, what the weather was like and how disastrous it was for farmers, Miriam broached the subject.

'Mary, I'm fairly free for a few days and Charles is busy. I could do with a change. Would you like me to come and stay with you say, from Thursday to Monday?'

'Oh darling, I would love it.' Mary replied enthusiastically.

'Mary was on the telephone this morning,' she told her husband at lunchtime. 'She said she would love me to go and stay there for a few days. I didn't think you would mind so I said I would go on Thursday and stay until Monday. Is that all right with you?'

'Fine' said Charles absentmindedly. 'How was she?' Mary didn't answer, she didn't have to for Charles was already lost in the latest edition of the Church Times and an article which was enthusiastically discrediting all the man's reported thoughts

⋆ ⋆ ⋆

If there is anyone worse than a pompous Government Minister it must be a pompous Bishop, Forbes thought to himself as he watched the Potter programme. They are so bloody sanctimonious too.

Forbes had moved fast following his decision to change his image. Rather, in the case of his two mistresses he hadn't moved at all. Notes explaining 'pressure of business' and 'Parliamentary responsibilities' designed to both impress them and keep them quiet for a while, had been sent to both of them. So far it had worked.

He had spoken with the Party Whips office and explained that 'personal problems' which had held him back for some years had now been resolved and he was now able to play a more active role in the party. The whips treated this metamorphosis with scepticism but welcomed it, although they had no intention of making greater use of him. He was too shallow for that.

He had almost made his final decision about the chosen subject for his personal 'crusade.' It would be the man, he thought, and his role would be that of a supporter. Detailed enquiries had shown that it was the ordinary people, the voters, who were sympathetic to the man. He would be too, he decided.

He watched the Potter programme and concluded that the doctor seemed to be a sensible and reliable man on whom he could rely. Contacting him would be the first step in his new campaign.

The following day he went to the House of Commons earlier than usual, being seen around more was part of his reformation plan. It was Wednesday, Prime Minister's Questions day and he planned to ask a sycophantic supplementary congratulating the Prime Minister on something or other to attract his attention and remind everyone he was around.

He arrived in time for lunch and went straight into the Member's dining room which, as it was still early, was almost empty. He sat down, ordered a drink and idly contemplated the menu.

'Excuse me sir,' said a voice. He looked up. It was a House of Commons messenger holding a pink envelope. 'A letter for you sir, hand delivered.'

Forbes thanked him and examined it closely. Both the fact that it was pink, and the handwriting, clearly indicated it was from a female.

He opened it, scanned through it quickly and looked at the signature. It was signed by two people.

He could not believe what he had read. He felt himself blushing deeply, his nerves tingling. He held the letter down on his lap, out of sight, and looked around to see if anyone had noticed his reaction. No-one was looking at him.

He looked at the letter again and read it slowly

*Dear Edward*

*Both Karen and I thank you for your note. If you are going to take on added 'parliamentary responsibilities' we suggest you are more careful with your correspondence.*

*You must learn to take greater care in placing the right letter in the right envelope and not mix them up as you have on this occasion. Pauline and I found it very amusing.*

*We understand from Pauline that she received the same message verbally about a week ago. Shame on you Edward ! You don't really expect the three of us to take this lying down? We've all done that for long enough ! Ha! Ha!*

*Your will be hearing from us.*

The letter was signed by Karen Thomson and Pamela Swift.

Edward looked at it in horror, his mind flashing through the appalling implications. They knew about each other ! For how long? How did they know about Pauline? What the hell will they do? What could they do? What a bloody mess!

He could not understand how he had made such an elementary mistake, putting the letters in the wrong envelopes. How could he be such a bloody fool? Then another awful thought struck him. The letter was hand delivered ! Christ ! She, or they, must have come to the House, might even still be here ! He looked around again. There were no guests in the room. He stood up.

'Forget it,' he snapped at the waiter who came to take his order.

He went out and made straight for the terrace where most guests were likely to be on a beautiful hot day.

He looked around nervously. My God ! There was no doubt about it. Clearly one was Karen, vivacious. with long brown hair, a pale face and slanting green eyes. She had long legs and a stylized body. The other was unmistakably Pamela, full-fleshed, a luxurious woman of abundance and sensuality in every pore and curve. Large breasted with violin shaped hips she oozed sex. They were both sitting at a table with......Oh ! No!...... Randle Carter, Labour Member for some obscure constituency in the North of England, a vociferous critic of almost everything and everyone and a well known moralist !

★ ★ ★

There is a well established adage when the British weather is discussed that suggests that if it rains on 15 July, St. Swithin's Day, it will then rain for 40 days. St Swithin, a 9th century Bishop, died in 862 and was buried in Winchester Cathedral. It was therefore of no surprise to Martin when he arrived on the outskirts to find it was pouring with rain.

Martin had arrived on the scene through sheer luck. He had telephoned his office dutifully each day to report his lack of success in finding the man. His News Editor became increasingly annoyed with him but it was an annoyance tempered by the fact that no other Fleet Street reporter had found the man either.

On this particular day Martin rang in as usual to be greeted by the news that Charlie James wanted to speak to him. Martin was just about to explain that he had still had no luck in finding the quarry when James came on :'Thank God you rang,' he said heartily. 'I wasn't sure you would know he was in Winchester. Have you seen him yet?'

Christ, thought Martin, the man was in Winchester and he had no idea.

'We got a piece on the tapes which just says he's there. I rang you at your hotel but they said you were out. I'm glad you got there in time. Let's have a story, about a thousand words as soon as you can. I'll hold the page if necessary but I'd rather not. I'll wait to hear from you,' said James as he replaced the receiver without waiting for an answer.

Martin looked at his watch. It was just after two o'clock. He had just returned to London. It would take him a couple of hours to get to Winchester even if he was lucky with the traffic. Even then it would be impossible to find the man and write the story in time for the first edition.

He would, he decided, have to resort to an old ruse he had used before, find as many people as possible who had spoken to the man or heard him and then write it as if it was a personal report. Tricky, but he might get away with it.

His dream faded even faster than it was concocted. An hour and a half later he found himself on the A31 at Kingsworthy, some three miles from the centre of the town. A long stream of red car lights stretched in front of him indicating a monumental traffic jam with no sign of movement. There was nowhere for him to go, nothing he could do. Other drivers were sitting with a glazed look of acceptance on their faces. Most had switched off the wind screen wipers, perhaps hoping that what they could no longer see would eventually disappear.

Cars and people choked the thoroughfares like a clutch of blood clots massing in vital arteries slowly squeezing the very life blood of the city.

Rumours that the man had been asked to come to somewhere near Winchester to see a man who had an incurable disease had spread through the area with all the rapidity of a bush fire out of control. There was no formal announcement, no advertisements appeared in the press, no loudspeaker vans roamed the roads and avenues making staccato announcements. People knew by word of mouth alone that he would be in the city very soon.

The chaos had escalated until the Chief Constable, unable to cope with the deteriorating situation. took over all available car parks and open spaces and ordered all drivers approaching the city to park and abandon their vehicles unless they could prove that their business in the city was vital. The latter relaxation seemed totally irrelevant because even if their journey was absolutely necessary, a matter of life and death even, they could go nowhere such was the impress of people.

Hit by a common problem the crowds that thronged the street reacted in a manner generally described as typically British - by joking. The rain, not heavy but determined, did nothing to deter them. Although there were isolated incidents of bad temper the vast majority resorted to back chat and ribaldry.

'Watch that speed limit,' shouted one driver at an elderly man walking slowly past him. 'Give us a lift,' yelled another.

'You should laugh,' replied the gent,' I'm about to start collecting ground rent.'

Peals of derisive laughter greeted the arrival of a traffic warden who was looking like a hungry vulture at a car parked and abandoned by its driver. He solemnly took out his notebook and started writing.

Why don't you have it towed away,' someone shouted. You can't nick him for parking, the car was built there,' shouted a young man who had been waiting in a bus queue.

Nearer the city centre the tempers of determined pedestrians were shorter. They had been waiting to move for much longer than those in the outskirts and the heat, the effort required to push and shove to make progress were having their effect and many of them were releasing their pent up frustration. Drivers who had been stationary for hours were showing their frustration in a cacophony of horn blowing.

'Let's hope a fire doesn't break out said one bystander to another,' the whole bloody city would burn down.'

Martin suddenly decided that he had enough and turned off the road and parked in someone's drive. It was empty and unlikely to be needed in the short term. He did not care. He had to get his story somehow.

But the cheerful acceptance of the situation was beginning to deteriorate. Large groups of people were obviously antagonistic towards the man and what he was reported as saying on the Peter Potter Investigation were making their feelings known on a increasing scale.

The rain was now getting heavier but still did nothing to dissuade the several groups demonstrating holding hastily constructed banners critical of the man although the boards and paper sheets began to look bedraggled and sad.

Devout Protestants and Catholics, antagonistic about what he was saying about the church, formed agitated groups; militant Muslim groups were remonstrating against his reference to Muslim terrorists, completely forgetting his stated view that Islam was peaceful and that he had said the fanatics were a small minority. Others, probably the strongest and most vociferous were angry that anyone was claiming to be another Jesus Christ even though he had claimed no such thing, or even vaguely suggested it. All were pushing and shoving towards an unknown target.

The centre of the city and its close environs were like a cauldron shortly coming to the boil. A violent overspill seemed inevitable. The shouting of slogans, the violent arguments between groups and individuals caused a cacophony of sound that seemed to obliterate the ability to think.

* * *

Martin's problem was to decide what to do. Not knowing exactly where the man was made it difficult to decide in which direction he should launch himself. Anyway, he thought, any route would be as difficult as the one he had tried. He began to worry because he kept hearing snatches of conversation suggesting that the man had been arrested and taken away by the police.

They only thing they could do with him, Martin thought, would be take him to the police station which, Martin knew, lay somewhere to the south of him, on the edge of the crowds. They could, of course, take him to a private house or some other building but he knew that policemen are creatures of habit, not endowed with too much imagination. Anyway, he would be safer in a police station.

Although drained of energy with sweat pouring from him and his sodden clothes dishevelled he decided to make his way to the police station and began to edge his way away from the seething mass. The scene was incredible, one he never thought he would see in England where crowds had a tradition of being well-behaved and controlled. The continuing rain seemed to have no cooling down effect.

Still more people seemed to be arriving and on the periphery of the crowds lay lines of the injured, laid out flat like the dead on a battlefield; injured children crying, separated from their parents, anxious mothers and fathers looking for lost offspring, tender residents nurturing the victims and doing what they could to make them comfortable. Sadly he walked away through the scene. There was nothing he could do to help and he had a job to do.

Eventually he reached the police station. Although there were large numbers of people milling around outside, the building itself looked deserted and calm. It was clear that if the man was being brought here he had not arrived yet, He knew he was in the right place when he saw a small posse of reporters outside the main entrance

'What do you expect to find?' the Telegraph Today's Grant asked him, smiling broadly.

'Well, I hope the man is here.'

'We have no idea but we think he is but you won't get anything in there,' he nodded towards the door. They won't say anything,' was his disappointing reply.

Martin decided to try anyway. Two police officers standing on either side of the door moved to stop him but a shirt sleeved sergeant, his stripes sewn on his white shirt just above the neat roll in his sleeves, approaching the two officers looked at Martin suspiciously: 'And what do you think I can I do for you?' he asked in a deep Hampshire voice. Martin identified himself as a reporter and was sharply told to 'go and join the others.'

'I hear you have arrested the cause of all this trouble?' he said, looking towards the scene outside.

'Depends who you mean.,' said the sergeant pompously, carefully straightening the charge book that lay on the counter in front of him. 'There are all sorts of trouble makers, some of them even work on newspapers,' he smiled.

'I've been trying to get to see the man who it seems is attracting these crowds but without much success,' he said, looking down at his clothes for corroboration. 'There's a rumour going around that he has been taken into protective custody, is that right?'

'I've no idea,' the sergeant replied stiffly.

'Come off it sergeant. If it's true my paper will find out fairly quickly and I'll be in trouble if I don't even know where he is. I'm only trying to do my job,' Martin pleaded.

'I don't know what has happened. All I know is that if the crowds got out of control we were going to bring him in for his own safety. Whether there was any trouble or not I don't know. I've been stuck in here all day.'

'Well it seems there was trouble. This crowd is certainly almost out of control. What I really want to know is, if they do take him into custody will they bring him here?'

'Good question. Could be,' he replied enigmatically. 'On the other hand they could take him somewhere else.'

'For God's sake,' Martin said impatiently. 'I'm not going to assassinate the bloke. I just want to save myself some trouble. If they are bringing him here I can wait. If not I'll have to chase all over the bloody town looking for him.'

The sergeant leaned forward conspiratorially. 'Between you and me son, the plan was to bring him here if possible but they may be forced to take him out of town. I honestly don't know what they will do,' he smiled as if to show that he really was doing his best to help.

Martin looked at his watch. It was almost three o'clock. He had no idea that time had passed so quickly.

'Where are you?' the News Editor asked when Martin got through to the paper.

'At Winchester police station. Have you any idea what's happening?'

'You're the reporter, you tell me.'

'It sounds daft but I can't get anywhere near him, there are millions of people here, the situation is totally out of control,' Martin said, ignoring the scowl from the police sergeant.

Martin explained what had happened and confirmed with James that he would wait at the police station until they brought the man in. If he turned up elsewhere it was just too bad. Martin walked to join the other journalist s who were as ignorant as he was.

'Snotty nosed little bastards. I'd like to get my bloody hands on them again.' Fred Thomas snarled angrily at the world in general, ignoring his wife who sat next to him on the wooden bench quietly crying into her handkerchief.

'I'd like to get my hands on that bastard who hit me,' Fred muttered to himself. 'I'd kill him.'

Joyce continued crying, tears streaming down her face as she used the handkerchief to try and muffle the sound of her heavy sobbing. The unhappy couple were sitting at a bus stop hoping to get somewhere where they could get transport back to Birmingham. The rain had stopped by now and Fred, soaking wet, his coat torn, his shirt open at the neck, sat with his elbows on his knees ignoring others waiting hopefully for public transport that was totally unable to navigate the streets.

He was also ignoring the swelling that was growing with alarming speed under his left eye. He had not wanted to fight although he had no intention of avoiding it if was necessary. He had only come to listen because Joyce insisted and had almost nagged him to death. It nearly drove him round the bend when the man started speaking about the value of principles laid down two thousand years ago and the need to remind the world of the need to maintain them. A lot of religious crap he thought.

As the conversation with the man and the people gathered around him was continuing his attention had wandered. He thought it would be a cheap day out for all Joyce wanted to do was to listen to the silly bugger . He wouldn't have to spend a fortune shopping.

His thoughts were suddenly interrupted by someone shouting. This is more interesting, he thought, more like a bloody union meeting. Joyce was angry and upset but Fred thought it brightened up the whole afternoon.

He was quite enjoying himself listening to the wise cracks and heckling until those yobboes pushed their way to the front and started telling everyone to shut up.

'What about free speech,' he had yelled at them in true union fashion. Joyce told him to keep quiet but he did not listen.

Fred began shouting back with gusto until some chap came up to him and told him to shut up or fuck off. A heated argument followed until the man took a swing at Fred and Fred took a swing back. He would have left it at that if the man, in trying to avoid Fred's blow, had not accidentally bumped into Joyce sending her reeling. That had got Fred really mad and he started punching out in earnest. He had hit quite a few people, some of them totally innocent, but someone suddenly landed one right in his eye. He'd put his hands to his face in agony and taken another punch in the stomach before Joyce had pulled him away.

Fred wanted to go back immediately and sort the whole crowd out, but the police had arrived and arrested some of the participants in the fight, missing Fred himself as Joyce had pulled him away.

'I'll get the bastards,' Fred thought to himself. 'I'll find out who they are and I'll get them.'

* * *

'Oh Harry it was really terrible. I never thought I would see anything like it in England, it was terrible,' Mabel Gregg said tearfully.

She was in a state of disoriented torment. Faced, for the first time in her life, with a major crisis after finding out about Harry's sexual exploits, she had returned to her Mother's home in search of sympathy, understanding and a place to sleep.

The truth about her husband's sexual activities had been broken to her by a 'friend' who stressing that she 'was not one to talk but' had passed on the gossip at the police station.

It was his habit, she explained, to closely examine a number of women he met while on patrol. Her information was sketchy but she was able 'only to be helpful' to name several.

All Mabel got from her mother was a place to sleep. Balancing precariously on the edge of seventy years of age, she was brought up in the 'grin and bear it' school of matrimony.

A wife married for better or for worse. If it turned out to be worse that was just too bad. She did not exactly say 'you've made your bed now you must lie on it' but everything she said had that implication. Whatever the husband did was no excuse to break up the family, even if there were only two of you and no children to worry about.

So Mabel's husband had had 'connections' with other women. So what? Men were like that, little better than animals when it came to sex. Mabel would have to put up with it until he was too old to function. Mabel's father, she found out for the first time, had put himself about the neighbourhood where they lived when they were first married but he'd eventually , she explained permanently clutching her handkerchief, grown out of it.

Mabel put up with the lecture for several hours and was continued sporadically over the next day. It was when Doris had told her that she was going to Winchester with her friend and the local Women's Institute was going to Winchester to listen to the man she decided it would be a good way to escape her mother and volunteered to go with them. It was a decision she later regretted. She never got close to the man because of the crowds and the appalling weather. It was the latter that eventually drove her back to her husband and the peace and quiet of her own home.

When she walked into the house her appearance was such a shock to Harry that he said nothing. Her hair, normally neat, was wet and in disarray, her coat wet and creased and her face tear stained and grubby. She sat in her chair leaning forward, playing anxiously with her hands, relating the events of the day.

'We got the bus to Winchester, Doris didn't really want to go but Mrs Gilbert....'

'Was she with you?'

'...yes, the three of us were together. Mrs Gilbert said we ought to go and see him and see what happened. We got there all right but we got into the middle of the crowd so it was difficult to see him because there were too many people, there were thousands of people most of them wet and bedraggled. A lot of them were trying to listen to what he said but a lot of long haired youths and girls were laughing and giggling. Most people were listening quietly until he said something about the church and organized religion…'

'What did he say?' Harry asked, interrupting the flow of words.

'I don't really know,' Mabel replied. 'I couldn't hear the actual words because we could not get near enough. I only caught the sense of it from what people around me said.'

'Well, what happened?' Harry asked impatiently.

'There were some very serious looking people standing at the front, they looked quite old and they should have known better but they started shouting at him. I don't know what they meant but suddenly some scruffy youths started joining in. They were laughing so I don't think they were serious. Then someone at the back threw something at the man. I think it was a stone but I don't know for sure. Anyway it hit someone standing near the man and he fell to the ground.'

'Knocked out?' Harry asked with interest.

'No I don't think so. The shouting increased something awful and then another group of young men pushed their way to the front, ever so rude they were. Then the fighting started. It was awful, shouting and screaming. I was frightened to death, so was Doris, but I thought Mrs Gilbert was going to join in.'

'She would,' Harry said scornfully.

'Anyway, we managed to pull her away and get to safety. Someone trod on my foot and it still hurts. Doris lost her hat and a lot of old people got knocked down. Luckily the police came and calmed everything down so we decided to leave before trouble started again. Otherwise, Mrs Gilbert said, someone would have got killed.'

'What happened to the man?'

'I don't really know we didn't stay to find out. I think he was hit by something. His friends pulled him away from the fighting and I didn't see him again. Mrs Gilbert said it all started because he began criticizing the church.'

'Mrs Gilbert,' Harry sneered. 'That bloody woman thinks she knows everything.'

'Oh Harry, don't be so rude. She could just hear better than I could, that's all.'

⋆ ⋆ ⋆

The scene had changed. The tempo had increased, the crowds thickened and there was more noise. Martin looked on in horror. Booing and cheering increased in intensity as a large black car slowly edged its way towards the police station, crawling through a churning mass of humanity.

It was not the size of the crowd that disturbed him, he was getting used to that, it was the attitude of the people in the crowd. Shouting and screaming men and women, the snarling faces of most of them, brandishing fists at the car, some banging on the windows and bodywork and the none too gentle efforts of the police. The booing and shouting reached ear splitting proportions as the car neared its destination. Gone was the good hearted banter of earlier in the day.

It took the car twenty minutes to travel the last fifty yards of its journey. It stopped almost opposite Martin and the other reporters. The crowd surged forward and he found himself fighting for his life.

Suddenly a posse of policemen, some fifty strong, charged their way out the police station and brutally formed a narrow corridor from the car to the building. Faced by the uncontrolled violence of the crowd the policemen, some in riot gear, drew truncheons and began wielding them at anyone who got in the way. The booing and shouting was joined by screaming as the victims reeled back. The noise was almost unbearable but there was little Martin could do to suppress it. He could not get his hands up to his ears for the press of people around him. Martin suddenly realized that the young policemen were as frightened as he was. The whole scene was one of uncontrolled fear on both sides of what was now a pitched battle.

Struggling violently to keep his feet Martin was punched in the ear, then kicked in the groin by those around him. The crowd was fighting back and it didn't care who it was fighting.

Suddenly Martin felt his mind detaching itself from reality. The noise seemed to fade into the distance. He felt he was going to pass out. Still half-heartedly fending off those fighting around him he saw the car door open and two hefty police sergeants leap out and stand on either side. The corridor of policemen narrowed slightly as the crowd pressed in, becoming more frenzied as the man himself, seemingly calm and unworried, slowly stepped out of the car and look around before being hustled into the police station.

It appeared for a moment as if he was about to speak to the crowd but he was given no chance as a policeman took each arm and almost lifted him off the pavement, up the steps and through the door.

For what seemed like an age Martin felt as if he was in a time warp. The noise and struggling around him faded into the background as all his concentration was centred on the figure that stepped out of the car, the man on whom almost all his thoughts had been concentrated for what seemed like an age.

He man was tall, just over six feet, Martin estimated. His hair was golden brown and wavy, reaching almost his shoulders at the back. He was clean shaven. The face was striking, aquiline with dark brown eyes emphasized by their pure white setting. Laugh lines spiked into his temples. The skin was bronzed with deep creases outlining the cheeks.

Even in his state of semi-consciousness Martin smiled to himself when he saw that the man was wearing a pure white sweater with a neatly rolled neck - the garment that had provided the clue linking him with all the so-called miracles. He wondered how he managed to keep it so pristine. As he moved up the steps Martin noticed he had light brown slacks, brown socks and open toed sandals. He was an impressively calm figure, an oasis of serenity in a sea of turmoil.

As the man was led into the police station by his escort Martin fell to his knees, sound came back into his consciousness, the struggle began again. The police cordon quickly withdrew releasing the pressure of the crowd and as the whole mob lurched forward he found himself groveling on all fours, hands trampled on, ribs kicked and head buffeted as others struggled to keep their feet.

In a moment of panic he realized that he could be trampled to death by the milling, unheeding hysterical crowd. He felt the air above him being shut off, the pressure around him intensifying. With an inhuman surge of self preservation he forced himself backwards, clawing and gripping anything that came to hand. He grabbed the pocket of a man's jacket which came away in his hand. A sudden kick in the small of his back knocked the wind out of him and after what seemed several minutes, but which could only have been seconds, fighting for breath he began to struggle again.

Slowly he was able to hoist himself up to a crouching position and then, when the crowd gave another swift lurch, he forced himself upwards onto his feet and he could see daylight and breath freely again.

Gasping for air he looked around. Somehow he had been pushed towards the police station. Frantically he tried to edge nearer but the struggling around him grew in intensity. He hardly knew what was happening when he felt a hand grab him by the scruff of the neck and tear him from the crowd into the doorway of the police station. The Sergeant he had spoken to when he first arrived stood puffing by his side.

'I saw you go down and thought you were a goner. When you suddenly reappeared I thought I'd better grab you.'

'Thank God you did, I thought I'd had it,' Martin panted.

Still fighting for breath, his body bruised and sore, his clothes filthy and torn, he was helped back into the calm serenity of the police station where only the presence of a large number of policeman and the steady background of shouting outside reminded him of the drama he had just survived.

* * *

'Where have they taken him?' Martin asked when he had got his breath back.

'He's with the Chief,' the Sergeant told him.

'Can I see him?'

'Blimey, haven't you had enough,' he gasped. He shook his head. 'The Chief won't let anyone talk to him.' he said.

'Is he under arrest?'

'He was brought in for his own protection. There is no charge against him but I think he'll be asked to leave the city as soon as possible.'

'Was he really in that much danger?' Martin asked. ' It seemed to me the trouble only started when he was arrested.'

'It started long before that. They reckon a group of ruffians were waiting for him when he arrived and started causing trouble. They didn't give him a chance. We got the tip off last night that there might be trouble and when things looked ugly we brought him in. He will be released shortly and taken to a place of safety.'

'How will you get him out?'

'We have our ways,' said the policeman mysteriously.

Martin decided he was not going to get anywhere, he would not be allowed to see the man and he would do better outside checking on what was happening.

He walked into the outer office and was surprised to find that it was full of reporters. All of them from almost every other national newspapers were there.

'Here's the bloke who should know. What's going on?' said Frank Faulkner when he saw Martin.

'Why should I know?' Martin asked.

'Well, you've just been talking to the sergeant.'

'I know no more than you,' Martin replied, 'in fact, probably not so much., he will be leaving soon as far as I can find out. I've no idea when.'

'He's what?' Grant snapped. A tall, blonde man with a strongly chiseled face and determined jaw never asked a question amiably. He was always on the attack but he was rarely rude.

'He is being asked to leave the city and I think he will do so tonight.'

'What for? Where is he going? When?.' The questions were fired at Martin with the rapidity of a drum roll.

'They're kicking him out into the hands of the mob,' Grant declared angrily.

'The mob will have dispersed by then,' said Faulkner, 'the pubs will be open soon.'

'Why do you think he'll be torn to pieces?' Martin asked. 'Why all this trouble?'

'I've no idea really' Grant replied. 'None of us has been able to get near him.' He looked around at the other reporters for confirmation.

'But according to people we've been talking to he's upset almost everyone in sight. He's alleged to have attacked the church for failing in its duty, he's had a go at the Pope although I don't know what he said, he's attacked racialism of every sort, he doesn't like permissiveness of any sort, says there's too much greed and so on ad infinitum. You name it, he doesn't like it.'

Grant went on: 'Some think he's absolutely bloody marvellous, others say he's a phoney and a crook. I've heard him called a nigger because he's dark skinned and a hooligan because he's got long hair. People really are bloody awful. The tabloids haven't help with their bloody stupid headlines like 'Has the Messiah Returned?' 'The Second Coming?,'

'Is Healer From Outer Space?' Fucking stupid if you ask me.' said Grant, looking at Graham.

'Hang on a minute,' snapped the Daily Sun's Graham, 'I don't write the headlines. I've never written anything about miracles.'

'Any more miracles?' Martin asked.

'Not that we've heard of. Frank spoke to a bloke who claimed he'd been cured of asthma, chap from the Daily Sun reckons there's a rumour he's raised someone from the dead in Birmingham. Except that as far as we know he hasn't been to Birmingham and they're better off dead there anyway. It's all a load of crap if you ask me,' Grant declared.

Martin was overcome with disappointment. What had all started so excitingly and full of promise was now deteriorating into sensationalism and sordidness. He had to find the truth about the man.

'When is he going and where?.' Grant asked.

'You'd better ask the Chief,' Martin told him.

'The Chief isn't seeing anyone,' the Sergeant interrupted. 'I told him you were here but he says he has nothing to say. And you've got to wait outside. He wants you all out.'

Reluctantly, and not without critical comment, the reporters shuffled out into the heat. It was slightly calmer as Faulkner had predicted and the weather had fully relented as if to mark the fact that the man was safe. The police had been busy and pushed the remaining crowd to both ends of the road and blocked it off. The reporters stood around outside wondering what to do.

'What a bloody life,' said Grant. 'Once again, gentlemen we wait,' he added, sitting himself down on the step.

Although it was early evening the atmosphere was still hot and humid so that beads of perspiration stood out on their faces even though they were doing nothing. Heat does not sustain impatience or encourage activity and gradually its soporific effect swept over them as they sat about and waited. Occasionally police officers interrupted their siesta as they walked in and out. For two hours, punctuated by sporadic inquiries as to what was happening, they waited patiently. It was Grant who suddenly came to life.

'Where the bloody hell is he?' he asked everyone in general. 'I can't wait here all bloody night.' He turned quickly, almost tripping over a prostrate body, and disappeared into the police station. He was back in less than a minute.

'The bloody place is empty, ' he declared. 'He's gone, the buggers have got him out!'

* * *

Miriam Cartwright was fast losing her temper. The last time she did that was thirty years ago when she was fifteen and saw a boy ill-treating a puppy. She had smashed the boy with a piece of broken tree branch and got into lots of trouble.

Now the anger welled up inside her again. It was an anger fed by frustration. She was a geyser about to blow. There was a fat self-satisfied Bishop pouring scorn on the man, on what he had done and on what he was going to do. And Charles, sitting alongside her, was agreeing with him!

'Absolutely right,' said Charles, supporting one of the Bishop's more outlandish remarks.

'Rubbish,' he responded to something Porter said.

'The man's a complete fool,' was how he described Craddock. That was something Miriam could agree with.

'I don't know how you can support the Bishop,' Miriam said, shaking her head, trying to keep cool. 'neither of you have met the man, all you know is what you hear or read from third parties and yet you condemn him out of hand.'

'There is no question that the man is a rogue,' Charles replied.

'How do you know?' Miriam insisted. 'Just suppose, just suppose for a minute that someone like Jesus did come back. How would you know?

What would you do? I bet you wouldn't believe him for a start.'

Charles pondered for a minute. 'Such a thing is not likely to happen,' he said at last.

'How do you know? Just suppose it did. What do you think would be the response?'

'Well.....he would have to prove who he was I suppose. He would make contact with the Archbishop of Canterbury if he was in this country. He would have to do his work through the church.'

'Why?'

'Well, if he was from God...Oh ! this is ridiculous.....then he would have to work through the church, God's church.'

'What about Catholics, Muslims, Buddhists, Jews and all the other religions. Would he have to contact them all?'

'This is a stupid argument.'

'No it isn't. You believe in God. Right. Suppose God took one look at the mess in the world today, the wars, the disease, famine, violence and thought I'd better send someone to remind them' what do you think would happen? I know. He would be treated just like the man is being treated now and how the last one was treated. The ordinary people would go and listen and learn. All the officials would call him a charlatan, try to stop him and would probably kick him out. You would hate him. Why? Because he would be trespassing on your territory. Only those who've officially joined the club can talk about Christ.' Miriam stopped for breath. It was the longest speech she had ever made. She waited for the wrath of Charles.

He said nothing for almost five minutes, just sat looking at the television screen. The sound had been turned down when the item on the man had finished. Miriam watched him closely. Waiting for the next outburst.

'When you come to think about it,' he said slowly and deliberately, 'You are absolutely right. We would not recognize him. We are all too concerned with our own affairs. You are quite correct,' he continued, speaking slowly and with deliberation, 'We do not have open minds. We would not accept him because we would not know. I doubt if he would arrive and say 'Hello, I'm the second Coming, the new Redeemer. But Miriam,' he looked at her with love and devotion in his eyes, 'I cannot believe for one moment that this man is such a person. However, I must apologize to you for my attitude the last few days. I was wrong and it was unforgivable of me.'

Miriam was stunned and near to tears. Charles never apologized. His reaction was so unexpected when she had built herself up for a battle royal. She was completely deflated.

'Thank you,' was all she could say as she dabbed her eyes with her handkerchief.

Charles put his arm around her. 'Sorry old girl,' he smiled. 'I'm afraid I've been as bigoted as that Bishop. Barnaby was always a bit of a pompous twit. I'm sorry I was so nasty about your article and so unreasonable thereafter. Unforgivable, absolutely unforgivable.'

'I forgive you,' she sobbed.

They sat quietly together, each concerned with their own thoughts. After a while Miriam stopped sobbing and looked up at her husband.

'I would like to go and hear him speaking somewhere,'

'Oh, I don't know,' Charles replied, shaking his head. 'There always seems to be trouble in the crowd when he is around and I wouldn't want you involved. I think it is too dangerous.'

'I must satisfy myself about him or I will always wonder. I would be very careful,' she said, looking at him lovingly. Suddenly she had a bright idea.

'You could come with me, then I would be all right,' she said brightly.

'Oh, no.....' Charles started, he was about to call the idea ridiculous., but paused. 'Why not?' he said. 'I don't do much for you. And it would make up for treating you so badly. We'll go together and make our own minds up. First., we must find out where he is.'

* * *

Once, when Hereford United had miraculously reached the fourth round of the FA Cup and had been drawn at home to Manchester United, seven or eight thousand supporters from the northern city had invaded the little cathedral town and brought total chaos. Fred Salmons, a staunch supporter of the home team was driven to a fear he had not known before as rampaging noisy mobs of youths, so-called supporters, roamed the streets.

He had sworn that for the rest of his life he would avoid crowds. It was a promise that he had kept until the day Doris had persuaded him he ought to go with her and see whether the man everyone wanted to see was the same man who had told him his legs were not broken.

Fred Salmons, an inoffensive and generous little man, did not like to deny his wife or children anything. His philosophy regarding his legs was simple and straight forward. He jumped, he thought he broke both his legs but they were all right and that was that. He wasn't at all bothered about whether a 'miracle' had been performed. The only miracle that would impress him was one that provided the right numbers on his lottery ticket and enough money to stop him worrying and enable him to take care of his family's needs. As far as he was concerned he was a happy man, his lined face usually had a smile, or at least the hint of a smile, on it and his brown eyes were friendly and alive.

One of eleven children of a waste disposal operative, what was known in more honest days as a 'bin' man, he had been brought up to be concerned about others, mainly his brothers and sisters. He always had to put their needs first. As a young msan he had contributed his share to the family income working first as an errand boy, then a storeman and latterly a school caretaker. He had philosophically accepted the fact that he did not have a job because his place of work had burned down. He was still being paid by the convent and knew he would be given another job soon. The temporary accommodation in a council flat suited him well. He wasn't over bothered.

His main interest above all else, except Gladys, was stamp collecting. Although he liked to have a few bob on the horses on Saturday, and to watch them lose on television, he was quite happy to take Doris to Winchester if she wanted to go. If that's what she wanted, that's what they would do.

They had joined the crowd on the outskirts of the town when it was still comfortable and then had been caught up in the maelstrom in the same way that Martin had experienced. He had grabbed Doris's hand and had not let go once. Although their hands were stiff and sweaty but they dare not let each other go.

They had been early so that they were towards the front when the man arrived. Salmons had been astounded when he saw that the doctor who had insisted that he legs were broken was there, talking to the man who was clearly the one who had told him his legs were all right.

'Jesus Christ Doris, **it is** the same man !' he told her, gripping her hand even more tightly.

'And that's the doctor with him.' What could it mean' he asked himself. Who were these people and why had they been involved with him?

'I told you it was the same man,' said Doris. 'But I don't know why the doctor is here. Funny isn't it?'

People around them had been listening to what they were saying and began asking questions. Fred, who didn't really like talking to strangers, began to tell them what had happened but soon Doris had taken over and was explaining to an increasing number of inquisitive listeners how her husband had been miraculously healed by this mystery man.

'They weren't healed,' Fred whispered. 'They were never broke.'

'Shhh,' she replied. 'It's better how I tell it.'

A few of the listeners, particularly the women, were enthralled by Doris's story. The men were more cynical, some smiling sarcastically as she continued her tale. Suddenly they noticed some young people laughing and jeering and they began to be jostled as the crowd tried to move away from the man and possible trouble. Once again they were being pushed and shoved, still clinging closely together.

Eventually they reached the steps of a doorway to an office block . Standing on the top step they could clearly see both the man and the doctor and what was happening.

'He looks very nice,' said Doris. 'I don't remember seeing him at the fire. I'm sure I would have noticed.'

'It's him all right,' said Fred. 'I recognize the jumper...and the face.'

They stood watching the two men talking to those around them. The jostling had temporarily stopped although the original trouble makers were still there laughing among themselves.

Suddenly the man looked up towards where Fred and Doris were standing.

'He's looking at us,' Fred said nervously to Doris. 'He's smiling at me!'

Whether or not the man was smiling at Fred, the caretaker was completely transfixed. His eyes could not leave the man's face. He felt very strange. There was something magnetic about the man. Fred felt a strong urge to walk over and talk to him. What about he had no idea. But it was impossible. There were too many people, he would not be able to push his way through with Doris and he certainly was not going to let her go.

'I've got to see him again,' he said aloud to himself. Doris looked at him quizzically.

'What did you say dear?' she asked. 'Nothing,' said Fred not know why he had said it.

★ ★ ★

# Part Four

# OMEGA

THE PETER POTTER INVESTIGATION HAD alerted the world to the story that was developing in England, the riot in Winchester and the excessive descriptions of who the man was and what he was alleged to have done in the media, had intensified the interest. Press representatives from all parts of the world had arrived in London and were covering the story from every angle, bearing down on anyone who had, or said they had, any contact with the man. The interest was reflected throughout every part of the country and was the predominant subject of conversation in pubs, clubs and wherever people met together. No-one was without a view.

As usual self-confessed experts came out of the woodwork and gave their opinion of who he was, his validity as a healer, and what his arrival meant to the church and the world in general, even though they had not had any contact with him and all the information they had got was what had been passed on second and third hand.

John Porter was now generally accepted to be the man's official spokesman although he never made this claim. He felt it had fallen to him because he was the only person the man was continually in contact with. It was no surprise to anyone that he decided, against his better judgement but forced upon him by the pressure of questions and his desire to make sure that facts given were correct., to call a press conference. He was very much afraid that the story was getting out of hand and claims were being made which were not true and had never been confirmed.

His attitude in public was reserved and uncertain. His narrow, well defined face with a nose that was slightly too big, was generally expressionless. He rarely smiled but a twinkle in this eye was a recognizable indication of a pleasant and friendly personality under the severe façade.

In was indicative of the interest in the man that although no announcement had been made the fact that a press conference was to be held, and its venue were quickly widely known, largely by word of mouth.

Martin heard about it from Frank Faulkner when he met him accidentally at Waterloo station. Faulkner had been told by David Grant of Telegraph Today who had picked it up in a betting shop where the odds of the man being what was becoming known as 'the Second Coming' had dropped from 1,000-1 to 10-1 in only three days.

Unaware of the growing media interest, Porter who was, after all, a doctor who had no experience of dealing with the press. On advice from Grimshaw he had booked a room to seat around 50 people in a five star hotel just off Victoria Street in London. The hotel had been originally built during the early inter war years by a speculative builder as an expansive home for a wealthy city family or a parliamentarian who wanted to live near his work. It was eventually turned into an hotel when it finally occurred to the developer that neither wealthy industrialists or politicians wanted a large home in the centre of London. As a hotel it had changed hands many times and had escaped serious damage during the 39-45 war years. Each owner wanted to impress his personality on the place and had altered it or added annexes or incorporated neighbouring offices so that by now it was a warren of rooms of different shapes and sizes and winding corridors.

The room was typical of the meeting rooms available at hotels, rectangular with a long table at one end and neat rows of chairs, the walls hung with boring scenes of London probably printed some 100 years earlier.

Porter envisaged a sort of well organized consultation meeting, similar those held in hospitals to agree treatment of a patient and future policy, with participants politely asking questions, listening to the answers and then writing accurate stories which would make everything clear. Journalists, he thought, would ask polite questions in the search for the truth. This belief lasted only a few minutes after his arrival at the hotel. Six television teams had their cameras and crew waiting outside, each wanting a position which would give them a clear view of the so-called platform. Naturally they wanted plugs and space for their cables and tried to clear away the chairs from the first two rows and set up, thus hiding the platform from view of the journalists sitting behind them. The representatives of the latter made their feelings known in no uncertain manner. Porter quickly found out that journalists and cameramen were not soul mates.

Porter and his small team and the management of the hotel were overcome by confusion and partly solved the problem by moving the event to their largest conference room which held around 200 people. At least it had a number of electric plug points available for the television crews. Porter, with the help of more experienced management representatives did a deal with the television crews to set up their cameras at either side of the room giving them a clear view of the platform and allowing the journalists sitting in the centre seat to at least see the person they were going to question.

Martin watched with deep misgivings and tried to advise Porter how it should be done but found it difficult to make the doctor understand.

He was surprised to find that Porters 'team' comprised Arnold Grimshaw and Ruth Morton, both participants in the initial events involving the man. Martin had no idea that they had met each other or that Grimshaw and Morton were now active followers.

It took much longer than expected to get all those concerned into some sort of order, to calm down the arguments between cameramen and reporters and to ensure that television crews stayed in their allotted spaces. It was a new and baffling experience for Porter.

Eventually the platform party settled down and Porter, looking like a nervous bridegroom waiting at the altar and having second thoughts, stood to face a mass of expectant faces.

'As most of you will know, Porter began, somewhat relieved that he had the opportunity to return momentarily to the profession he really knew about, 'I was the medical practitioner who diagnosed a fissure in the lower limbs of the janitor at an educational institution in Hereford following a conflagration and subsequent incident which required medical attention….'

'Could we have an interpreter,' shouted a baffled American journalist. 'I haven't understood a bloody word.' Porter looked shocked.

'He was the doctor who diagnosed that the caretaker at the school fire had broken both his legs when he jumped out of the of a burning building,' Grimshaw explained with a broad grin.'

'Thank you,' replied the American sitting down again, 'can we keep to one syllable words in future.' Everyone laughed, grateful for the interruption..

'I'm sorry,' said Porter, blushing with embarrassment, 'but I'm not used to this sort of thing. I will try and speak English in future,' he added, nodding to the American. 'I said that the man had broken both his legs but it transpired, sorry, turned out, that both legs were perfectly sound. I do not know how I made such an elementary mistake but in view of subsequent events I might eventually be forgiven.

'You have all covered the events I am talking about, the curing of the crippled boy, the escape from what might have been a fatal accident and the fact that only one person, the bomber himself, was killed during a terrorist bomb here in London. These events have led many of you, and the public, to believe that there is a person currently performing what are being described as miracles.

'I am now in close touch with the man under discussion and can say categorically that he makes no claim of miracles being performed. He describes himself as a teacher who is simply trying to remind us of the message given to the world 2,000 years ago. During that time the world has changed and advanced in many ways and much of what was said at that time is what you would describe as out of date. He says he is really updating.. His message is exactly the same was it was 2,000 years ago but much of it has been interpreted inaccurately with personal feelings and opinions allowed to infiltrate.

'Are you saying that he is what we would describe as 'the second coming?' Is he claiming to be the new Jesus Christ?' asked Noel Green, a well known trouble maker from the News of the World.

'He certainly is not,' snapped Porter, upset by Green's aggressive attitude, something he was certainly not used to.

He went on, glancing angrily at the reporter,' I would like to introduce you to my colleagues on the platform. On my right is Mr Arnold Grimshaw and on my left Mrs Ruth Morton. Mr Grimshaw is one of the survivors of the London terrorist bombing where only one person, the bomber, was killed, while Mrs Morton and her small daughter survived what should have been in most cases a fatal car accident. They have since met the man and have been so impressed that they have decided to join and help him. They are both prepared to answer questions later.

'Why isn't the man himself here?' asked Grant for the Telegraph Today..

'As I have said before he will not talk directly to the media because he has no confidence that his words will be accurately recorded. He fears that personal views and interpretations will dilute, even alter the message.' Porter was interrupted by mumbled conversation among the journalists and one quiet cry of 'shame' and another 'he knows us too well.'

'He would rather talk to small groups of people in the certainty that his words will be passed on quickly and accurately mainly because the people will listen to what he says and are not interested in exaggerating or searching for a headline.'

'May I point out, ' said Faulkner with a touch of sarcasm in his voice,' that the original story of Jesus Christ was told by four Apostles, Matthew, Mark, Luke and John. They were the reporters of their day and their stories differed in some respects but I've not heard any criticism of that largely because the fact that they differed was confirmation that the stories were genuine. If they had told exactly the same story it would have looked like what we would call a put up job and lose credibility.'

Porter gave Faulkner a friendly grin. 'But they reported what they had seen and heard, as far as we know they did not embellish the story with their own opinions or interpretations. It was pure reporting and we certainly don't get that in this century. You all have too fertile imaginations now.' Faulkner smiled back but said nothing.

'Why England? Why has he chosen this country,' asked Jeremy Clark of the News Mail.

'Because the original message has been ignored or abandoned by practically every section of the community here. Churchgoers, for example, give lip-service to the Ten Commandments but very few people bother to observe them,' replied Porter with emphasis. 'The population has largely lost the church going habit and the Ten Commandments are looked upon as religious decrees and therefore not relevant to them.

'Let me give you some simply examples 'Porter continued. ' The statement that there should be no other God seems to have no place in modern life. Money is now the modern Deity. The directive not to take His name in vain is ignored, the Sabbath day has disappeared, replaced by the seven day working week, honoring your father and mother is no longer of prime importance, the precepts not to kill or steal are no longer considered important while the instruction not to commit adultery has certainly gone by the wayside It has all been in the name of progress and has almost become a national pastime to break the rules of decency, moral obligations, responsibility and accountability.. All these changes have come about under the excuse that we now live in modern times and one has to be modern. Why do things have to be so appalling because it is 'modern'?'

'But this does not only apply to Britain. Standards in every country have fallen or are falling. All the other apostles such as Muhammad, Buddha, Confucius and the others sent out the same message or something similar but they are largely getting the same treatment in the name of progress.

'What is the worst example is the fact that all these 'teachers' gave the same message about not to kill but the world has been at war for over 5,000 years and in the last two hundred centuries, since the birth of Christ and others the fighting has largely been caused by religious differences. That is a shocking fact. Everyone agrees with that statement but none of the nation's leaders does anything to stop it..

'That was a devastating attack on modern life but probably an exaggeration,' said Faulkner,' although it contained some truth.'

'So what does he suggest we do about it,' asked the BBC's Eric Tomson, a highly respected commentator.

'He updates the ten commandments but instead of using a negative approach he adopts a more positive attitude.

'First he explains that there is only one Deity, which is an embodiment of the ideal way of living. It is an intellectual concept described in different ways according the religion.

Referring to what he calls Christianity he mentions the much used phrase 'God is everywhere' and confirms that this is true because God, the basic essential of humanity, is in all of us. There is one Deity but many Gods because everyone has a different vision in their minds. The popular imaginative perception is governed largely by drawings and pictures they have seen. But these drawings and pictures have been and produced by artists using their own imaginations. There is no definitive image of who we are pleased to call The Almighty. The concept of God is given reality by what he describes the Basic Rules of Life, the modern interpretation of the Ten Commandments.

'As I have said they are not commandments, they are a code. By coincidence there are ten of them. The first affirms the Basic Rules as a standard for your beliefs. It tells you to be honest with yourself and with others; to give attention to and care of, your parents; to avoid lying and cheating; admit your mistakes and try to correct them; to respect and give consideration to your neighbours; to treat others as you wish to be treated; to work for the benefit of your family and community; to honour your marriage vows; It suggests that adultery is a violation of several rules.'

'What about homosexuality?' asked Grant, interrupting.

'In my own view homosexuality is intellectually unacceptable. The man knows what I think but has not commented. The trouble is that there is an ambivalent approach recorded in the Bible with different interpretations given by different groups. There is nothing more I can say on this subject.'

'He says that if everyone obeyed these basic rules most of our troubles would disappear,' Porter continued.

There was a stunned silence as the journalists considered what had been said. They had dozens of questions to ask but they were stunned for a second time when Porter spoke again.

'I have explained what the man has said. I have no intention of answering any questions on his view of the Deity or the Code. For me to answer questions would be to put my own interpretation of what he has said. I am in no position to do so. That is what he wants to avoid.'

There was a rumble of dissention as the journalists were denied what they considered their God given right to ask questions. Faulkner, trying to re-establish a semblance of order stood up, silence fell.

'I understand your difficulties even though your decision is disappointing. But you did say we could question Mr Grimshaw and Mrs Morton on what they believed happened to them and why they have joined the man.'

Faulkner pointed out.

'You are quite right,' Porter replied, 'I will ask Mr Grimshaw if he will step forward.'

Arnold Grimshaw, soberly dressed in pin stripe suit, white shirt and blue tie, looking very much the city gent, did not look happy. It was a new experience for him, facing some of the world's top journalists and having to answer questions. In the bank people sought his advice on a one-to-one basis, and he always knew more about the subject they were discussing than the person to whom he was talking. He certainly knew what he was about to discuss but he was nervous of the questions and reaction. He looked hopefully at Porter who was only too happy that his role was temporarily over so he remained still, looking the audience.

'Why do you think the fact you were unhurt when the bomb went off was a miracle. Several other people were also unhurt.' asked Jeremy Clark gently, aware of Grimshaw's nervousness.

'I didn't think it was a miracle and have never said it was. Miracle was a word introduced by you, the media. I just thought I was damn lucky because I was on the bus and quite close to the bomber who was killed. Everyone else thought they were damn lucky. I thought nothing more of it until someone wrote a story about a man in a white sweater was at the scene and said that a man similarly dressed had been seen on other occasions,' said Grimshaw confidently.

'So why are you with him now?' Clark persisted.

'I heard he was speaking close to where I live so I went to hear what he had to say. I liked what he said. I felt he put into words many of the thoughts I had so I decided to stay with him for a while and see if I could help him.

'What sort of thoughts?' asked a voice from the back.

'That things are on a sharp decline in this country. That no-one seems to care very much about anything or anyone as long as they get what they want. I am in the banking business so I know that everything is determined by profit. Not only to those of the banks who decide policy and what will give them most profit, but all those who work for them who never question the decisions. They are as bad as those who lead them. Whenever you query a bank decision you always get the reply 'that is the way we do it' which means that they are conscious of being part of the team. There is never any consideration of the effect their decisions will have on other people. Money is their only god.'

Noel Green, News of the World was quickly on his feet but Porter was even quicker.

'Mr Grimshaw has explained what happened to him and why he is here today. We are now entering the area of opinions, views and explanations and that's not we are here for. I am going to ask Mrs Morton to come forward.'

Ruth Morton, a cheerful 30-year-old in a colorful dress and with a broad smile under a considerable mass of blonde hair, jumped up enthusiastically.

'This is a new experience for me. It's the first time that 200 men and women are actually waiting for me to speak and prepared to listen to what I say. Normally they are trying to shut me up and change the subject.' The serious tension that had so far enveloped the assembly suddenly changed midst a wave of laughter.

'I know exactly what you mean,' said Robina Carter of the Express & Star, smiling broadly.

'I have the same two questions and I will certainly be listening to the answers. What happened to you and why are you here?'

'As most of you know,' sad Morton, looking round the room,' I was driving my small daughter home when I was hit full on by a car being driven at around 50mph. I was bashed into a large tree which quickly re-designed the car.' Another wave of laughter.

'My four-year-old daughter, in the passenger seat, was knocked unconscious. I thought she was dead.. I had become an untidy heap, my head jammed between the gear stick and the handbrake with my legs twisted above my head. Despite reports to the contrary I do not think I was knocked unconscious for I seemed to be quickly looking at the lifeless body of my daughter.

'Help was quickly on the scene but they could not get me out of the car because the driver's door was rammed up against the tree. They could not use cutting gear because there was petrol floating all over the place. They did manage to free my daughter and confirm that she was still alive.

'It was while I was contemplating death and what would happen to my family, who would look after my daughter - I don't have a husband - when I saw a man's face at the window. It was quite incredible. I was injured, shaking with shock, fearing the worst when I looked into his eyes. All fear fell away. I knew immediately that they would get me out, my daughter was safe and so would I be. From being in the shadow of death I was in the sunlight of life. I even joked with the firemen trying to free me telling them watch where they put their hands..

It was when I was free and had spoken to the police that I saw the man again, standing nearby. I went over to talk to him and say thank you. He said he was happy to help and her agreed to meet up again. He explained briefly what he was trying to and we arranged to meet and talk. After a long discussion with him later I decided to try and help him,' Morton said with finality, acknowledging the unexpected applause..

'As a teacher I am very interested in young people,' she went on as an afterthought, 'I was able to talk to him about my views on crime and lack of respect among the young. I am a firm believer that parents are responsible for their children until they are 18 and they should accept that responsibility. I believe that they should be held responsible if their children get into trouble with the law. If I was in power I would give serious thought to introducing a law which would send parents to gaol if their son or daughter was a habitual offender so that they would serve the sentence imposed on their offspring. If this happened parents would become much more interested in what their children were getting up to and, one assumes, the children would be much more reticent about getting their parents into trouble if they thought that one of them would end up in prison.'

At this point several journalists leapt to their feet to interrupt but Morton pressed on. 'This might cause a problem if there was only one parent but it could be overcome by establishing residential homes for the parentless child. They would be purely residential, there would be no punishment, but the child would be taught the finer points of living in a community. They would leave the home when their parent was released. The man said he thought it was interesting and was a pragmatic approach but he did not comment further,' Morton sat down having said her piece. The media leapt to their feet anxious to ask more questions about this revolutionary idea.

'I think that is all we can do' said Porter, stepping forward. 'We are getting away from the point. No more questions thank you all for coming.'

'But that does not give us time to find out what the message is,' complained Tony Graham of the Daily Sun.

'We have done what we said we would do, and that's the end of it,' Porter replied with all the authority of a doctor giving instructions for treatment.

The room became full of the buzz of discussion as the journalists began to dissect what had happened and what had been said. Some tried to stay behind in order to catch Morton and question her but were moved on by Porter who took her by the arm and moved her into a back room and closed the door.

'You said too much' he admonished her. 'This meeting was not called to allow you to expound your views. I am very annoyed.'

'I'm sorry, ' she replied, quietly. 'I got carried away. I feel very strongly about children.'

⋆ ⋆ ⋆

Taking Morton into a back room did not solved Porter's problem. They talked about the man and how they felt about him and what he was saying for over an hours.

'It's time I went home,' Ruth said eventually. It had all been very exciting and tiring. What she desperately needed was her bed.

'Of course,' said a sympathetic Porter. 'I shouldn't have kept you. Have a good night's sleep and I will be in touch with you morrow. You'll be at home?'

'Yes, we're still on holiday,' she smiled.

She went out into a clear, dry night. Stars would have been visible if it were not for the city lighting. It was good to be out in the fresh air so she decided to walk up Victoria Street and look in shop windows on her way to her temporary lodgings near Victoria Station.

As she stopped to look in a brightly lit dress shop window young woman approached her slowly.

'Miss Morton?' she asked gently.

'Yes,' she replied nervously.

'I'm sorry to talk up to like this but I'm Robina Carter of the Express & Star and I was at the press conference at which you spoke. I would like to talk to you about what you said. Could we go for a drink somewhere?

'It's very late and I'm very tired. I would like to get to my hotel as soon as possible.'

'I understand but I would like to ask you whether you meant what you said about parents being sent to prison if their children misbehave.'

'Of course, otherwise I wouldn't have said it. But I didn't mean in every case, only for habitual offenders. But I do think parents should be held responsible for what their children do.'

'But wouldn't it cause a lot of trouble?'

'I'm sure it would but we've got to do something about discipline. Kids think they can do what they like and an awful lot of parents don't care. We've got to take a look at education in general, for at the moment, it is falling apart for all sorts of reasons,. We've got to take seriously what the man is saying. Discipline, responsibility by parents, teachers and children themselves. If we don't we might as well give up, education will collapse.'

Carter smiled. 'Thank you,' she said. 'I won't keep you. You have been very helpful. Can I walk you back?'

'No, thank you. I am not far away.'

* * *

'So what did you think of that?' Frank Faulkner asked Martin slipping his note boom into his pocket.

'Interesting,' Martin replied.' Plenty to write about and it will really stir the critics up'

The national newspaper group had moved together by force of habit into the nearest pub in Victoria Street and were now sitting round a table enjoying drinks bought, out of character, by Graham.

'There'll be a bloody great outburst,' laughed David Grant of Telegraph Today, 'All the churches will be in a frenzy They'll be outdoing themselves trying to shoot him down..' 'And Christ knows what the reaction will be to Morton's idea to slam parents in the nick if their children don't behave themselves.' Graham laughed. 'There will be hell to pay. I know we will have some fun with it. It's a crazy idea. She can't really believe that we will take it seriously. It's a bloody good story in itself'

'It is not something the man said ' Faulkner pointed out seriously. 'It's only Morton's idea.'

'But according to her he didn't condemn it,' Graham snapped.

'It's not such a daft idea when you think about it,' said Simon Walker of the Sunday Express & Star. His remark caused some laughter among the other journalists for Walker was well known as a vocal critic of practically everything.

'Don't look so bloody shocked,' he responded. 'It would certainly make parents look a lot more seriously about what their kids were up to. It would at last introduce responsibility to a lot of them. On the other hand if the kids thought that their parents might have to do time it might, I say only might, make them think.'

'But a lot of them don't give a damn about their parents,' Frank Solo of Channel Television News, a welcome member of the group because he once worked for the Express & Star, joined in. Don't forget their parents were brought up just as badly as they were.'

'It certainly wouldn't work for everyone' Grant agreed, ' but it would make them think and that would be a first.'

'Well, you can't argue with his supposed reason for being in England. We really need someone like him when you look at the state we're in. Trouble is they are all the victims of the permissive society when everything was allowed,' Solo continued. His words were greeted with a low groan by his companions for his favourite subject was to complain about the permissive society.

'It's no bloody good you all groaning. I'm right. No-one seemed to realize that if you removed standards in one area you sooner or later reduce standards in another, and before long you've got anarchy. The Swinging Sixties and the pill wiped out all the old fashioned morals and values were thrown away and replaced by free expression, free love and generally doing what you bloody well like. Young people were given all the freedom they wanted and cast away all restraint. Instead of a disciplined moral society we've now got AIDS, broken homes drug addiction a society steeped in insecurity and misery.'

'Give it a rest,' Faulkner interrupted impatiently. 'We've heard it all before.

'The current excuse of moving with the times only means abandoning the culture and practices build up over a thousand years using the excuse that it's progress, Solo continued unperturbed. 'Almost everything described this way is a retrograde step. I shouldn't think the man will argue with that.'

'It's all too deep for me ' Grant admitted. 'I think I'll wait and see how the row develops. If they are not careful ideas like Morton's will take the emphasis away from the man.'

'Not a chance,' said Faulkner. 'The church will never let what the man is saying remain undisputed.'

'He did give the Ten Commandments a going over,' the News Mail's Jeremy Clark contributed.

'He's quite right of course, Faulkner joined in. 'This country really is going to the dogs. In fact it's already there. The basic rules of decency, politeness and consideration no longer apply, every part of our culture is under attack. But we're not here to discuss the future of the universe. We're supposed to be finding out the truth about this bloke. At least, that's what I'm doing."

'It was a bloody advertisement for the seven deadly sins. Adopt one now and feel at home.' Clark suggested.

'What do you mean?' Martin asked.

'Consider it,' said Clark. What are they, sloth, lust, pride,' he said holding up a finger each time,' anger, envy, gluttony and coveting other people's property,' he ended triumphantly. 'No-one feels they have to work that hard to earn what they are paid, Less work, more pay. There's more lust to the square inch than ever before, in every walk of life, screwing is a popular pastime. This government is full of pride in what has achieved.

But it doesn't stand critical examination. If you criticize someone all you get back is a stream of angry invective..'

'We're always having these deep philosophical discussions which don't get us anywhere. It's a waste of time and time for another round.' Grant commented. Faulkner took the hint and bought another round. They all looked upon him as the senior man present and in that role he was expected to put his hand in his pocket.

'But what we say is basically true,' Clark insisted. Some of the others nodded their heads in agreement.

'The man's right about lack of leadership in churches and the major religions. They're all too concerned with their own welfare and pay little regard to the validity of other religions including the fact that Christians, Jews and Muslims all have the same God.'

'No,' said Robina Carter of the Express & Star quizzically. 'Is that true?'

'Sure it is, they just go a different way about it.'

'His concept of God fits my way of thinking,' Martin told them. 'And his criticisms of the churches.'

'The leaderships of almost all organizations are where the trouble lies. Whenever anyone achieves a leading position their only objective is to maintain the status quo. When they put forward suggestions on behalf of their members they are really putting forward proposals designed for their own benefit,' Simon Walker of the Sunday Express & Star joined in. Some of his companions looked doubtful.

'It's true, Walker insisted. 'I used to cover trade union organizations and know that many of the demands they made, ostensibly as demands of the membership were no such thing.

'Either the members didn't know what was being decided or they were not about the subjects on which the membership really had any strong views. They were really what the leadership wanted and the only way they could stand a chance of getting them was to say that they were following the demands of the membership.'

'This all very well. Its an interesting debate but its irrelevant. The question is: So where do we go from here?' asked Carter.

'We persist in trying to talk to the man himself and question him. If he's genuine he will talk to us. If he refuses, for whatever reason, we can assume he is frightened about what we will find out.'

There was some agreement among the journalists gathered but many of them had their doubts. But none of them was prepared to let the others know what they intended to do next., not while there was still a chance of an exclusive!

★ ★ ★

Working in a coal mine is highly dangerous. The constant presence of disaster through roof fall, gas and explosion could be frightening if you thought about it. The dust ladened atmosphere made it extremely unhealthy and unpleasant. And you were never paid enough.

But it was a damn sight safer than being here with this sodding great crowd of people, Dai Griffiths thought to himself as he was pushed inexorably in a direction he did not wish to go. He began to feel far more claustrophobic than ever he did a mile beneath the earth on a pit face probably no more than five feet high.

He had come to Winchester with Gladys. She had desperately wanted to see the man that everyone seemed to be talking about and Dai was not happy about her going by herself.

They had got the bus to Cardiff and the train to Winchester. Dai was surprised that the train was so crowded and thought there must be some sports event in the town that was attracting them. It soon became clear from the conversation of those around them in the carriage that they had all come to see this man who had performed 'miracles' all over the country. All over the country, Dai thought to himself. I've only read about four. I must've missed something.

Suddenly he found that Gladys was talking to the people around them explaining how her husband had once been one of the miners rescued from a pit disaster but was now a docker. How they now had a family problem and they thought the man might be able to advise them. People began asking him questions he did not want to discuss . Dai did not appreciate people who they did not know being told the family history and problems. He was not in favour of gossip, an art at which Gladys was a master.

They arrived at a wet Winchester in a station that was already crowded with people. They had no idea where they were supposed to go but it didn't matter because they were carried along by the flow of people, most of whom seemed to have some idea of their objective.

Dai noticed that they were walking towards a big church which Gladys said was a well known cathedral. It had come as a surprise that a little place like Winchester had a cathedral. He had always thought you could only find them in big cities..

Despite the crowds they got close to what Dai still thought of as a big church and quickly their attention was drawn by the people around them, to a small group of people dominated by a tall man who was clearly doing the talking. Dai listened as best he could but when he caught the words 'church and God' he quickly lost interest. Something to do with religion, he thought to himself and began to look around him.

He caught sight of a group of young people, all about Megan's age, and began to think about the problem he had with his pregnant daughter. When he had returned from the pub the night before, Gladys had done what he told her and sent Megan away. She didn't tell him where at first where she had gone but eventually he found out that she'd been sent to her grandmother's house in Cardiff. He was still angry that his daughter had let him down and made the family a laughing stock.

He had examined his motives many times, trying to convince himself that he was right in cutting her off from the family. He was unrepentant. She had been brought up to know right from wrong. Although not religious he was a God fearing man he told himself illogically. Sex was prohibited outside marriage, there was no excuse for it and she was far too young anyway. She had been taught what was right and what was wrong. She thought she knew better even though she was only just seventeen. Well, she'd made her decision she would have to live with it. The fact that she had refused to tell her mother who had fathered the child incensed him. He wanted retribution on the dirty little bastard.

Gladys had done her best to persuade him to change his mind and have Megan back, but he was adamant. I know I'm right, he told himself.

The whole question had upset him more than Gladys understood or he would admit. At one stage he had, without thinking it through, suggested that Megan should had an abortion. That would be the perfect solution, no scandal, no unwanted child. He had regretted it the moment Gladys heard the word 'abortion.'

'Dai Griffiths have you gone mad,' she snapped, a look of horror on her face. 'Are you suggesting taking a human life so that you won't have to face a scandal? Her ashen face had a look of disgust he had never seen before.

'It's not human yet,' Dai replied defiantly, already realizing that he was out of his depth.

'She's too young to have a child, she's only seventeen,' he added lamely.

'That's true,' Gladys replied in a more placatory mood,' but the fact is that she is having one and we have got to agree what to do about it,'

'Abortion' Dai replied. 'Lots of women have them and they end up okay. I don't see the problem. We can't look after a child at our age. I don't want a screaming child about the house.'

'As usual, selfish to the last,' Gladys sneered nervously, she was not used to arguing with her husband on this scale. She also felt guilty about calling him selfish. That was the last thing he was.' Abortion is wrong. It is murdering an innocent child. The man says that in his Code of Life, as he calls it, no-one should kill. It's quite clear and that's that,' she added with finality.

'Well, women have them if there is something wrong with the baby, or they've been raped and no-one objects.'

'I've said all I'm going to say and that's the end of it,' was the response as Gladys looked at him defiantly.

'Quite right,' said a man standing next to him.

'Pardon?' Dai asked, suddenly shaken out of his reflections..

'I said he is quite right,' said the man nodding in the direction of the group. 'He's just been talking about tolerance. Those young buggers over there ought to listen, they might learn something. You've got to be tolerant, try to understand the other bloke,' he added knowingly.

'You have,' Dai agreed nodding heartily..

Martin had followed up on his last remark when they first met ' let's get back to me liking you' with another meeting and the mutual attraction became obvious. It might have been Candice's loneliness and Martin's lack of female company that brought them together but both knew that it was an association without a future. Candice had a husband with whom she was in love; Martin knew he was not a marriage breaker even though he found it difficult to think about anyone or anything other than Candice. He was also aware that he was jeopardizing his job and his career.

Now, having a late dinner with her when, he was aware he should be out like the other reporters trying to locate the man, talk to him and find out what he was about. But he could not leave her. Whenever she could be free to see him he had to be available.

Every morning he got up early and grabbed the newspapers looking through them nervously to see if he had missed anything. So far he had been lucky for none of them had anything new, they were usually full of ill-informed speculation or repetitions of already well publicized facts.. Up to now he had been able to satisfy his own newspaper with daily stories which were themselves little more than fudges of details already used. He knew this could not last for much longer. He quickly found out that he was right.

Looking at his watch he saw it was nearing midnight. 'Do you mind if I nip out and get some of the early editions just to make sure I haven't missed something?' he asked

Candice nodded her assent. She knew that Martin was in love with her but she was also concerned that he might be seeing so much of her because he wanted to find out what she knew about the man, through her husband.

She knew something was wrong immediately she saw Martin returning with a bundle of newspapers. His face was white and he was agitated and worried.

'What's wrong?' she asked.

'Look at this,' he said, thrusting the paper in front of her.

'Man Had Sex with Chambermaid' the Mirror headline screamed. The story told of an interview one of its reporters had with a chambermaid called Helen Green who worked at the Red Lion Hotel in Cambridge. 'Mystery Man Inspires Violence,' shouted the Mail. 'Youths Smash Meeting' the Sun blared, but both were thrust to one side..

'That's where you stay, the Red Lion' said Candice, shocked.

Martin nodded, his attention still on the Mirror story which described how the man had stayed there before going to the meeting at which Grace Golder was given her sight back and how, the night before, he had persuaded Helen to stay in his room when she arrived to turn the bed down in the evening. Within minutes, she alleged, she wasn't turning down the bed she was lying on it being seduced by the man. She described him as being 'very gentle and very sexy.' The story driveled on with near explicit descriptions of what had taken place.

This cannot be true, Martin assured himself. It must be a pack of lies.

Frantically he got out his address book, found the number and rang the hotel.

'Armstrong here, is the manager there? Do you have a chambermaid called Helen Green?' he asked when the manager picked up the phone.

'We certainly do not, We've seen the story Mr Armstrong and it is completely untrue. A complete fabrication, utter nonsense. We have no Helen Green and as far as we know the man in question has never stayed here. We know almost everyone who has been here in the past week or two, they're all regular customers, except you Sir,' he added laughing. 'But a number of journalists have stayed here recently, I think you know most of them. But the story is a pack of lies.'

Martin thanked him and replaced the receiver.

'No, there's no such chambermaid and the man hasn't been there,' he told Candice.

'Why do they say it then?'

'Nothing else to write about my love, they have to make something up. But it means I will have to get back on the story. Have you any idea where the man is?' Candice smiled and shook her head.

⋆ ⋆ ⋆

A parachutist having fallen halfway through a ten thousand feet drop without his parachute opening could be forgiven for feeling less than confident about his future, a mountaineer surmounting a flying buttress and seeing the rope that is holding him frayed and about to break would not be too optimistic about his prospects. Their feelings could hardly be compared with the lack of confidence and pessimism experienced by Edward Forbes as he sat in the Members' bar at the House examining his life.

He felt it was slipping out of control and that the thread that had kept it on a smooth and steady course was about to break.

Since the day when Pauline had climbed out of his car issuing dire threats for his future he had lived his life on a knife edge, expecting her to strike at any moment. So far nothing had happened. He had not seen her again or heard a word from her. It was, he felt, the calm before the storm, not the peaceful end of the affair.

In his quieter moments his mind had audited the current situation and the options for the future. What could she do? Denounce him in public? That would be embarrassing but he felt sure he could talk his way out of it. He could say she had tried to seduce him, he had refused and she was a women scorned and we all know what they are like. That was no problem. The real danger was that she would sell her story to the News of the World or some such scurrilous rag. They would embellish the facts to make it far worse. The story would be picked up by all the other papers and he would almost certainly have to resign. The precious members of the North Sussex Conservative Association would demand it. Scandal would terrify the old women of both sexes in the constituency.

It was this latter prospect that made him so nervous. He had almost had a spontaneous heart attack two days previously when, at a Conservative Ball in his constituency, he had seen a well known News of the World reporter heading towards him. He thought of avoiding him by hiding in the loo or making a quick getaway but he could do neither as he had to present the raffle prizes at almost any moment.

'Good evening Mr Forbes,' the journalist had greeted him.

'Hello,' he replied, trying to hide his nerves.

'I'm sorry to interrupt you during a social occasion but I wonder if I can ask you a couple of questions?

'Well it is a social occasion but if you insist, and if you are quick.'

'It won't take a moment. My paper is doing a feature on blood sports this week, we're against them, and we're doing a poll of Members of Parliament of all persuasions to get their views.'

Christ, thought Forbes, this is even worse than be asked about my private life. If I say I'm against them then all the hunting crowd in the constituency will be upset. If I say I'm in favour, all the bloody animal lovers in creation will descend upon me.

'I think this is largely a matter for individual conscience,' he replied. 'I have no wish to impose my views on other people. There is a lot to be said both for and against the argument and the answer needs very careful consideration,' he replied.

'Yes, but you must have a personal view,' the reporter persisted.

'I can see the point of view of those who are in favour of it and I can understand the feelings of those against it. I do not think I wish to say more at this time. Now, if you will excuse me, I have duties to perform,' he said, smiling and edging away. The reporter. a look of disgust on his face, watched him go. Forbes visibly relaxed.

Since that evening he had been constantly on edge looking for hidden meanings in everything said to him. He jumped whenever the telephone rang and reached a high peak of nervous tension whenever the House of Commons usher brought him a message.

But the severance of contact with Pauline had another unexpected effect. He had gone off sex. It was a conclusion he reached with horror. It had been his life's work and suddenly he had lost interest.

Not only did he not wish to start the new affair he had planned and which had led to his ending with Pauline, he no longer wanted to continue with Karen and Pamela. His decision was not made out of any high moral sense. The danger which had become apparent with Pauline's response was totally unacceptable when it was multiplied by three. He realized for the first time how vulnerable his affairs made him. The problem he had to solve was how to end them without the reaction he had got from Pauline.

There was also another aspect of the situation which, again, involved an agonizing reappraisal of his life. The fictitious suggestion to Pauline that he had to sever relations with her because he might be given a government appointment had proved to be more than a feeble excuse. It had take root in his mind and developed from fiction into ambition.

He was forty five years old and had frittered away most of those years in self indulgence. He now saw a government post, even a minor one, as an attractive prospect. It would give him a certain standing and open up avenues he had not previously explored. If he played his cards right he could get his K. Sir Edward Forbes sounded right, Lord Edward Forbes even better.

The problem was that he had not only to change his image, and to do it quickly. He had to take more interest in what was going on, spend more time and speak more in the House and get himself invited to more speaking engagements in the country.

First thing he needed was an issue, a topical subject on which he could become an expert and the natural source of quotes when the press needed one.

What was there? He knew nothing about economics, very little about defence, the environment or foreign affairs. Anyway they were as dry as hell and everyone took them far too seriously. He needed a real live subject.

Forbes was in no doubt as to what was the live subject at the moment. It was this man whom people said had performed miracles and was causing trouble all over the place.

From conversations he had heard in the House and in his constituency it was clear that the popular view had polarized either enthusiastically for the man or determinedly against.

Initially he had to decide which side he would take or whether he would adopt a compromising role. He discarded the latter idea. Despite the popular view which talked of 'typical British compromise' he did not believe that the mass of British people really felt that way. It was wishy washy. They liked strong, definite views and actions.

Pushing aside the ever present problem of Pauline it was clear that he had to find out about the man, who he was, what he did and the veracity of his message if he had one. Then he would have to take view as to which argument would eventually prevail and prove most popular. It was little use picking the side that was going to lose.

* * *

Clive Carrington, in his late fifties, had become the doyen of chat show presenters. His list of guests was impressive and included the famous in every sector life from politics, stage and screen to sport, pop music and business from all over the world.

The main reason for his success was his polite and gentle approach, he was never aggressive or antagonistic. His manner was reassuring and relaxed but he still got the information or the answers he wanted. His favourite approach was his introduction to most of his questions with 'as I understand it …' which led the interviewee to believe that Carrington understood that he could be wrong and so drop his defences. This approach often drew out more information being extracted than was intended.

In a week that was dominated by stories and rumours about the man it was expected that Carrington would cover the story in the best way possible. He was scheduled to interview the Home Secretary about the failure of the Government to act in a number of important area but his studio audience of two hundred and the two to three million viewers were in for a surprise.

'Good evening,' the smiling face appeared on the screen. It was a rugged face with a permanent smile under a well cut mass of grey hair which was unusual when most men of his age were carefully laying their hair over the steadily increasing bald patches.

'In a week during which most news sources, newspapers and television at home and abroad have been devoted to the activities of the man who is reported to have performed several what are being described as miracles. I felt sure you would want me to do my best to find some of the answers to the many questions surrounding the story.' A mild applause rippled through the audience.

'Opinion is sharply divided between those who hoped that his presence has some deep religious significance and those who either believe that the man is a charlatan, or in fact just an innocent observer who just happens to be around when something extraordinary occurs or the man is, in fact, nothing more than four or five different innocent observers and that the incidents have no connection.

'Naturally I have tried to persuade the man to appear on this programme but, as you probably know, he refuses to have anything to do with the media. I think he is wrong but he is adamant for what he believes are very good reasons.

'But I have had some good fortune. A Hereford doctor, John Porter, who, it seems, has become the man's official spokesman has agreed to come on the programme to explain some of the things that have been reported so that we can get a clearer understanding of events. Ladies and Gentleman, Dr John Porter.'

The audience in the studio broke into loud and enthusiastic applause.

John Porter, who had been thrust from the relative obscurity of his country practice into the maelstrom of the news world, appeared at the top of the studio staircase and began a self-conscious walk down to the chair opposite Carrington. He was dressed in a dark blue three-piece suit with blue tie, a white shirt with a neatly folded white handkerchief in his jacket top pocket with black socks and highly polished shoes. His appearance contrasted sharply with the usual casual, tie-less appearance of most of Carrington's celebrity guests. Porter who, on earlier public occasions had been a bag of nerves and insecurity now gave the appearance of a man in total control.

The two men shook hands while the applause continued, and then sat down with Carrington smiling broadly at his guest.

'Welcome,' he said. 'It is good of you to come. I suppose the best way to begin this conversation is to start at the beginning. How did you come to be involved with who we are simply calling, the man?'

'It's a pleasure to be here,' said Porter going through what he thought to be the niceties, 'but I am not sure I will be able to answer all your questions. I can tell you some of the things he has said and what he describes as the purpose of his visit. But I will not be able to explain to you what he means because that would mean I would to some extent have to give my own opinion and that is something I will not do,' Porter said confidently, beginning to settle down.

'As I understand it you made his acquaintance because when you gave a wrong diagnosis on an injured patient,' Carrington said sympathetically.

'Yes, it was a bit embarrassing. At least, it was on the face of it. I was called to attend to a school caretaker who had escaped from a building on fire by jumping from the third floor on to a concrete playground. I examined him and diagnosed two broken legs. I am an experienced doctor and I know a broken leg when I see one. I can tell you that both his legs were broken, badly broken, below the knee. However, while waiting for the ambulance to arrive he suddenly got up and walked to where his family was waiting. When we got him to hospital he was x-rayed and both legs were found to be sound, with only some bruising. He gave as his reason for walking that while he was lying on his temporary bed of coats on the school playground he was told by a man, who virtually no-one could remember seeing, to get up and go to his family.'

Porter turned from Carrington and looked at the audience. 'The whole incident caused me great concern as well as considerable embarrassment. I worried about it for several days and even thought about giving up the medical profession. It was while I was worrying about it that I read the story about a crippled boy being told by a man to put away his crutches and go and play with his friends. When I then read a newspapers story about two more incidents I began to wonder. When I saw the man was described as wearing a white sweater I remembered that the caretaker had used the same description. That decided me that I had to follow it up and try and find out who the man was.' Porter ended.

'And you did?' asked Carrington.

'I was lucky, a friend of mine who understood my problem rang to say that he had heard where the man would be.'

'So you met him and decided he was someone special?'

'Not really. He seemed like a normal man. He told me what he was doing. He was quite specific. He did not say what he was trying to do. He was more positive than that. He said he was doing it.'

'Which was?' Carrington continued the questioning trying not to stop Porter's eloquent flow.

'As I've explained before, on the Peter Potter programme, he says that humanity was given guidance about the way to live 2,000 years ago, including the Ten Commandments before that and by almost every other prophet of the time, said has been almost totally ignored. He is now simply trying to remind people of the truth.'

'As I understand it he has been very critical of the church and the leadership of all religions,' smiled Carrington, 'and has upset a large number of people.'

'All religions were given the same message of love, peace and understanding. They all preach the message and pay homage to their leaders but they do absolutely nothing to control the extremists and fanatics within their religions. They do nothing to bring religions together, to spread understanding of each other's beliefs in a gesture of cooperation which is the only way to live. They throw up their hands in horror and, in effect, say it is nothing to do with us. They talk a lot but spend all their time maintaining their own positions and looking after their own interests, They believe that if they stress the differences they have with other religions they will win more support and strengthen their own positions' said Porter, gaining in enthusiasm as he warmed to his subject.

'But am I right in thinking that what he is saying about religion and God is much more far-reaching, almost revolutionary. Isn't he doubting the existence of God and the very basis of religion.

'He is doubting the general conception of the Deity, yes,' said Porter, becoming concerned that he was about to become involved in something he did not clearly understand himself. 'It is not easy to explain and needs a lot of lateral thinking and the abandonment of many preconceived ideas.

'He makes the point that the whole question of religion is an intellectual concept which is totally subjective. Whatever the religion the concept of God is totally in the mind of the believer. There is no definitive description which every one can recognize, no incontrovertible proof that such a Deity, as we now understand it, really exists.

'All we have is second, third or even fourth hand knowledge. The words of the leading religious prophets, such as Jesus for the Christians, were reported by apostles who naturally gave them their own interpretations as they understood them. These, in turn, were, and are still being, interpreted by religious leaders, many of whom have their own agenda influencing their translations.

'In every religion the physical descriptions of the Deity are the results of the imaginations of artists, sculptors, writers, religious leaders and images in the minds of everyone who professes to be a follower. We each have our own image, it is unique to the believer. Conclusively, it is a mental exercise.

'You can see this in the fact that religious students go to a university to get a degree. What do they do there? The listen to tutors who use the Bible to give their own interpretations of what Jesus is reported as saying and what he meant. That is an important point, they tell their students what they think he meant, or what someone else has told he meant. What they say then becomes the definitive definition.

'He points out that the mind is a powerful instrument which few people understand. No-one makes full use of the power of the mind which can, in fact, influence the degree to which something happens or does not happen. Today we talk about the power of positive thinking and almost everyone has at least one example of how it has helped them. He says that it can be used in greater depth and to greater purpose. And that we should give more thought to developing it.

'When, he says, someone prays to their God what they are really doing in concentrating their minds on the problem to a greater or lesser degree. Porter, looked around beginning to feel exhausted. He had spoken for longer and in more detail than he had expected. But he felt confident he had given an accurate report.

'Are you really trying to tell us that he says there is no God?' Carrington asked aghast.

'Certainly not,' Porter replied sharply. 'Absolutely the opposite. What he is saying is that God is in everyone. The religious believe, and repeat it interminably, that God is everywhere. The man agrees with that because, he says, the idea of God is within each of us whether we recognize it or not. The way they manifest it is through adherence to the basic rules. If they acknowledge them they are giving the image a substance,' Porter explained patiently.

'This is a lot to take in,' Carrington said thoughtfully, leaning back in his chair. 'And the questions pile up. Where, for example, does your theory….'

'Not mine, 'Porter interrupted sharply. ' The man's.'

'Well, anyway, where does it leave the church, it is an integral part of millions of lives.'

'The man's view is that there is a vital place for the church but not as it is at the moment. He sees it more as a place where ideas can be exchanged, problems and their solutions discussed and where the basic rules can be explained and interpreted.

'He believes that much more use could be made of church buildings, usually huge edifices supposedly devoted to the work of God but in fact only used two or three times a week.Mostly these are for services which, with the best will in the world, can only be described as unproductive aimed mainly at giving the Minister the opportunity to express his or her view on a given subject. What effect these sermons have is debatable but if, for example, they were followed by a discussion involving the congregation they would have a useful purpose. Everyone has problems and most people have to face them alone. They would find much consolation and help from people in the congregation who have faced similar problems and overcome them.

'For most of the time the church lies empty while homeless people sleep on the streets. Many good people work hard to provide temporary homes for the needy. They have to raise money for rental and running costs as well as find helpers willing to give some of their time. It would be, he suggests, a glorious opportunity for church to make a more useful contribution to the community and its members,' Porter declared.

Carrington, still with an uncertain look in his face was about to say more when Porter began to speak again.

'All the problems that people face, every drama that has ever happened in this world has been due to human error, by mistakes made by human beings he says,. not by some powerful God intent on punishing people. They have happened because people have ignored signs, logic or rules.'

'What about natural disasters?' asked Carrington, anxious to get back into the discussion.

'There is no such thing as a natural disaster,' said Porter, stressing the word disaster. Major events, such as earthquakes, massive floods, tsunamis, hurricanes and tornadoes, to mention only a few, only become disasters when human life or property is involved If, for example, there was a massive earthquake in the middle of an unpopulated desert or some obscure mountain range no-one would know about it and when people did learn about it experts would explain it was part of the continuing development of the Earth.

'It is when people ignore the fact that they are building on a place where continental plates meet and are subject to earthquakes, or on the coast or low lying land seriously liable to flooding or in areas where hurricanes, tornadoes or typhoons are seasonal, that disasters happen. Nothing to do with the Almighty. It is usually the 'it won't happen to us' philosophy that causes the trouble.' Porter ended, exhausted.

The audience had listened in almost total silence while Porter was speaking, when he concluded there was an outbreak of uncertain applause.

A substantial number seemed to agree with what he had said, fewer applauded out of politeness and other sat in silence, still trying to take in what had been said.

Carrington himself seemed uncertain.

'Well I had hoped to get answers to some of the questions being asked. I find that the answers have only brought new questions and expanded the range of the subject. I don't think anyone can honestly give a knee-jerk reaction to what has been explained to us. It needs considerable thought and much more discussion. I thank you for coming and talking to us,' Carrington looked at Porter. 'I am sure we will be discussing this again.'

He was greeted by a strong murmur of discontent but he had no choice. It was timer for the advertisements.

* * *

Seduction is too strong a word implying a degree of gentility to described what Fred Thomas had planned for Sharon. All that was on his mind was a quick screw. He wanted Sharon because she was a sexy piece and had a good figure and because she would add to his list of sexual conquests. His target was one hundred by the time he was forty. He was three quarters of the way there in age and two thirds of the way in women. He still had plenty of time.

He had thought of a ruse to get Sharon into the storeroom and he had given the storeman a bribe for the use of his secret 'office in the packing cases.' All was planned in great detail. Trouble was that on the day the plan was due to come to fruition Fred felt awful. He hadn't been fully fit for several days but he had fixed his mind on having Sharon and he wasn't going to miss it.

The following day however sex was the last thing on his mind. He felt sick. One moment he was hot, the next shivering uncontrollably with cold. He could not keep any food down and he wanted to do nothing but sleep. Late in the day he was so bad that Joyce called in the doctor.

'This could be flu,' pneumonia or something more serious,' he said. 'I'll have to get you to hospital in the morning for tests.' Fred looked concerned. 'It won't be for long, just for a few tests, they may kick you out the same day.'

★ ★ ★

The grass and the trees were a lot greener than she remembered. Even though it had not rained for several weeks until the recent cloud burst, and farmers were already crying drought and water was rationed in some parts of the country. To Grace Golder, it was a blaze of colour.

It was only a few days since her sight was restored but she had already accepted the fact that it was permanent. At first she had been fearful that it was only a temporary phenomena, that any moment she would be plunged back into blackness and loneliness. Now she knew it was all right.

In the same short time she had almost driven Alice to distraction with her constant exclamations of wonder at the sights she was seeing for the first time for fifteen years. Television fascinated her. She had watched very little in her sighted days but now, after so many years unable to watch, it opened up a new world for her. She watched every nature and travel programme and even the cricket. Only a few things, including some films, were disappointing. She said that her imagination was more colourful and more accurate than that of some directors and producers. Some people were better looking than she imagined, others bore no resemblance to her mental image.

When she wasn't watching television she was out in the town shop window gazing or sitting in the park watching children playing. It was also very pleasant to be able to pick up a book and read it and to be able to actually see the food she was eating. Her life had changed totally.

But while she was engaged in this orgy of self gratification through sight she had not forgotten the circumstances of its return. The picture of the man's face, the very first thing she had seen, was engraved on her memory forever. The picture of the kind brown eyes, the gentle smile which revealed two rows of perfect white teeth, the weathered brown skin and the brown wavy hair would never fade.

When the shock, but not the excitement, of her sight returning began to fade she turned to thinking about him and who he was. Why was she able to see when she looked at him, why did he give her a feeling of strength, why did she feel so utterly at peace with the world? She thought about these questions and discussed them with Alice far into the night.

Together they read everything they could about him but generally ended up angry at what had been written. They failed completely to understand why his presence had caused so much trouble in Winchester.

'We have to try and find him,' she told Alice.

'I thought you would say that soon,' her friend replied.

'Well I simply have to thank him for what he did. And I want to know more about him , what he is doing and why. Perhaps we could help him.'

'I agree,' said Alice. 'The only snag is how do we find him? No-one seems to know where he is. The newspapers can't find him until he appears and there is trouble. Then they miss him, he's gone before they can speak to him.'

'Do you remember that doctor who was with him? ' Grace asked. 'What was his name.. Potter or something like that?'

'Porter,' Alice told her. 'He was the doctor at that fire in Hereford.'

'Well he must be in the book. We'll ring him. He might know where the man is and he would tell me.' Alice nodded.

'We'll do it now.,' said Grace.

★ ★ ★

Kenneth Innocent lay staring at the wall. It had been a traumatic three days. Mary lay by his side breathing heavily in a drugged sleep. A sleeping pill had been the only way to drive the worry and fear out of her mind so that she could rest.

A tall, 27-year-old West Indian medical student with a patrician face which implied self-confidence, He had faced problems, including that of race, all his life. It had started when he was in his teens when a smart-alec fellow student at school had asked him whether his parents were monkeys.

Innocent had looked at him kindly and with all seriousness replied: 'No, you must be thinking of my grandparents. They were asked to come to Britain in the 1950s to do work your parents could not do.' Personal attacks of that nature had soon ceased. His sporting skills, at football and athletics, soon made him a school favourite. These skills had assured him a favoured position ever since.

His parents were, in fact, both solicitors with a successful practice in

Brighton where they had been since before he was born.

It had started two nights before when they were making love. Kenneth lay beside her, his leg thrown across her body as he prepared to take her. He was fondling and kissing her breasts as she held him, ready to guide him when he was ready to enter. Preoccupied as he was with what he was doing it did not at first register in his mind what he had felt. And when it did he was not quick or alert enough not to react.

'Why have you stopped?' Mary asked him sharply.

'Stopped what?'

'Playing with my breast,' she said.

'I haven't,' he replied, kissing her breast gently.

You have. You stopped for a second. Why?'

'I didn't stop, I just changed position.'

'You did, you were stroking my breast and you suddenly stopped. I know you did.'

'I don't think so,' he lied.

'You felt it didn't you?'

'Felt what?' Kenneth asked, falling back away from her all thoughts of loving making driven from his mind.

'The lump on my left breast.'

'No, what lump?'

'For God's sake Kenneth, don't lie to me,' Mary shouted, sitting up quickly. She put her hand up to her breast and rubbed it brutally. 'There is a lump there. It wasn't there before. I felt it yesterday. ' There was panic in her voice as she looked at him appealingly.

Kenneth put out his hand felt the breast clinically like a fussy customer examining fruit. There was a small pliable lump on the left hand side.

'May be nothing,' he said calmly and hopefully.

'Oh Kenneth, don't be so bloody stupid. I've got cancer and you treat it like a joke.'

Kenneth sat up quickly.

'You haven't and I didn't,' he said. Mary started to cry and leaned forward and put her head on his shoulder.

'There may be a small lump there but it is not necessarily cancer,' he said gently. 'It could be all sorts of things.'

'Such as what?'

'I don't know. I just know that just because you've got a lump it doesn't mean you've got cancer. I've heard of women finding lumps there that weren't serious.'

Mary was beyond comfort. 'They will cut it off,' she sobbed, 'and you will hate me.'

'Now don't you be bloody stupid. Of course I won't.'

'You will. All men like women's breasts and you won't like it if I'm deformed.'

'For Christ's sake Mary, I didn't fall in love with your left tit. I fell in love with all of you. and I still love you. I'd love you if they cut everything off,' he added smiling.

'There wouldn't be much left,' Mary replied, trying to smile. 'Kenneth my darling, what are we going to do?'

'Very simple. We'll go to the doctor first thing tomorrow morning and see what he says. He will probably tell you it is nothing to worry about and send you on your way rejoicing.'

'But you won't love me anymore if I've only got one.'

'Don't be silly, think of the attention it will get !'

They talked deep into the night with Kenneth trying constantly to reassure her. Eventually they fell asleep wrapped in each others arms.

The following morning the doctor confirmed that there was a lump and although he said that it was not necessarily serious he was not very convincing and failed to allay Mary's fears. She became even more concerned when he arranged for her to go to the hospital that afternoon for tests. They were now awaiting the results.

Kenneth looked at the sleeping figure. She was beautiful, her dark curly hair accentuating the whiteness of her skin. She had the neat figure of a schoolgirl he thought, and then he realized that she was in fact, little more than a schoolgirl. She was far too young to have to go through this.

He dreaded the verdict. If the tests proved positive he knew the affect on her would be disastrous and no amount of comforting from him would help. If they had to remove the breast she could be disfigured both physically and mentally. The physical side could be taken care of, the mental would be much more difficult. She was terrified that he would go off her and leave.

Of course he wouldn't. He would love her even more if that was possible. He had told her a thousand times it would not make any difference to him and he knew that in reality it would not. He liked her breasts, he liked looking at them, he liked fondling them but their love was not based entirely on two well shaped, full tits.

He would have to prove it somehow.

It was a disappointment to him, that something should arise that might endanger their marriage. He had thought that after all the problems of the past they had assured the future. He was black, a West Indian, She was white brought up in a strict Protestant family. Her Christian parents quickly consigned to the shelf all their convictions that everyone was equal, white or black. It was not that they did not like Kenneth, it was more a question of what the neighbours would think for mixed marriages were not welcome. There was something about black people that was different, although apart from colour they could not say what it was they could be friends but marriage could not be considered. But they had a problem. They loved their daughter and it was obvious that she was in love with her man and all they wanted was her happiness. But, because of his colour, this did not seem possible. They could of course pray that Mary would change her mind. But who could they pray to? They had a sneaking feeling that God would have none of it, for they had a feeling in the back of their minds that he would not recognize colour as a problem. They had always agreed with that view, until they had to deal with it themselves. They pretended for a while that nothing mattered and just lived in hope.

Kenneth could see their problem, and had some sympathy with their mental agony. It was nothing new to him to have to deal with the hypocrisy of colour

He lay there thinking and finally made up his mind. First thing tomorrow morning, he decided, before the results of the test come through, he would ask her to marry him.

* * *

Despite the fact that he was engrossed with his decision to abandon his medical practice for a while and assist the man in his work John Porter could not get his wife Candice out of his mind. She had changed recently and he was not sure why. While at one time she was deeply involved with him in his work, now she was pre-occupied and distant. She spoke little of his work, was only vaguely interested in the man and, more often than not, was out when he telephoned.

On the other hand Porter knew that he had ignored her since the night of the fire when the man first came on the scene. He thought she understood that he was worried about his wrong diagnosis, then he had become fascinated with the man when he met him.

Although he tried hard not to think about it, he could not rid his mind of the thought that Candice might be having an affair. She was a very attractive woman whom men had always admired. Some had made a play for her attention but had been clearly made to understand that she was a married woman who was in love with her husband. He thought she was. He was certainly in love with her, but not sure that she understood this. He was not demonstrative although he remembered birthdays and anniversaries but her rarely surprised her with a romantic gesture

Problem was, what should he do? Should he face her with his fears or ignore them and hope that it, or they, would go away? He did not want to face her with ill-conceived allegations which might be wide of the mark. That could lead to disaster and the end of the marriage, God Forbid. He determined to let well alone, act as if everything was normal.

Immediately he made the decision the doubts came back. She seemed to like the journalist they had recently met. They had appeared very friendly right from the start. No, she couldn't, she wouldn't. She was too faithful. Or was she?

Porter decided that he had to be much nicer to her, more thoughtful, spoil her, show more care. Kill her with kindness, he thought, that would beat off any competition. It would make her feel guilty and therefore vulnerable.

His uncertainty about Candice was mirrored in his thoughts about the man. He was still mystified by his agreement, or was it his own decision, to act as the man's spokesman. When he was alone he was consumed with doubt. Yes, the man had persuaded Salmons to walk and the legs proved not to be broken. But could there possibly be another solution. He could not think of one but there may be something beyond his comprehension. The crippled boy and his cure could have another solution, nerve damage which had repaired itself with the passage of time. Morton and Grimshaw could have been pure coincidence. There was, however, the fact that he was sure he had seen Grace Golder regain her sight.

All doubts disappeared when he was with the man. His body seemed to change, to become complete in some strange way, his nerves were calm, his outlook unquestionably optimistic, there were no questions just a smile of friendship and total belief.

He had surprised himself when he made the offer to help. He seemed to have made a spontaneous decision without prior thought.

⋆ ⋆ ⋆

The normally combative and aggressive Fred Thomas sat on a park bench staring at the world. A group of small boys were playing football with a tennis ball, their jackets roughly folded, placed on the ground as goalposts. A small pack of dogs of varying sizes and makes were sniffing at each other excitedly, deaf to the calls of their owners. Two cyclists, a man and a woman, rode slowly past him having ignored the sign at the park gate which commanded 'NO CYCLING.' A couple walked by him talking quietly and unthinkingly discarding a chocolate wrapper on the path. In the background traffic raced along the busy main road which was edged by offices and apartment blocks. White clouds scudded across the sky but the breeze which activated them was not at ground level and like the many days before the weather was heavy and hot.

But Fred did not see the children, the dogs, the cyclists or the litter louts. Neither did he notice the traffic or the weather. He was looking into space with unseeing eyes, his mind too occupied with his thoughts, reliving the last hour.

He had arrived at his doctors feeling tired as had become usual over the last few weeks. He had no aches or pains he was just consumed with lethargy and an occasional feeling of nausea. The doctor had telephoned him earlier that morning with the news that he had received the results of tests and would Mr Thomas please come in and see him. Too tired to feel over concerned Fred had driven slowly to the doctors. He waited twenty minutes before being called in and told to take a seat. The doctor smiled at him but it was a weak smile, his face quickly resuming a stern and concerned look

'The results of your tests are here Mr Thomas,' he said, lifting a sheaf of papers. 'I'm afraid the news is not very good.' Fred tried not to look too worried although his stomach was churning. He was sure he was going to be told he had cancer.

They show that you are HIV positive. I am sorry to say that you probably have Aids,' said the doctor in a gentle but authoritative voice.

The overwhelming surge of relief that it was not cancer collapsed suddenly and gave way to the horror of the verdict.

Images of aids victims flashed through his mind.

'What does that mean?' he asked the doctor weakly.

'Put simply, you have an advanced immunity deficiency, that your body can no longer combat viruses and disease.'

'What is the cure?' Fred asked, prepared to put up with anything to get well again.

'There is no cure as yet, ' the doctor replied, showing concern. 'But of course research is going on all the time.' Fred did not know what to say, the import of his message had still not impressed itself on him.

'What I am going to do is to send you back to the hospital to see the AIDS experts.. They will carry out more tests to find out how far the disease had advanced, what treatment you should have and they will explain what they know about the disease and what you should do.'

Fred nodded. His mind was racing, trying to remember everything he had ever heard about AIDS. Suddenly the thought occurred to him.

'You have to be a bloody homosexual to catch it,' he announced sharply.

Fred felt his body begin to tremble. It was a shiver of fear. The truth was going to come out. He had once had a homosexual experience and although it was now more acceptable than it had been years ago he was still ashamed of it. He had done it out of curiosity. Then, as he liked it as a viable alternative to screwing a woman all the time as it was exciting and dangerous. Most of all he had liked the idea of a youth being in love with him. It gave him a feeling of power.

It had started at a party when he noticed a young man, fair skinned and effeminate, staring at him as he spoke. The boy had never taken his eyes off him and Fred was so gratified by this that he had taken the boy to a pub afterwards and then given him a lift home. At the youth's insistence he had accepted an invitation for a night cap drink. Slowly it had dawned on him what the young man was after. Fred had thought about homosexuality but had no strong views on it but had decided to do it for fun. He had enjoyed the subservience of the youth and his obvious skill at knowing exactly what to do. He had enjoyed it.

The affair had lasted only three months and Fred, who had also continued laying women whenever the opportunity arose, had become bored and dropped the boy. It could have been difficult but fortunately someone else came on the scene and took the boy's attention from him.

Fred's attention suddenly came back to what the doctor was saying.

'That is a common fallacy,' the doctor was saying,' you can become HIV positive through normal sexual relations if the other partner has it and you do not take precautions. We will need to ask your wife to come in for tests...'

'No,' snapped Fred. 'She must not know, Christ, she must not know, that would be disastrous.

'I'm sorry Mr Thomas but we must tell her. She must know whether she has been infected.

'No, she's not. She is perfectly well, very fit in fact, there is nothing wrong with her.'

'She can carry the disease without knowing it or it affecting her,' the doctor explained patiently. 'Do you mind if I ask whether you have had any extra-marital contacts?'

'No,' said Fred. 'I don't mind you asking and no, I haven't' he lied.

The doctor made some notes, checked where Fred would be so that he could let him know which hospital would want to see him. He stood up, muttering some hopeful remarks which Fred didn't hear, and bade him goodbye.

Fred walked straight across the road and into the park and sat down. This was the end. What the hell was he going to say to Joyce. How could he possibly tell her that he'd been with a bloke and that he had given him AIDS. At the back of his mind he remembered he had heard that you could catch it off the lavatory seat, but he knew that it was highly unlikely. What the bloody hell was he going to do?

He sat for over two hours going through it all in his mind. Was he going back to work. Would this affect his work? Christ, he had forgotten to ask the doctor how long he had left. He had not bothered to think about it but he knew that people with the disease did not last long, especially if it was advanced. Death. He had never bothered to think about it. He had never been frightened of it or thought that it could happen to him. But he did now. He knew it could be a painful death. Not him, Not fucking him. He would kill himself first.

* * *

It was a tumour. It was malignant. There may have to be a mastectomy. And quick.

The news could not have been worse. The dreaded thoughts that had been suppressed by both Mary and Kenneth on the ground that 'it could not happen to us' had become a cruel reality.

The people at the hospital had been very kind. They had pointed out that it was better to lose one breast than one life. Mary was unconvinced. Certain as she was that she would be deformed, that Kenneth would no longer love her and would leave her, that she almost believed that death would be the wisest choice.

However, arrangements had been made for her to have the operation on the following Monday so that they faced almost a week of agony and worry. Mary had already informed her office that she would be away for some time. The fact that schools were on holiday enabled Kenneth to plan to spend the whole of his time with her.

The problem facing Kenneth was to occupy their time so that Mary's mind would, as far as was possible, be taken off the impending ordeal. They spent their days shopping, walking, a theatre trip, playing cards and Scrabble and planning and cooking complicated meals which neither of them felt like eating. They made love passionately as though each occasion was the last.

They rarely watched television for, it being the summer schedules, they thought the programmes boring and banal. They were both convinced that programme planners believed that no-one with any sense spent their time watching television during the summer so they didn't need to waste time planning interesting programmes.

It was Kenneth, at a temporary loss about what to do next, who switched on the television to watch a repeat of the Peter Potter Investigation in the hope that it would be controversial and catch Mary's attention.

They listened in silence and switched off immediately when it finished. Kenneth waited for Mary to speak as he knew she would.

'What do you think?' she asked eventually.

'I don't know,' Kenneth replied quietly. 'We don't know enough about him to form an opinion. He could be what the Bishop says, a charlatan.'

'But he has healed people,' Mary said, her voice full of hope.

'So they say.'

'But if he can......'she could not finish the sentence.

'Darling, I know how you feel. But please do not start putting too much faith in this man.

We don't know who he is or what he is. We don't even know where he is. He may not be able to help.'

'But anything.....'she pleaded. Kenneth himself had been full of hope as he listened to the programme but he dare not convey this to Mary. It was all so questionable. He knew that some people had strange powers. He had listened often enough to his parents discussing the amazing powers of voodoo in the West Indies. He just did not know.

'Can we go and see him?' Mary asked plaintively.

'Of course we can if you want to,' he replied. 'But please, please do not let your hopes get too high.' He walked across the room and took her in his arms. 'I love you very much,' he murmured,' and I do not want to see you any more hurt than you are. After all, I have to look after you now that you've promised to marry me.'

Mary smiled. 'If there is anything left to marry.'

'Don't talk like that,' he snapped. 'You'll be fine. We'll get married and you'll probably produce children like a rabbit.'

'I don't want children that look like rabbits,' she laughed.

'I didn't mean that. I mean we'll have three or four.'

'Oh, you coloured men. You're so virile,' she teased.

'So they say,' laughed Kenneth. 'So they say.

★ ★ ★

The decision of the man to talk only to people and not the press created major problems for both the reporters and himself. To satisfy the voracious demands of their papers the reporters had to get all their stories second or third hand. This led to extensive misreporting, greater exaggeration and the use of imagination to an even greater degree than was usual with the ladies and gentlemen of the media. For the man it meant that his plan to avoid distortion of his words by misreporting went sadly amiss and exacerbated rather than eradicated the problem. Porter, whose life had been devoted to dealing with patients, was not equipped with methods of how to deal with the media so was unable to advise him properly.

The constant flow of news reports about the man, whatever their voracity, kept the nation and the rest of the world informed about his activities. As the stories increased and grew in importance as the word spread so did the criticisms of him. As more and more people met him, began to accept him as probably being someone special, so did the number of detractors increase.

The number of reports of 'miracle healings' grew daily as the man moved around the south of England but they were usually second hand and unsupported by real evidence. It was becoming increasingly difficult to determine which were genuine and which the results of enthusiastic publicity seeking.

It seemed to Martin and his fellow journalists that news editors, faced with nothing but support for the man in the stories filed from the field had excelled themselves in trying to redress the balance.

As the Telegraph Today reporter, David Grant, told anyone who would listen: 'They don't give as damn about what the man is really trying to do, or whether it is right or wrong. All they care about is a good story and at the moment criticism makes better copy than support.'

It was true that criticism was a bandwagon that everyone jumped on when the man had passed. Comment from towns and villages, particularly from those who had not spoken to him or had missed him, even when the welcome had been rapturous and enthusiastic, contained little but statements from people who claimed they were shocked at the man's erroneously reported presumption and disgusted at his presumed association with the Prophet of two thousand years ago.

The bandwagon carried heavy battalions of churchmen, the various denominations uniting under a banner of dislike and disbelief. The Vatican began pouring our a steady stream of exhortations to Roman Catholics not to listen, go and see or talk about the heretic in England. The Church of England, represented in newspapers and on television and radio by a series of self-important pious men, each trying terribly hard to be reasonable but attacking every word he was reported as saying, every thought he was said to have transmitted.

Never in its long and checkered history had the Bible been quoted so often. Even avowed agnostics used it in support of their arguments that the whole thing was so much rubbish. But while the Establishment in its various forms was plainly opposed to the man and the ideas he represented, mainly because he had no background and, what was worse, no obvious qualifications, the man-in-the-street was not so sure.

The new concept of a God who exists only in the human mind proved difficult to accept. Even those who thought they knew what he meant had a little corner of doubt in their mind. A Gallup Poll carried out for the Guardian showed that ten per cent thought there was something in what he said, ten percent thought it was all rubbish, thirty five per cent said they didn't know and forty five percent had never heard of him. Interestingly, of the don't knows and the 'never heard-of-him,' eighty percent said they would be interested in knowing more.

The television programmers had gone berserk. Peter Potter had acted as a catalyst. News services interviewed anyone willing to express a view whether they had any relevant background or not. Those taking telephone calls were battered by people with every sort of view, most of them inarticulate knowing that they wanted to say something but were unsure how to express themselves. One thing their calls proved was that the current British education system was even worse than its most vociferous critics said it was.

Breakfast programmes and their over cheerful presenters fell over themselves to recruit so-called celebrities with differing views. Well known comedians and soap actors suddenly became experts in spiritual matters. Chat show hosts, anxious to prove themselves more pleasant than the much disliked Peter Potter, put on serious faces as they asked ridiculous questions designed to provide wise answers. The suspicion increased that most the off-the-shoulder interrogations were, in fact, well rehearsed.

'So who do you think the man is?' was the popular over-used first question. The answers, mostly delivered with apparent authority, fluctuated between a clever charlatan, a hypnotist, a psychiatrist, a madman, someone mentally unbalanced to a religious sage A small number thought it was all coincidence and fewer thought that there was no one man but several.

Foreign newspapers covered the story with equal enthusiasm as the British press. The Italian press was, of course, totally opposed and had been advised by the Vatican not to cover the story. The French and German media agreed that if any country needed help from the Deity it was Britain, while the Americans took a more ambivalent view, except for the vocal members of the 'Bible Belt,' for although his activities were widely reported in the American media the public did not feel so transfixed, after all, it wasn't happening in America. There seemed to be a general reticence to use the phrase 'a Second Coming.'

London, it seemed, was filling up with up with people from all over the world who had heard about the man and wanted to see and listen to him or, in a number of cases, to strongly oppose his views.. The main roads into London were carrying heavier loads of traffic each day, flights into Britain were fully booked and it was becoming increasingly difficult to drive around London. There was a clear atmosphere of expectancy in the air.

* * *

Dai Griffiths and Fred Salmons had become good friends since their meeting at the station buffet at Winchester. Dai had persuaded Fred to come with him to Reading where, they had discovered, the man was going to talk to a group of young people, and although Doris had objected when he telephoned to say he wouldn't be home she had eventually and reluctantly agreed.

The two men were sitting under a tree with two six packs of lager, talking and listening. They had arrived early, talked to the man briefly and spent the rest of the afternoon and early evening listening to him talk to the young people. Both had been impressed by what he said and both were beginning to believe that he was not just an ordinary man with the gift of the gab who could do a bit of faith healing.

'There's a lot more to this than we think,' said Dai knowledgeably.

Fred had agreed but could not put into words exactly what he was thinking. He knew he didn't know the words that could express his feelings accurately. They sat and watched the youngsters, many with wild and imaginative dress, drinking and occasionally, getting it off with each other, but in a very moderate way.

'They're not a bad lot,' said Fred eventually. 'Just shows you can never judge by appearances. I wouldn't give you tuppence for the lot but when you talk to them you find they do really think and they do really care.'

'Yes,' Dai had replied, his mind on his own youngster. Did she really think. Did she really care?

'You got any of your own? 'he asked Fred.

'Only five, mainly little ones. All good kids, no trouble. How about you?'

'Two, bigger, nothing but trouble.' said Dai feelingly.

'Oh dear, what sort of trouble?'

'Son who thinks he's too good for his mother and father and a daughter who thinks she knows it all.'

'Oh, they all think they know it all. We did when we were their age.'

Dai considered whether to tell Fred about Megan. He hadn't told any of his friends and he didn't really want to talk about.

'She got herself pregnant,' he suddenly blurted out.

'Bloody hell,' said Fred. 'Still, that's always a danger these days in this bloody permissive society.'

'I think its disgusting,' Dai declared. 'I threw her out.'

'You did what?' asked Fred, shocked.

'Threw her out. I didn't want a daughter of mine bringing shame on the family. She went to stay with her grandmother I think.'

'You only think?' said Fred. He was shocked by Dai's attitude but did not know whether he ought to say anything. He liked Dai and he didn't want to upset him.

'What would you have done, Dai asked him.

'Don't know really,' said Fred. 'But I wouldn't kicked her out. Doris would have played hell. You got to stand by your kids when they're in trouble. No matter what it is. That's what I think anyway. I could be wrong of course.'

'You mean you would have let her stay at home and have the baby?'

'I expect so. Doris would have loved it once she got over the shock. Sod the neighbours, that's what we say.'

Dai was taken aback by this attitude. He had looked upon Fred as a bloke after his own heart, they got on and understood each other. He didn't see how he could accept such a terrible thing.

'What's your girl going to do?' Fred asked him.

'I've no idea. I don't know whether Gladys has.'

'Well these days they can get rid of it fairly easily. She'll have to do that if you won't have anything to do with her.'

'Get rid of it?'

'Yes, have an abortion. You can do that now if you get your doctor to agree, its pretty easy I think.'

The idea of an abortion had become impossible now that Gladys had spoken.. Gladys would never allow it. God, the neighbours would be even worse. An abortion in devout S. Wales!

They would never live it down. Neither would they ever live down an unmarried mother. What the hell was he to do? God, he would have to think about it.

'Think about it,' said Fred. 'Take the girl back and talk about it with her.'

* * *

The man had spent several hours on the fringes of a pop concert on the outskirts of Reading. It was quickly obvious to Porter, who as usual was escorting him, that while the Establishment and several other groups were cynical about the man and his message there was no such reticence among young people.

The pop concert had been widely publicized, it was in fact, an annual event with many thousand young people, and a few more mature adventurists, gathering in a field outside Reading to hear and cheer a plurality of pop groups of every description. In many years the caprice of the British weather had shrouded the venue with either baking hot weather which created a crowd of sun baked, sun burnt, enthusiasts or, more often, it had been flooded by continuous torrential rain which flooded the site but failed to reduce the general enthusiasm. On this occasion rain showers had dampened the ground but more rain was forecast.

'He speaks our language,' one young man told Porter. 'Older people have no idea how boring the traditional church services are. They haven't changed for years and there seems to be some great fear that if they altered anything they would be insulting God.

We're sure that when Jesus was talking about God he did not envisage marching around in fancy clothes, muttering incomprehensible phrases carrying strange instruments with prayers intoned by someone else.'

Another young man, in faded jeans and multi-colored shirt, joined in. 'What has all that nonsense got to do with religion and the way we live?' he asked. 'Why is it that laughter has disappeared. If you dare to laugh in church those around you glare angrily as if it was a sin to be happy.'

'It's always mystified me,' a young man in a multicolored shirt and torn jeans, said to the group in general, 'When Jesus told Peter that he was the rock on which his church would be founded did he have any idea what he was letting himself in for. First, he got a bunch of people who believed in God and what Jesus was saying. Then he had to face the fact that one lot disagreed with another on some messages in the Bible, so they divided and formed two different organizations. Then small groups found that they didn't agree with other interpretations so they broke away too.

'And of course, they all had to have their own places of worship so they built hundred of churches at great expense, but paid the builders poorly because they were working on behalf of their God. . It became a question of not worshipping God but building the best possible churches, largely to satisfy their own egos.

But you can't have thousand of worshippers and hundreds of churches without an organization. So you had to have bosses, a Pope or an Archbishop and they had to have staff, bishops, suffragan bishops, archdeacons, deacons priests, clergymen, ministers Synods and others. You also had to have routines, services laid out to be followed each week, baptisms, confirmations, communions, and then you had to divide everything into parishes.

Being human beings they had to criticize each other and disagree. And to learn not to worry about what Jesus originally wanted, to live according to his words of peace, love and understanding.

The young man, who had gained the rapt attention of those around him added 'I don't suppose that if he had been able to point these difficulties to him Jesus would have replied, 'that's your problem sunshine.'

'Unlikely,' said a laughing Porter, 'but I see your point.'

'And why are other religions looked upon as the work of the devil?' asked an enthusiastic girl in what seemed to Porter to be a pocket handkerchief and a wide belt. 'We are all supposed to be worshipping one God even though we might have different views about him.'

'Porter was lost for answers to questions he had often asked himself.

* * *

The man had shown great interest not only in the music but in the young people attending, many of them showing great interest in what he was saying.

Guided by Kenneth Innocent he spent over two hours walking through the imaginatively dress young people and answering their many questions

'He fully sympathized with the multitude of questions about the church and its complete failure to understand how young people felt about its boring and meaningless dialogue. He nodded agreement when the accusations were made that that religious leaders had not moved an inch away from the rules laid down 2,000 years ago, even though the world had moved out of all recognition. To repeat endlessly that God is looking after all of us it totally ridiculous when one considers the tragedies which strike people an families over which they have no control..' His young guide explained to the followers in the party how the man had reacted. There was no doubt about the man's popularity when he eventually left to enthusiastic cheering and clapping.

* * *

Edward Forbes had watched the proceedings with increasing interest. The fact that the majority of young people seemed impressed with the man and what he was saying was very interesting. He congratulated himself that he had come out in support the man. That should get him the young people's vote at the next election and prove that he was not, as most of them thought, a useless old fool.

* * *

# Part Five

# CATACLYSM

'Good Afternoon. Here is the one o'clock news this busy Thursday' said the smiling face of the newsreader against a backcloth showing a photograph of the Pope and St Peter's Square. Martin leaned forward to turn up the sound, sat back in his chair and put his feet up on the coffee table that stood in front of him. He had arrived in London and was spending the day with Frank Faulkner of The Daily Times whom he had met earlier in Cambridge.

'The Pope.' the newsreader continued. 'In the Vatican today the Pope, after blessing a crowd of some hundred and fifty thousand people in St Peter's Square, said that the church could not accept that the man currently said to be preaching in England had any religious validity. The Pope told his audience that nothing could alter the basic truths preached by Jesus Christ.

'The police are still searching for contacts of the suicide bomber killed when he tried to kill the passengers on a London bus, all of whom escaped with minor injuries. It is believed he was part of a England-based terrorist cell of supporters of the terrorist Al Qaeda.'

The newsreader went through several other news items, all bad news, from various parts of the world.

'Those were the main points of the news,' he went on. 'Now for more details of the Pope's message over to Alistair Graham in Rome.'

The picture changed again to show a short, dapper man standing in St Peter's Square accompanied by several self important pigeons.

'A warning that any claims made by the man being described as a religious teacher now touring part of Britain were extremely dangerous and misleading was given by the Pope today after blessing a massive crowd in this historic and impressive square.' Graham looked around as if to reassure himself that it was important and impressive.

'Reports that I have received,' said the Pope, 'are both disturbing and alarming. The true message of God was given to us two thousand years ago by Jesus Christ. Any claim made by the man regarding any relationship with God should be regarded with the utmost contempt." Caldicott, who had been reading from notes, looked up at the camera.

'Later a Vatican spokesman said that Roman Catholics should ignore both the man and what he was saying. Told that there had been an number of eye witnesses to the healings made by the man the spokesman declined to comment.

'But here, in this land of deeply religious conviction and weeping Madonna statues, the fact that miracles are said to be being performed in Britain have caused little surprise.

'The people themselves are showing considerable interest in what is happening and do not seem willing to accept that there is nothing in the stories being circulated here. There have been many reports of miracles and religious sightings here over many years. This is Gerald Caldicott, News at Ten, Rome.'

The picture changed again, back to the studio in London.

'Here in London the scene is becoming increasingly chaotic as thousands of overseas visitors arrive each day to attend the meeting scheduled to be held in Hyde Park on Saturday. It is rumoured that the man will speak about his work and who he is. Traffic is at a standstill in an area three miles around Hyde Park and police have warned all motorists to keep clear of the area. A temporary ban on all commercial vehicles in a specified area around central London has been imposed by the Department of Transport from midnight tonight. The ban will not be lifted until Monday. For further news over to Andrew Hudson at Scotland Yard.'

'Here at Scotland Yard,' said Hudson, speaking from what was clearly the traffic control room,' there is grave concern about the size of the problem. The crowds started arriving almost without warning and the arrival of the visitors by almost every mode of transport coincided tonight with the rush hour home. The AA says that every road is blocked and some vehicles have been stationery for over five hours. On the motorway approaches to London there have been several meetings of angry commercial drivers who have been stopped from completing their journey. Those carrying perishable goods have been turned around and sent back to their point of departure. This will almost certainly mean shortages of some types of food in London over the weekend. At the Channel ports vehicles are being turned back to the Continent and this has caused trouble among the drivers.' The picture changed again to show Heathrow Airport. ' London's three major airports are facing the worst traffic conditions in their history,' said a voice-over,' as plane loads of visitors arrive every two minutes. At Gatwick the authorities have put landing restrictions on charter flights from all parts of the world with many being diverted to airports throughout Britain, some as far away as Edinburgh and Glasgow. Visitors will then face long rail journeys into London on trains already packed with British travelers.'

The picture switched back to the studio.

'In the centre of London many businesses have closed down until after the weekend or are continuing to operate using skeleton staff to keep offices open on Friday. Like the Stock Exchange and major banks they will use staff who live within walking distance of their office.

'Meanwhile there are continuing reports of healings being carried out by the man in many parts of southern England. A 52-year-old man in Monmouth claims he can now walk after being crippled since birth, several blind people have claimed that they can now see after talking to the man, while a man suffering from Parkinson's disease says that since he met the man in Gloucester all the symptoms have disappeared.

'But from Norwich come reports that Philip Green, the crippled boy healed by the man in the Norfolk village of Harwood, has had a relapse and is now seriously ill in Norwich's Royal Orthopaedic Hospital. It is said he will never walk again. It was a report on the healing of Philip that first brought the activities of the man to the nation's attention.'

The newsreader then turned to other items of news ending with the message 'because of the situation in London there will be news reports every half hour throughout the day. Parliament will be discussing the situation this afternoon and we will bring you a report on their debate and its conclusions as soon as possible.'

★ ★ ★

Martin felt the blood drain from his face. The news of Philip Green was shattering. It could not be true. He was absolutely certain that the little boy was cured forever. It must be a report put out by someone who is trying to denigrate the man and his work.

For a moment Martin felt totally out of control of himself. His hands trembled, his stomach turned to jelly. He did not know what to do. The experienced, nerveless professional journalist disappeared. He felt a whimp. He did not have Miriam Cartwright's telephone number, nor that of Philips' parents. What could have been the most important story for over 2,000 years was falling apart. Or was it? He had not heard any news about Grace Golder. She had not, as far as he knew, lost her sight again. But would anyone have told him if she had?

Dr Porter. The name suddenly sprang intro his mind. Because of Candice he had his telephone number. He would know. Trembling he dialed the number.

'Porter here,' said a strong, comforting voice.

'Dr Porter, this is Martin Armstrong of the Examiner. I'm sorry to trouble you but have you heard the BBC news about Philip Green?' Porter momentarily told himself that this was the journalist who was very friendly with his wife. Is that how he knew the telephone number? He put those thoughts aside.

'You are the fourth reporter who has telephoned me about it. Yes, I've heard the story. It is total rubbish.'

'Are you sure?'

'Of course I'm sure,' the voice snapped. 'I've told the others. At the moment Philip is on holiday with his parents in the south of France. He has not been anywhere near an orthopaedic hospital. The hospital has confirmed that,'

'I wonder where the BBC got the story?' Martin asked himself as much as Porter.

'The Daily Sun is publishing a story tomorrow. The BBC found out about it but did not bother to check with me,' Porter told him sneeringly.

'I bet it was that bastard Tony Graham,' Martin thought aloud.

'Well, that's what your profession is like,' said Porter, a tinge of regret in his voice. 'If you haven't got a story you make one up so you've got a headline.'

'Not all of us,' protested Martin.

'Maybe. Is that all, I must go.' Porter put down the phone

Martin heaved a monumental sigh of relief. He sat thinking. The story wasn't true. He was angry at being so upset. He decided to ring the newspaper and talk to Graham. Then he thought about it. Graham would refuse to talk to him or, more likely, would not be there. He would wait for the next news bulletin and see if there was a retraction. What a bloody life.'

★ ★ ★

Parliament, that mixture of the egocentric, largely inarticulate, wrangling and cliché- reiterating ambitious, after days of ignoring the problems caused by the man's presence, at last turned its attention away from the childish and largely meaningless political infighting to normal life and recognized that something untoward was happening in the outside world.

The subject came up at Question Time when several Members, among them the representatives of Hereford, Oxford, St Alban's, Paddington North and Sussex North, drew the Home Secretary's attention to the unfortunate demonstrations that had been inspired by the man and asked what steps were being taken to protect the citizens of 'this great capital.'

The Home Secretary, a tall, dominating, superior figure man who looked with lifeless eyes upon Question Time as an affront to his dignity, said that the Metropolitan Police had an excellent and long record of dealing with large crowds. They were fully aware of the situation and quite capable of dealing with it.

Honourable Members, who knew the Minister's dislike of questions, usually made a point of peppering him with supplementaries and this occasion was no exception. Several sprang to their feet as he sat down.

'No one would argue with the Right Honourable Gentlemen's remarks about the Metropolitan Police,' said the Member for Hereford, after successfully catching the Speaker's eye, 'but is he aware of the many thousands of people this man is attracting and the tremendous passions he is arousing? In my own constituency, where this religious charade began, considerable damage to property and persons was caused, not only by hooligans and vandals who seized the opportunity provided by chaos but by the very size of the crowd and the unreasonable passions expressed by the man's audience.'

The Home Secretary, half rising from the Government bench, declared:' I can only repeat my previous answer.' His reply was accompanied by a cacophony of jeers and shouts.

Another scramble, this time the Member for St. Albans was victorious.

'Does the Minister plan to take any action under the Race Relations Act?'

'No, sir,' the Minister replied amidst further jeers and shouts.

'Is he aware,' St Albans continued, holding his ground, 'that this man is deliberately inspiring racial hatred; that only yesterday he made a vicious attack on our West Indian friends?' Cries of 'shame' from some Honourable Members.

'I was under the impression that he himself was of a pale brown hue,' the Minister replied. 'To put Members' minds at rest I can say that I am receiving daily transcripts of speeches made by this man. So far I have seen nothing that calls for action by my Department under the Race Relations Act.'

'I would not wish to challenge the veracity of the Right Honorable gentleman's answer but I find it difficult to believe that he is receiving daily transcripts of the man's speeches when, in fact, he isn't making any. As I understand it he is only talking to small groups of people. Does the Home Office have transcribers in every group?' the member for St Albans observed amid laughter.

The Minister stood up to ironic cheers. 'What I meant was that people who have listened to him have informed us what he said.'

'I see. It's government by gossip,' St Albans added as the laughter continued.

Up leapt the Member for Oxford: 'I am very perturbed by the Minister's answer to my Honourable Friend. He seems to be completely ignorant of the violence that has been inspired during the man's journey around southern England, and completely unaware of the many thousands of people who are arriving in London daily to see this so-called prophet when he arrives. Will the Minister reconsider his reply and show greater awareness and concern for the dangers and a greater sense of responsibility towards the ordinary citizens of London? The question was accompanied by resounding cheers throughout the chamber.

The Home Secretary, slightly flushed with anger, stood up slowly, looked around the House, placed his hands firmly on the despatch box and squarely faced the Opposition benches.

'Any Member of this House, even those who occupy the benches opposite, must be fully aware of the tremendous and alarming influx of visitors in the capital. The daily journey to this House is enough to convince one of this fact. But I repeat,' the Minister said slowly and deliberately, 'that the police are fully experienced and fully capable of dealing with the situation.' He sat down again with a gesture designed to signify that as far as he was concerned that was that.

Honourable Members did not agree,

'If what the Minister says is correct, would he explain why the crime figures in the Greater London area have risen so appallingly during the past few days?' asked Paddington North.

Another cheer from members mingled with cries of 'shame' and 'resign.'

'I would take issue with the Honorable Member on his assumption. The crime figures which, I agree, are always too high and always will be as long as there is a single crime, have not risen unduly,' said the Minister. He sat down amid cries of 'Oh !' from Members.

The Member for Paddington was up again like a flash, received an acquiescent nod from the Speaker and launched forth again.

'Do I understand that a record of two murders, fourteen robberies with violence, seven pay-roll hold-ups, fifty six muggings, six cases of rape and forty-three assault cases in a week is the normal state of affairs in this city?'

Cries of 'shame,' 'disgusting' and 'resign' rang through the Chamber again. There was a flurry of activity in the Press Gallery as reporters rushed out to telephones to report the horrific figures and their replacements rushed in.

The Home Secretary was obviously taken aback.

'I will need notice of that question,' he said quietly and sat down again. Shouts of dismay and further exhortations to resign echoed round the historic Chamber. Appeals for an answer were practically screamed at the Minister from both sides.

'Will the Minister answer the question?' asked Paddington North, on his feet again.

The Speaker called for order. 'I think I am right in assuming that the House attaches some importance to this subject. It therefore seems to me to be advisable for Members to conduct themselves with greater decorum so that both the questions and the answers can be heard with some clarity,' he said.

Finally, worried by the trend of the questioning and the strength of feeling the Home Secretary rose again reluctantly.

'Before commenting on the figures given by the Honourable Member, which I do not recognize, I would wish to confirm their accuracy. He stopped and uncharacteristically gave way as Paddington North rose again.

'The Minister can rest assured that the figures are correct but in order to save his time and the time of Members, would he guarantee that when he has confirmed their authenticity he will make a further statement explaining what action he is going to take to re-establish law and order?' he asked.

'I will look at the figures but I can give no guarantees,' said the Minister sitting down again.

When he was bored, as he so often was, Forbes unexpectedly romantic side came to the forefront although no-one was aware of it. He liked to contemplate about where he was sitting and the long and significant history that surrounded him. Every day when entering through Westminster Hall he liked to reflect that this was where Charles 1 was tried and sentenced in 1749. He made a point of looking at the mark which showed where the doomed king had stood, even though he had looked at it hundreds of times. When he walked through St Stephen's entrance and into the Porch he never failed to imagine the hall as it was when it was used as the House of Commons debating chamber in the 1700s, and where Spencer Percival, the only British prime minister assassinated, was shot in 1812. At one end of the current chamber where he now sat was the public gallery. He tried to present an impressive figure to those watching as if he was engrossed in the issues being debated. At the other end was the Press Gallery which he tried ignore out of contempt for journalists and what they might really know about him.

Forbes had decided that he might speak on the subject of the man if he could catch the Speaker's eye. He knew this would be impossible from where he usually sat, in the back row at the end furthest away from the Speaker. He had arrived early and chosen a seat below the gangway, three rows back. It was the seat favored by the Member for Nottingham West who, when he eventually arrived glared at Forbes. He was about to say something but on second thoughts, noticing Forbes' challenging expression, moved away. Totally unused to actually listening to a debate in the House with the aim of joining in, Forbes listened with concern at the trend the questioning had taken. He began to wonder whether it was politically wise for him to publicly support the man. To his credit he only wavered briefly for he had been impressed when he met the man in Reading and had decided that he was prepared to stick his neck out in support of him. He had met Grace Golder and was convinced that it was through the man that she regained her sight. As the Minister sat down, Forbes stood up quickly trying to catch the Speaker's eye before he terminated the subject.

'Mr Edward Forbes,' shouted the Speaker.

'Mr Speaker,' Forbes opened to ironic cheers from his backbench colleagues for a speech or statement by him was an unknown event.

'I am appalled by the attitude of some Members of this House who are trying to imply that this man is personally responsible for the violence and the crime now prevalent in this city.' Forbes looked steadily at the Speaker concerned that if he paid attention to the heckling he would lose his nerve. He shuffled from one foot to the other and could feel beads of sweat forming on his brow.

'No word of support for him has been spoken in this House' he insisted. 'That is quite shameful. There has been no word about the actions he has taken to restore sight to the blind and mobility to the lame.' Forbes was interrupted by jeers from some Members and a shout of 'rubbish' from the Opposition benches.

'I can confidently say,' he continued seemingly unperturbed but with his heart beating rapidly,' that this man has done more good for ordinary people in this country in the short time we have been aware of his existence than Members of this House have done in a lifetime. And I include myself in that allegation. I do not know who he is. I do know he is not a charlatan. I do know that many of the hundreds of people he has spoken to feel richer for the experience.

'He preaches tolerance - that does not inspire violence. He has said that the world needs to be reminded of the value of human life - that does not inspire violence. He has taught that we should remind ourselves of the strictures laid down in the Bible and make greater efforts to observe them - that does not inspire violence. What this man should receive is the full support of this House. We should take urgent steps to ensure that he is heard without disorder and disturbance. Will the Minister now take control of the situation and discharge his responsibilities to this House and the British public?' Forbes sat down to a loud mixture of cheers and jeers but he noticed that much of the enthusiasm for derision had dissipated.

A London Member, well known for his witty comments rose: 'Mr Speaker, on a point of order. May I say that the man we have been discussing has already performed one miracle which we can all see for ourselves. He has given the Member for Sussex North the ability to string a number of sentences together for the first time in his career in this House.' He was going to say more but the Speaker interrupted.

'That is not a point of order, he said, amid laughter

'Has the Minister given any thought to the message the man has been giving that there is no God?' What does he see as the implications to the Church of England?' asked an obscure Member from an even more obscure constituency.

'He has not said there is no God, ' a voice from the bank benches shouted. There were shouts of 'Quite right' and 'Yes he has' from various part of the House.

'Order, Order,' shouted the Speaker.

The Minister rose again and looked at his notes. Clearly his departmental team had not prepared any background to help him give an answer. The dominating and superior attitude burst like a balloon punctured by a pin. He looked again at his notes, turning over some pages..

'This is not a question which, I believe, is a matter for the Government,' he replied pompously. More shouts of derision from the bank benches.

'On a point of order,' Forbes rose again. The only chance he had of speaking again was to raise a point of order. He knew it was not a genuine point but the Speaker would not know that until he had made it. 'The man is only making use of the greatest freedom this country still retains, the freedom of speech which it is up to this House to protect. One would think that the only choice the Church of England has is to support him to the full. He is.......'

'That is not a point of order,' the Speaker shouted above the din with emphasis.

Several members rose but the Speaker announced the end of Question Time. There was to be a Government statement on another matter.

An embarrassed Forbes was about to leave the chamber but instead he sat firmly in his place, a look of horror slowly spreading across his face. As he moved to stand he had glanced up at the public gallery and was petrified to see all three of his former mistresses, Pauline, Karen and Pamela, sitting together in the front row of the Stranger's Gallery watching him. Good God ! he thought, are they going to make a scene? To Forbes' enormous relief as the Government spokesman began his statement the girls stood up and walked out,

Forbes' sat back with relief but he was becoming aware that his transformation from a political joke into a thoughtful statesman had gone further than he anticipated. He was now taking matters very seriously. Despite an expedient decision to support the man which he had made for political reasons he had begun to consider the man and what his presence could mean, and ask himself what was the point of it all. He had been very upset by the reaction of his Parliamentary colleagues on both sides of the House during the Commons debate and the fact that they criticized and attacked the man although he done nothing wrong. All the reports of his activities and his words, whether you supported him or not, were of the good he was doing

Forbes began to study his colleagues and he did not like what he saw. Who were they?

What was their purpose.? He concluded that they were all professional schemers, as he had once been. They had schemed their way into being selected as candidates, they had schemed their way to being elected by telling the voters what they thought they wanted to hear, whether they believed it or not. They schemed their way into favorable positions within the party hierarchy and the House. They always did what was expedient, with one eye on being part an active part of the government with a position of some importance. For most of their political lives they were nothing more than votes in suits. Their sole duty was to support their party, no matter what. They schemed with each other to select someone who would help them, to be the leader of their party and they schemed to remain in favour.. Yes, he admitted, he had been a prime schemer, although a lazy one with no great ambitions.

Even though he initially studied the man for the wrong reasons he was fast becoming convinced that there was something in what he said. He had the right ideas and he was broadcasting the right message.

Forbes was as aware as anyone else that Britain was fast declining. Inefficiency pervaded every area of government. The National Health Service was falling apart, education was failing abysmally, making money was the primary objective, not making life better for the British people. Britain was being run by a bunch of ill-equipped amateurs.

Forbes sighed deeply. He did not recognize himself. Was he getting old, or had he just woken up. Whatever it was, whatever the man said or did, the task of changing things in time might be impossible. Nevertheless, he felt he was on his own road to Damascus

★ ★ ★

Outside in the streets the scene corroborated the views of the questioners rather than that of the Minister. The scenes in Winchester when the man last appeared were repeated a thousandfold.

The seven million people population of Greater London had more than doubled by sightseers and those who were being described by some of the British press as 'pilgrims.'

Despite their more cosmopolitan character most of them were just as content as those in Winchester to wander aimlessly through the streets, seeing the sights and window shopping, awaiting the man's arrival rather than expending energy by going to look for him.

But the aimlessness was becoming more organized. It seemed that every visitor had the same idea, to go to the Palace of Westminster in Parliament Square and then to admire Westminster Abbey. Then up Birdcage Walk to Buckingham Palace then down the Mall to Trafalgar Square which became a whirlpool as they crossed the people who had walked up Whitehall from the Embankment on their way to St Paul's, the Tower and Tower Bridge. Piccadilly Circus resembled 'white water' falls as they all met again on their way and turned into a slow flowing river, that streamed down Piccadilly on their way to Hyde Park. In this way they managed to cause maximum damage to normal city life and disturb the largest number of inhabitants.

Unfortunately the river was not entirely smooth flowing as tributaries ran off the main stream as some searched for genuine amusement, and others went to off to make amusements of their own by arguing with those who objected to their presence, breaking shop windows if the mood took them, or arguing and fighting amongst themselves if they could find no other diversion.

At night the West End became a living hell for citizens out for genuine pleasure. Thousands with nothing else to do, many with absolutely nowhere to go, caused impenetrable obstructions.

Police closed Piccadilly, the Circus, Regent Street and Shaftesbury Avenue in a futile attempt to keep some traffic moving. Genuine pleasure seekers, and the number had been greatly reduced by the traffic problems, had to run a gauntlet of sarcasm and ribaldry on their way to theatres, cinemas and restaurants, and drunken abuse on their way home.

Nightlife, particularly respectable night life, was slowly grinding to a halt while the casinos and night clubs reveled in freedom from police attention. They had far more important things to do.

★ ★ ★

While the crowd thronged the street in a semi orderly manner the newspaper industry was engaged in a frenzied war to produce the most newsworthy story.

Frank Faulkner, as became the most important member of The Daily Times editorial staff, tried to produce the most responsible report. He described in detail the five incidents that has introduced the story indicating that only two of them involved any evidence of healing. The first and third, although interesting, could have been a question of a mis-diagnosis of a doctor and the other involved a near escape. People had near escapes nearly every day of the year. It had to be said, wrote Faulkner, that the boy had been unable to walk for a number of years and there was plenty of evidence that Grace Golder had been blind for more than 15 years. The fifth incident was, a matter of a near escape.

Faulkner pointed out in the man's favour that everyone who had contacted him spoke of his calmness and serenity and the aura of peace that emanated from him. The man certainly had something about him, Faulkner added.

On the constant criticism that the man had refused to speak to the media Faulkner pointed out that although Jesus Christ had spoken to groups of hundreds of people he had not had to deal with a voracious media, Faulkner admitted that many newspapers were quite prepared to be economical with the truth and were prone to exaggeration.

David Grant of Telegraph Today chose the man's reported remarks on the church and religion and his suggestion that the church had little relevance with the basic code upon which human activity should be based, as his target. The man had been reported as saying that the prophets of all religions when launching their relevant code were certainly not launching organizations which would build huge and expensive, in time, money and edifices, with a hierarchy only concerned with maintaining its status. It was quite wrong for religious leaders to complain about the activities of their fanatics when it was their responsibility to control those fanatics. They were the ones who should be maintaining discipline.

Grant repeated the question, said to have been posed by the man - What does the church actually do to improve the lives of people? Serious sermons full of cliches were of little use. What did the church do about housing the homeless people in their parishes, or offer the poor real help with their difficulties?

Grant speculated that clearly some people did need a centre on which to base their lives a rather different sort of church was needed, a place where people with problems could go and discuss them with other people in order to find a solution, or people who had solved major problems could go and tell others in the hope it would help. Discussions could be led by a chairman, rather than a priest . People would leave feeling that something constructive had been achieved instead of just walking away self-satisfied that they had done their duty.

Grant, now obviously in sympathy with the man, could not really understand why religious leaders such as priests went off to university to learn religion when what they needed was experience of life so that they could useful help and advise their church members. Have you ever heard of an Imam being asked to give a sermon to a Church of England congregation, of a Buddhist or whatever, to explain what they think and discuss the differences?'

The News Mail, full of righteous indignation about the criticism of the man, had done the obvious journalistic thing and had sent a reporter to the south of France to find and interview Philip Green. The paper carried a photograph of a healthy looking Philip on his bicycle smiling broadly. It carried a full interview with Philip's parents confirming that he had not seen a doctor since the initial tests had confirmed he could walk without crutches.

The Daily Sun made no mention of the story they had previously published about the man allegedly sleeping with a hotel maid. Rather than making new accusations it concentrated on being busy seeking a scandal. It revealed that their reporters were looking into the man's background and finding people who had known him before and said it was checking stories ostensibly sent in by readers.

The only unqualified support came from the Express & Star reporter . Robina Carter, one of the most attractive and sexy members of the press corps, had obviously been told by tbe owners to follow growing public opinion that the man was genuine.

Unfortunately, as was the way with the paper, Robina's report was written as an interview with the man even though that it was widely known that he would not speak to journalists. She concentrated on the view that had been expressed that parents should be sent gaol if their children misbehaved and intimated that the man had said education in Britain was collapsing. She failed to make it clear that there view were expressed by

Ruth Morton, not the man. She explained that she had been undercover as a member of the public desperately seeking assistance. What she had done, in fact, was to talk to people who had actually spoken to the man, and then translated his comments as if they were answers to her questions.

It was thus that the man had described to her how he had seen Grace Golder in the crowd and realized that she was blind. He had spoken gently to her, telling her that she would see if she believed him strongly enough and, in fact, she was able to see. This ignored the fact that Grace Golder herself had said in several interview with other newspapers that the man never spoke to her.. The man had told her, Robina added, that the same thing had happened with Philip Green. Unabashed she went on to quote the man as telling her that most of the trouble throughout history had been caused by religion. Not the people themselves but by religious leaders putting their own interpretation on what has been said. This was a comment that had earlier been reported by Dr Porter.

Martin, whose story in the Examiner had been almost a repeat of his original story updated by subsequent events, read the stories with various degree of despair. He had a premonition that it was all going to go wrong.

* * *

Dai Griffiths picked up the telephone with all the hesitancy of someone not practised in using one. He dialed slowly and deliberately and waited with anticipation. He was one of the few people in his area not to have a telephone in his own home but his neighbour Emlyn, who was a bit above himself, had had one installed over a year ago. Dai knew that Emlyn's wife Bronwyn would go and get Gladys. He had a pocketful of coins so he wasn't too worried about how long she took.

Bronwyn was quite excited to learn it was Dai on the other end of the line. She knew it must be important otherwise Dai would not be using an instrument he hated.

'What is it? Are you all right?' asked Gladys immediately she took the receiver. She did not even confirm who she was speaking to.

'Yes, I'm fine,' Dai shouted. He really didn't understand how is voice could be carried so far if he didn't shout.

'Don't shout,' said the more sensible Gladys. 'I can hear you perfectly well if you just talk normally. What's wrong?'

'Nothing's wrong.'

'But it must be if you're using a telephone. Are you hurt?'

'No I'm not hurt. Just shut up for a minute and listen.' Distance made his nerve feel stronger. Gladys remained silent.

'Its about Megan.'

'What about Megan?' Gladys interrupted.

'For God's sake woman let me finish. I've been thinking. I know I've been wrong about her. I want her back home.....are you listening?'

'Oh! Dai, that's marvelous. What changed your mind?'

'Never mind about that. Tell her grandmother to let her know that she can come home as soon as she likes.'

'I'll tell her myself, she's here.'

'Where?'

'Well,' said Gladys hesitantly, not sure about what was happening. 'She's been staying with me while you're away. She's here with me now.'

'Put her on.'

'Hello Dad ,' said a cautious voice.

'Megan. I'm sorry I've been so nasty to you. But I was only doing what I thought was best but I was wrong, I see that now.'

'Oh! Dad.'

'Stay at home and have your baby, your Mother and I will think of something.' Dai heard his daughter burst into tears at the other end of the line.

'Oh Dai, that was nice,' said Gladys after a few seconds. 'But was has happened?'

'I've seen sense that's all. Anyway this phone call is costing me money so get off the line. I don't know when I'll be home but it will probably be at the weekend. Goodbye love'

'Goodbye.'

Dai replaced the receiver and turned to look at Fred who had been standing by his side.

'There. I've done it.'

'Good lad,' said Fred, patting him on the back. 'You'll not be sorry.'

'Do you know,' said Fred, 'I feel bloody marvellous. Let's go and have a pint.'

★ ★ ★

Innocent was ever aware that racism, whether the authorities admitted it or not, was still rife in Britain. It wasn't always blatant but it was there, underneath the surface. He was certain that if anyone was to blame it was the immigration authorities, strongly supported by ill-advised liberals who were guilty of gross intellectual laziness. They had never bothered to think the problem through and look at both of the argument and the consequences of any decision.

The thought it was politically correct to agree that Britain was, and always had been, the place refugees from dictatorial foreign regimes could seek safety. And they welcomed those immigrants who filled any job shortages in this country.

But no-one had ever given serious consideration to what would happen if they came to Britain in their thousands. We are good hearted souls and we welcome you all, they boasted.

But allowing thousands to come over here regardless, without any control, people from different cultures, with different habits, different languages and their own view of communities was a sure sign that our own democratic ways, and our way of life, established over a thousand years, would be engulfed and eventually disappear. Most of them, particularly Asians, came from countries with very large populations where it was essential to compete with many others in every area of life. There was no time for the politeness and pleasantries which were once a basic of life in Britain

This was not racism, Kenneth was sure. It was commonsense. A fact of life. Sure, welcome immigrants, political and economic, in numbers that could be carefully and efficiently handled.

It was essential, Kenneth had always thought, that when they arrive they should be given indoctrination courses, explaining the British way of life, what we would accept and what was unacceptable. He was not sure about an oath of allegiance. If they were earning enough money they would be loyal.

He realized that such a system would be expensive and take time but he was sure the effort would be worth it. He felt sure that other countries, such as America and, he thought, Australia did . If the man's message was as reported and his rules of life explained clearly that would do the job. It could be Britain's salvation.

★ ★ ★

Harry Gregg could not forget the man he had heard being discussed on the Peter Potter Investigation. The fact that he might actually have seen him at that road accident intrigued him. He was also fascinated by the thought that the man might really be someone special. The feeling that he had to see him and listen to him and if possible speak to him grew stronger each day. He did not know why. He could not explain it, even to himself, so he didn't try.

Since Mabel had discovered the existence of his many female friends his behaviour towards her had been impeccable. He returned home promptly when his duties were finished, and helped her whenever he could. He treated her gently and with consideration and tried to reassure her that he loved her.

Mabel's reaction was one of deep suspicion. Was he being nice to her because he was sorry, or because he had another girl friend and did not want her to become suspicious It was strange seeing him with a tea towel in his hands. He'd never done that before. Then he made her a cup of tea. She did not knew that he was aware of how to do it. But when he offered to clear the table after supper she felt he must be in an hypnotic state. He asked her if she wanted a hot water bottle in the bed but as it was a warm and sticky evening she told him she thought it was unnecessary.

But they did not make love. Mabel's forgiveness could not stretch that far, not now at least. She could not forget that he had been with other women, had lain with them and made love to them. She knew that if she gave way and let him try that when it came to that moment when she had to give herself to him she would be overcome with revulsion, she would never be able to forget that he had done it with so many other women. Many of whom she knew.

When he said he was going away to try and see the man again she believed him. He had been so kind and considerate to her that she could not believe he would be unfaithful to her again.

Harry looked back at a near escape he had on a visit to London. Sitting alone at the bar in his hotel he had spotted a sexily dressed blonde sitting alone at the other end. In the past the alarm bell s would have rung and he would be plotting seduction. It was a shock when he noticed that she was approaching him.

'Are you alone?' she had asked.

'Yes,' he had replied with a nervousness that was entirely new to him.

'Could we get together?' had asked. Leaning forward to reveal impressive twin peaks in a substantial range of mountains.

'I'm sorry but I'm gay. I wouldn't be of any use to you.' he had replied.

She had looked at him with disgust, flicked the cigarette ash at him and walked out.

Harry sat there sweating. He did not recognize himself. Him? Gay? Where did that come from? He wasn't sure how he felt at that moment, proud of himself or disappointed. Mabel would not believe him if he told her. But there was no danger of that.

What had changed him? He had no idea but somehow he felt that the things he had heard the man talking about had got through to him. He was well aware that his past was something to be ashamed of. When he listened to the man he felt completely different. He couldn't explain why but he had a strong determination to change. .

★ ★ ★

Martin awoke that last Saturday stiff and heavy eyed after an almost sleepless night. He kept going over and over in his mind the momentous events of the last three weeks.

At six in the morning he gave up the fight to sleep, got up, made himself a cup of tea. Fortified and slowly returned to consciousness. He went out quietly to look for a newsagent where he bought all the morning papers. Back in the flat he made himself another drink and sat back to contemplate the past and read what now was happening in the world.

It seemed an age since he watched a seriously injured school caretaker get up and walk away apparently unhurt. Then there was the story about the crippled boy who walked to join his friends after several years on crutches. Then seeing a picture of a man in a white sweater at a car accident, recalling that such a man had been described at the previous incidents. Then came the London bomb where the man was seen again on television standing on the edge of the crowd. Martin recalled how his mind had struggled with the coincidences and what, if anything, they might mean. And then came the decision when the blind woman seemed to have had her sight restored by a man described as wearing a white sweater. Then the nerve wracking decision to put his thoughts into print. It was one hell of a story. This conclusion was confirmed when he looked at the newspapers he'd just bought.

'PROPHET ARRIVES IN LONDON,' announced the News and Mail across three columns; 'PROPHET REACHES CAPITAL' said the Express & Star; 'SON OF GOD IN LONDON?' asked the Daily Sun, while The Daily Times revealed 'MAN ARRIVES IN LONDON.' The Morning Mirror, in large type which took up all the front page, told its readers ´ARRIVAL OF MYSTERY MAN BRINGS VIOLENCE.'

Despite the emotional headlines there was nothing of importance in the accompanying stories, they contained the usual reports on alleged healings, the usual criticisms and statements, including the latest from the Pope and the Archbishop of Canterbury. Neither could be described as open-minded or friendly.

From the Daily Times Martin learned that Moscow had made its first comment about the man. Pravda had described the man's journey through southern England as ´yet another plot by western capitalism to influence the uncommitted nations of the world´, and dealt at length with the scenes of violence along the route. Pictures of the riot which had followed a football match last season between Glasgow Rangers and Celtic, traditionally known locally as 'Protestants versus Catholics' had been published by the Russian press as an incident following one of the man's meetings.

Representatives of militant white organizations had described the man as ´a black racialist trying to ferment trouble´, while spokesmen from those representing coloured people called him 'a white racialist trying to foment trouble´.

Anti-Semites described him as 'yet another Jewish prophet.' Jewish groups disclaimed all association with him and said he was 'a tool of the anti-Semites attempted to bring further discredit to the Jews.'

The Daily Times, in a first leader under the heading 'What has he done wrong?' listed a number of mistakes alleged to have been made by the man. They seemed to Martin that all they had done was pick up on the mistaken reactions to what he had said rather than attempting to accurately interpret his words. It was what he had emphasized really concerned him.

But the news that really dismayed Martin came from Parliament and the Home Secretary. Clearly shaken by the battering he had received during Question Time, he had announced a whole list of precautions to be taken to ensure public safety during the man's visit.

The man would only be allowed to speak once in London, in Hyde Park. He would be allowed to walk from the house he was staying at in Paddington to Hyde Park but not allowed to leave by foot. After the meeting he would be taken by helicopter to Heathrow for a flight to a destination of his own choosing. A large platform was being erected in the park, and sound equipment provided. The Metropolitan Police would be responsible for law and order within the park but army units would be posted at strategic points in case there was trouble.

Martin understood the need for caution but the idea of putting the man up on a platform in front of a vast crowd seemed utterly ridiculous. The man never spoke to large crowds. In fact he had declined to do so. Martin doubted whether the man would accept these conditions and might even refuse to appear. That would cause more trouble that even his worst critics had predicted. As Frank Faulkner pointed out, when Jesus spoke to large numbers of people they all wanted to hear what he was saying, there was never any serious vocal opposition.

At nine o'clock as they had arranged Martin and Frank Faulkner left to meet the man and go with him to Hyde Park. It was pointless trying to use Faulkner's car because the streets were impassable and the whole area between Hammersmith and the centre of London were subjected to police closure. It took them almost two hours to walk the three and a half miles from Faulkner's house down Notting Hill and the Bayswater Road and through Sussex Gardens. They were not sure where the man was staying although they knew the name of the road. They need not have worried because when they finally reached their destination their problem was immediately solved.

A battery of press photographers and television camera men stood outside amidst the mass of people. The house itself was protected by a wall of policemen, looking apprehensive but trying to be cheerful by joking with the waiting throng. Martin and Faulkner pushed their way through to join the reporters they knew who had arrived earlier. There was a strong sense of camaraderie among those who had spent much of the last three weeks searching for the man and trying to get to him, without much success.

They waited for over an hour with a crush of people which, though noisy and cheerful, was slowly becoming impatient. Rowdiness was encouraged by several false alarms when other occupants of the house opened the shabby door of the terraced house to go either in or out. Several times the police guard had to push back the throng as it became too enthusiastic.

Martin was becoming more and more concerned for he feared that the high spirits would not last for ever and that impatience would lead to anger and anger to violence. He was also worried that the man would refuse to come out because he did not like the arrangements that had been made.

It dawned on him at one stage that maybe the man would not be able to get out of the front door and would therefore slip out by the back. It was Grant of Telegraph Today who pointed out that terraced houses of the sort they were looking at rarely had the luxury of a back door.

A section of the crowd began to sing the traditional British anthem 'Why Are We Waiting?' accompanied by the ribald remarks expected from any light hearted British assemblage. There was a stir of excitement when a senior police office accompanied by an immature army second lieutenant, arrived to talk to the police on duty. They talked for a few minutes and then the army officer turned to study the crowd around him. Standing thoughtfully, slowly tapping his cane against his boot he then spoke to to the police officer and quickly walked away.

Another ten minutes or so passed. Martin looked at his watch and saw it was after one o'clock. A small, uncertain cheer attracted his attention and he saw little Dai Griffiths, the Welsh miner, standing in the doorway looking out anxiously. Suddenly, noticing Martin standing on the other side of the barrier of policemen he had a quick word with one of the officers and walked across.

'He would like to see you,' Griffiths told Martin, his face worried and unsmiling.

'All of us?' Martin asked, looking at his journalist companions.

'No, only you. He says you were in at the start and was the first one to recognize his work. Will you come in?'

Martin felt a flood of self-satisfaction wash over him. He had always felt he was the first and that this fact had never been properly recognized. Now, at last it was, and by the man himself.

Watched by his envious colleagues and eyed with interest by the crowd he followed Griffiths across the road and into the dark interior of the house.

★ ★ ★

When his eyes had become accustomed to the dim light in the windowless hallway Martin saw a long passage which led past two closed doors on the right, bent sharply round the staircase and led to what was clearly a Victorian style breakfast room.

The hall was covered with a frayed carpet, the pattern long since vanished under an army of feet. As on the outside the woodwork was covered with a dismal chocolate brown paint. The walls were hidden by a peeling and faded floral wallpaper which did nothing to cheer the soul.

A tall umbrella stand, alongside which was an oval mirror stained at the edges by damp and age, stood just inside the door. On what would have been the outside wall if it hadn't been a terraced house, just before the staircase, hung a picture of a lonely stag staring out over the bleak highlands of Scotland. Monarch of the Glen, Martin thought inconsequentially.

Despite the heat outside, the temperature in the house was chilly for the sun had never reached any part of it. A smell of boiled vegetables permeated the atmosphere.

Dai Griffith led the way into a moderate size what he had heard called the breakfast room which clearly had not had any money wasted on it through modernization, which was bigger than Martin expected, was full of people standing drinking tea or coffee. It was untidy but clean. Fawn wallpaper did its best to reflect the light of a 60 watt bulb that hung shadeless from the centre of the ceiling. Two old armchairs, on a carpet, a rich plum colour showing signs of wear and tear but the edges retaining some pile. A sofa, covered by a pile of old newspapers, had been pushed against the wall.

An attempt to alleviate the dullness had been made by the lady of the house who had shoved half a dozen plastic flowers into a jam jar and placed them on the hob.

'This is my Aunty Bronwen,' said Dai indicating a small, tubby woman with black hair and a cheerful round face. Martin smiled, shook her hand and was about to say something when he had to stand aside to allow someone else into the room.

'Would you like some coffee?' Aunty Bronwen asked him in her lilting Welsh accent, thoroughly enjoying being needed.

Martin thanked her and began looking around the room as she scurried away. He quickly recognized John Porter, Miriam Cartwright, who smiled at him when he caught her eye, Ruth Morton, Grace Golder, Grimshaw, Harry Gregg, the policeman from the road accident. Dai Griffiths.

He was surprised to see Fred Salmons, the caretaker who, as far as Martin was concerned, started all this.

'I didn't expect to see you, he said, smiling. 'I saw you in Hereford.. Are you with the man?' he added, still annoyed that he could not use a name for the man.

'Well, I'm with him but I'm not sure I can be any help. I don't know what he is talking about most of the time but he's a good man. I know that.'

Martin nodded, not knowing what else to say. Asking him if his legs were all right seemed a waste of time as he was walking about without any sign of difficulty.

He was rescued by Miriam Cartwright who approached him as if he was an old friend.

'We meet again,' she said cheerfully. 'Surprising isn't it, what's happened since we last met?'

'Yes,' said Martin, reflecting about the uncertainty of that meeting, much had certainly happened since then. 'How is the vicar?' he asked, knowing of her difficulties. 'Is he still the anti-man?'

'Surprisingly, not any longer. In fact he is here somewhere. We had a few painful disagreements but it's all right now. He has seen that some of the comments made about the church have a degree of truth in them. He's asked himself whether, as a vicar, he has really done very much of God's real work. He goes along with the basic code and says he knows he has forgotten some of it in the past.'

'That's good news for you then,'

'Yes, everything between us is much better and he has promised to help where he can.'

Martin saw a small group of followers he recognized from previous incidents, talking together about the upcoming meeting.

'I didn't expect to see you all here, he said the group in general.

'We all made our decisions to join him individually and this seemed like a good place to meet and support him,' said Arnold Grimshaw, dressed as usual as a typical banker. All he needed was a pair of glasses to peer over and an overdraft he could refuse.

'He seems to have a hit a cord with you all,' Martin suggested.

'He has put into words many of the thoughts I have been dwelling on for a long time, and provided some of the answers to my questions. As a banker no-one is more aware of the fact that money has become the God. It seems that if you give people the ability to handle money they only use it to improve their personal positions. Ever heard a company or organization announce a profit of over a million or more saying they will use the money to reduce the cost of the products. It is always going to be used for further investment. Then they can make an even greater profit the next year which, again, would be used for further investment And so it goes on. You rarely see any benefits to the customers.'

'He's right,' Forbes intervened, adopting his new-found serious and knowledgeable approach 'He blames the hierarchy of the church for their dismal failure over the centuries. The leaders have always been more concerned about retaining their position and the status quo rather than spreading an understanding of religion and what it really means. The same could be said about politicians. Whatever they say they are only concerned with their own well-being and making sure they get elected at the next election. How many of them , from any political party, have ever made a strong stand on a principle. It might make them unpopular with their electorate and, more importantly, with the leaders of their party. Look around at what is wrong with the country at the moment, in almost every sector, and then try and think of a politician who has stood up and clearly stated the facts and what the solutions, some them difficult, should be.

'I'm a very good example,' Forbes continued, a slight smile on his face. ' I haven't done anything constructive during my years in Parliament. No-one seems to care. I haven't made a stand on any principle mainly because I haven't had any principles. All I could think about was making sure I got re-elected next time. From now on I'm going to surprise a few people, particularly my party leadership.' A few of those gathered around clapped gently.

'Well, I'm not interested in any of the arguments about whether he gave me back my sight.' Grace Golder joined in. 'All I am aware of is that I could not see for over 15 years. On the day that I met him my sight returned. That's good enough for me and I'm going to do everything I can to spread his message and help others. I don't know how but I will find a way.

Griffiths, the smallest man in the crowd, put his arm around her. 'I'm the same. My wife convinced me that I've got to listen to what he says and try and do it. I always listen to what my wife says, she's usually right, so I'm here to help.' A general outbreak of nodding.

'I'm like Grace,' Salmons said with feeling.. 'I know that when I fell out of the window I did break both my legs. The pain was bloody awful in both of them and I was about to pass out. But all the pain went when he spoke to me and told me to go and join my family. That's good enough for me. I'll do anything he asks now.'

'What everyone says is true,' Ruth Morton observed. 'We've got to learn to respect one another, be tolerant and more patient. Forgiving someone who has done something to hurt you is a bit of a problem but we've got to try.'

She spoke with strong feelings. Her view that parents should be held responsible for the crimes or problems caused by their children, including fines, community service or even detention had upset many people. She had been abused whilst out shopping, had eggs and rotten fruit thrown at her and windows had been smashed in her home. 'My plea for tolerance and respect has been ignored,' she complained. She looked pleadingly at Martin as if he could assist her but he had no idea how to react but put his hand on her shoulder as if to reassure her..

Thomas looked at his colleagues self-consciously. 'I've got a problem. It's my own fault. I just hope he can help me, ' he said shortly, making it clear he wanted no questions.'

'I agree with what he has been saying about the various religions,' said Kenneth Innocent, joined the discussion from the periphery. 'We all want exactly the same things, at least, the people do. The leaders have got to realize that we are all compatible and do much more to silence and discipline the fanatics.'

'I'm not sure what I can do,' said policeman Harry Gregg. 'I spend my life dealing with criminals and forgiving them is not my job. I certainly could not forgive some of them. I saw the state that Ruth and her daughter were in when their car crashed. That they are both alive is certainly a miracle but whether the man had anything to do with it I do not know. But I'm here to learn what I can.'

Porter had been standing by watching the discussion and when it seemed to be ending he walked over to him.

'I don't think you've met our leader,' he said, holding out a hand to guide the man towards Martin.

'No I haven't. And I've been trying for long enough,' Martin laughed as he shook hands with the man. Immediately he understood what people meant when they said they were captivated by his eyes translucent deep brown with distinctive whites, they seemed to hold and examine you as he smiled. 'I'm sorry you have had to wait so long,' he said in a low, deep voice. He smiled showing two rows of white even teeth. 'But I'm afraid the police will not let me leave.' Martin looked surprised.

'It's all right,' the man laughed. 'I'm not under arrest yet. They say they need time to clear a route to the park. I understand that there is quite a crowd out there.'

'You are certainly right about that,' Martin replied still staring at the man's hypnotic eyes.

'I wanted to thank you for your help and say goodbye,' the man added.

Martin felt himself blushing and for some reason he felt very nervous.

'I haven't done very much to help you,' he replied. Then, suddenly :'Why goodbye, are you leaving?'

'Yes, I do not think we will meet again after today.'

'You're going away?'

'Yes.'

'May I ask where you are going?'

'Just away,' replied the man mysteriously. 'I cannot explain further but you will understand later. Dai Griffiths and Grace Golder and the others will help John Porter carry on my work.'

'What will Dr Porter be doing?' Martin asked, worried by the tone of the conversation.

'Dr Porter knows where his future lies. I have explained to him and he understands. I'm sorry that I cannot give you a good story. There is nothing more I can say.' The man looked at Porter who smiled broadly.

Further discussion was thwarted by the arrival of the coffee and there was a moment of confusion as cups were gingerly handed round, during which the man and Porter moved away.

Martin felt very strange. Normally he would have moved after the man and pursued his questioning more energetically but this time something stopped him. It was feeling that not only would he achieve very little but that he shouldn't even try. He had never had a feeling like that before.

Martin began to feel uncomfortable and out of place. He didn't know many people in the room and those he did were busy talking together.

'You don't know Ken and Mary do you?' said a voice behind him. It was Dai Griffiths with an attractive young woman and a tall colored man.

'I've just met Kenneth, Martin replied..'

'I'm Mary Carpenter,' said the young woman taking his hand. 'I understand you are a reporter.'

'Yes, for my sins,' Martin replied. 'Are you with the man?'

'Yes,' said Mary, 'but we only joined him today. I believe he has helped us a great deal and so we now want to help him.

'May I ask how he helped you?' asked the reporter in Martin.

Mary smiled. 'It's a comparatively long story. I thought I had cancer, it was confirmed that I had and that I would have to have an operation. Ken and I went to see the man in Reading and although we met him we didn't have time to talk to him. The amazing thing is that afterwards when I went to the hospital for operation, they carried out pre-op tests and what they found was benign.'

'Good heavens,' was all Martin could say.

'I know that many other women have found lumps which turned out to be benign but I'm sure it was the man who cured her,' Kenneth joined in. 'Mary was very distressed that she couldn't talk to him and we felt all was lost.'

'That's marvellous,' said Martin, putting his hand on Mary's arm. 'Absolutely bloody marvelous. Mary smiled broadly, her eyes shining with happiness.

'By the way,' Martin said suddenly. 'What happened to that little boy from Norfolk. I heard that he had a relapse? Dr Porter told me that the story was wrong.'

'You should ask him,' laughed Kenneth. 'He's here.' He looked around the room. 'There he is, just going upstairs, looks all right to me.'

Martin watched as the boy, smartly dressed in short trousers and check shirt walked quickly up the stairs.

'He was going to come with us but his parents thought that the crowds were much too big.'

'So what I heard was rubbish?'

'Yes, the boy did go to the hospital for further tests and he was in for longer than expected so the rumours started going round that he was crippled again. The only reason he was such a long time was that the specialists couldn't believe what they found so they kept checking.'

Martin was just about to ask more questions when there was a harsh knock on the door. Aunty Bronwen answered it and came hurriedly back into the room.

It was the police, she told Porter. They say you can leave now.'

⋆ ⋆ ⋆

It was close on two o'clock when the man and his companions left the house to begin his journey to Hyde Park. The man seemed philosophical about the conditions imposed by the authorities and had not objected to speaking from a platform.

The mood of gloom that had overtaken Martin in the house was not dispelled by the bright sunshine that greeted the party as they emerged. The clear blue sky was seen by many as a good omen on the ground as the 'the sun always shines on the righteous.' Martin told himself that all would be well but his subconscious did not believe him.

The man, as usual, walked ahead with John Porter and although the police escort was drawn closely around the man and his party he was able to stop occasionally to talk to someone. He was followed by the small group of followers including Grace Golder, Harry Gregg, Miriam and Charles Cartwright, Dai Griffiths, Fred Salmons, Edward Forbes, Mary Carpenter, Kenneth Innocent and someone Martin did not know but was told he was Fred Thomas who had joined the man recently.

Grimshaw himself was surprised that he felt relaxed, a new feeling since he was married. He had gone about his business efficiently and accurately but always, in the back of his mind, and sometimes at the front, were thoughts about what Elizabeth was doing at home. Was she being the efficient housewife and mother which, on increasingly rarer occasions she could be, or had she succumbed once again to the attractions of the bottle. What would he find at the end of the day? What would he go home to?

Harry Gregg found himself in a difficult situation following the escort of policemen behind the man. He felt that most of them were more frightened than those in the man's party. They were, he thought far too rough when people got close when a more relaxed approach would have been more beneficial and efficient. It was the programmed 'if they get too close push them away' approach.

Martin made a mental calculation. Twelve people, he thought, I wonder if there is any significance in that. A posse of pressmen, including Martin, were closely following the lead group, pushing and shoving in an effort to keep in touch.

The police, supported by army units, had managed to clear a narrow path through the milling throng just wide enough to allow the man and his team to walk unhampered beyond the reach of outstretched hands. The heat of the sun which was high in the sky was making the atmosphere oppressive and almost unbearable.

Reaching the Bayswater Road the crowds became even denser and more difficult for the police to handle as people became more anxious to catch a glimpse of the man as he passed and before he disappeared into Hyde Park. They pressed forward, pushing those in front against the solid wall of police who lined the route. Slowly the party crossed the road, through Victoria gate and into the shade of the trees. The man stopped every two or three paces to talk to someone but it was almost impossible for him to converse against the din made by the crowd.

Martin looked around at a sight which to him was unique and would never be seen again. The sky which had been clear blue was now spotted with bobs of cotton wool cloud that was being propelled slowly overhead. But the wind responsible for its movement was not obvious at ground level so the heat was an overwhelming combination of hot sun and perspiring human bodies. In front of him stretched a massive sea of faces stretching as far as he could see. Nearly half a million people had crammed into the park that afternoon. It seemed quite incredible that the man was expected to talk to all these people at once. It was even more inconceivable to believe that they would all hear him.

For the first time since he first saw the man Martin wished he was elsewhere. He would rather have been anywhere than in this seething cauldron of humanity on this hot afternoon.

He looked at the ocean of faces set against the background of luxurious buildings in Park Lane, dominated in the distance by the towering Hilton Hotel. He looked at the gentle softness of the trees with their variegated greens and burgeoning browns. This was England, he thought, gentle. peaceful England. Nothing could go wrong.

Martin Armstrong was not the only person in the vast crowd who was sorry to be there. Harry Gregg began to regret his decision to come to London and join the man. He had originally planned just to see him but had decided to try and join him to help as much as he could as a sort of penance for the way he had failed Mabel so many times. He just had to do something that he felt was right. But his policeman's instincts told him that the size of the crowd was impossible, it could not be handled if there was trouble no matter how many of his colleagues were on duty. There was little the soldiers being held in the background could do either.

The small procession led by the man moved slowly towards a clearing where Environment Ministry workmen had erected a stout tubular steel platform which stood about fifteen feet off the ground. On its right stood a higher scaffold tower which had been constructed for the six television cameras allowed there by government officials. Slightly below, on an intermediate platform, stood several men and one woman with microphones describing the scene to their worldwide audience. The crews and their assistants looked strangely calm and unhurried sitting above the swirling sea of humanity.

Once again raised voices asked 'Why Are We Waiting.' The bush telegraph had told them that the man was in the park and they could not understand the delay.

But the man was not to be hurried. He spoke to anyone who wanted to talk to him. Sometimes they seemed to only want to touch him as though, by doing so, some great problem in their lives would be resolved.

Others wanted to question him about things he had already said. A few, their faces tired and worn with urgent difficulties, spoke to him intently in undertones, trying to shield their voice from those around them.

Most of the people who stopped him were women, middle aged and old, to whom family responsibilities for one reason or another had become overpowering. A few cried as they spoke and with these people the man stopped for longer periods, sometimes breaking the police wall to put his arm around their shoulders, a warm and understanding smile on his face.

Each one seemed to gain comfort from his words. One or two, their faces bright, their eyes sparkling, stood staring into space as though offering a silent prayer of thanks for the help they had received. The majority showed their relief in the meaningless chatter of the unburdened. They turned proudly to their neighbours and related the conversation while at the same time advertising their problems to the world in general.

After each conversation reporters and photographers tried to talk to them. Martin ignored them. The conversation he had previously with the man had made him feel that he was part of the day's events rather than an observer. For the first time in his working life his newspaper was not the most prominent thought in his mind.

He spent most of his time looking anxiously at the people around him trying to gauge their mood and looking for potential troublemakers. It seemed that representatives of every nation, every religion and creed and every colour had packed into the park. He saw clergymen by the hundred, bus drivers, cab drivers and city gents in their business suits even though it was a Saturday. There were farmers, rail workers, shopkeepers, men who could have been anything and those who could not possibly be doing anything constructive for society. There were married women with and without small children, spinsters young and old, old men and boys, workers and their families on their day off, holidaymakers seeking something new and different, and foreign visitors by the thousand English seemed like a second language.

The multitude included the serious and the facetious, the want-to-know mores and the couldn't-care-less, those who wanted to learn and those who thought they knew, those who listened and those who scoffed, the talkative and the silent, the extroverts and the introverts, the educated and the ignorant.

Here, in this three hundred and sixty acre park, was a cross-section of all nations, Martin thought. The man would not be speaking to half a million people, he would be speaking to the world.

The man and Porter eventually reached the wooden steps leading to the platform and by this time Martin had infiltrated himself close to them. Porter and the man stood in deep, intense conversation.

'What's the problem?' Martin asked.

Porter, startled by the voice, turned sharply but smiled when he saw who it was.

'Oh, it's you,' he smiled. 'We were discussing how we ought to go about this. He wants to go up and start talking but I think someone should go up first and set the tone.'

Martin looked quickly at the man. Clearly the man did not need an introduction.,

'I should let him play it his way. He knows what is best,' Martin told Porter.

'I suppose you're right but I don't liked the idea of him going up there alone,' said Porter.

Nothing more was said. The man smiled at them, turned quickly and walked up the twelve steps which took him to the platform.

★ ★ ★

A gigantic roar greeted him. It reverberated through the park shattering the eardrums with its intensity like a thousand waves breaking on a rocky shore during a hurricane.

The man, tall and straight, his white sweater looking brilliant in the sunlight, surveyed his vast audience, turning slowly so that he could look at and be seen by those in every direction.

Suddenly the noise was shattered by complete silence. It was total, as if a giant hand had unthinkingly switched off the volume. Incredibly it became so quiet that the birds could be heard twittering excitedly as if to tell each other 'he's here, here's here.'

'By your presence here you have indicated your eagerness to learn the truth,' he said, his voice echoing around the park, carried by the huge tannoy system.

'But to learn that truth, even to begin to understand it, you have to put aside all thoughts of yourself, all animosity towards others, all the preconceived ideas of generations.' He paused to let his voice reach every corner of the park. Silence was complete as his audience listened to words that seemed ghostlike as they echoed and re-echoed through the sound system.

'All the differences between men and women over colour, class, creed, way of life, all national and international differences, all past errors, the accusations and counter accusations must be forgotten. It must be as if there were no yesterday for there is, in truth, only today.'

The voice thundered out as a million eyes riveted on the solitary figure, the white sweater clearly visible against the green and brown background of trees and buildings.

As he spoke he continued turning slowly so that he was addressing the whole gathering.

'Only in this way will peace be brought to the world, to nations and to individuals,' he thundered.

Amplified a hundredfold by the relay system the calmness of the scene up to now was shattered as the message crashed around the park. Startled by the sudden shout babies scattered throughout the crowd, began to cry, dogs brought by unthinking owners started barking, birds suddenly scudded out of the trees flying around aimlessly a, murmur of conversation rippled through the crowd.

The spell was broken.

'I am not here to criticize any country, any people or any individual. I am here to point the way, to reiterate the articles of faith and to ask all people to renew their commitment. I speak to people of every colour of every..........'

'How dare you come here and start telling us how to live, who the bloody hell are you?' shouted a raucous voice.

The man began to answer and it was clear that large sections of the crowd were still anxious to listen but with the spell broken, those not in sympathy began to make the most of it.

Martin was struck once again by the hatred expressed in some of the faces. People who, by their previous verbal explosions had identified themselves as church-going believers, had abandoned their previously expressed love and understanding and were hurling abuse at the man. What the hell are they afraid of Martin asked himself. He is preaching their message.

The first sign of real trouble came from an area mainly occupied by Asians quite close to where Martin was standing. They began to yell abuse and wave their fists in the air. A group of white men began to move towards them.

'Shut your bloody mouth,' one of them, Fred Thomas, told the vocal Asians,' or I'll shut it for you.' Fred, whose anger was mixed with fear for the future, still harboured the grudge he had borne since he was punched at the Winchester meeting. He was determined to revenge himself on someone and he didn't really care who.

'You go mind your own fucking business man,' the coloured man replied, unafraid. 'This is a free country and I can say what I like.'

'And I'm free to ram those pearly white teeth down the back of your bloody throat,' replied Fred, raising his fist threateningly. The heat was not only affecting bodies it was distorting minds and tempers were becoming uncontrolled.

Fists would have been thrown there and then if two burly policemen had not moved in quickly. They were bigger than the potential adversaries and they stood between the two groups.

'Violence is not the answer to your problem, nor is it the answer to any problem,' the man went on. 'One nation, one man may prove to their or his satisfaction through his strength that he is better than his opponent. But that is not a victory. It poisons the loser's mind with thoughts of revenge and further violence.....' the man suddenly stopped speaking. He staggered backwards across the platform and clutched the handrail. He stood looking at the crowd, blood streaming from a cut behind his ear.

A jagged piece of brick clattered on to the floor, rolled a few inches and then lay still, the focus of a thousand eyes.

For an instant which seemed like an eternity to those gathered in Hyde Park time stood still. The scene froze with all eyes on a lonely island in an ocean of faces where the man was still reeling from the blow.

A moment later the illusion was destroyed as those around the man came to their senses and rushed to his side. Martin and Porter were the first up with Innocent close behind, his face frozen with shock, quickly by his side trying to steady him. The others tried to gather round the platform to stop the hundreds of people who were also trying to climb up to help.

Martin took out his handkerchief and placed it over a two inch tear in the skin at the back of the man's head. The blood formed an large irregular stain on the immaculate sweater which gave the illusion of a twentieth century stigmata. The man, deathly pale, his eyes still glazed by the force of the blow, was praying out loud but it was impossible to hear what he was saying in the clamour now being created by the angry crowd around the platform. Dozens of policemen attempted to climb to get among those fighting to protect the man.

'I'm all right,' he said eventually. 'I will carry on.'

'Like hell you will,' Martin replied unthinkingly. He knew that the man should be taken away from the platform as soon as possible but that this was impractical in the present circumstances.

He looked at the faces surrounding the platform and it seemed that without exception they showed pain, anguish, anxious concern or fear. Even the Asian group who stood nearby and had helped to start the incident looked worried about what had happened.

People began searching wildly for the attacker and though many were accused and hotly denied it the chances of finding the culprit were faint.

Shouting that it was a black boy who threw the brick, that it was a white youth, rippled through the crowd. Accusations flew thick and fast as the temperature of the assembly began to rise again.

Rumours about who it was or what group it was gained momentum and flashed around the park with the speed of a forest fire. Soon tempers were lost and the seeds of further violence sown. Adversaries clashed in a flurry of fists, those who attempted to force their way through the crowd, screamed for help, their shouts mingling with those of pain and fear from people knocked to the ground by fists that neither knew nor cared who they were hitting.

The noise of battle grew as half a million people fought and struggled for their survival, by one means or another.

Martin began to panic. There seemed no way in which the battle of Hyde Park could be halted. Isolated on the island platform he knew there could be no escape. Instead of fearing for the man, he began to fear for his own safety. He called to John Porter.

'Let's try and get him out of here,' he shouted, not knowing what the doctor was thinking or how he felt. Porter nodded his agreement and holding his arms around the man, began to propel him towards the steps,

The scene of battling humanity was made worse as people fought to find safety on the platform others fighting to get away became entangled with a group of soldiers ordered to protect those on the platform. At the top of the shaking steps two policemen, helmetless and with dishevelled uniforms, tried to add their weight to Martin's and Porter's efforts.

'Get get him under the platform, he'll be safer there,' said one of them. Martin and Porter nodded their agreement, there seemed no other way, and began gently pushing the man through any gaps made by the efforts of the policemen.

Slowly they fought their way down the steps and to the base of the platform. Porter went under first then turned to assist the man who was still partly dazed. As he bent down to get under the platform an angry man lunged at him but was stopped in his tracks by a powerful right hook from one of the policemen. The man was hurled backwards into Martin who lost his grip of one of the platform stanchions and fell sideways. When he finally regained his feet he found he had been pushed away from the platform by other struggling bodies.

Martin fought frantically to regain his position with the man but the maelstrom of humanity around him was too strong and he was gradually edged further and further way. He saw he was being pushed towards a large oak tree with low branches on which some young people had already sought refuge. He slowly fought his way towards it. Just as he got there he was struck a blow in the stomach but as he fell again he felt the tree at his back. With a surge of energy he did not know he still possessed he pushed himself upwards, stretched out his arms and, using the bodies around him as steps, battled his way up into a branch which had been lowered by the bodies already seeking sanctuary.. He rested his head against the trunk of the tree, breathing heavily and badly bruised and tried to regain his wits. Hardly understanding what he was watching he saw that the area around the platform was still the scene of a bloody battle which police and now soldiers seemed powerless to stop. On the outer ring order was slowly being restored by groups of soldiers isolating small clusters of people and then moving them away from the centre.

They had no chance of reaching the platform quickly.

Martin tried to think what to do next. He could not reach the platform and although he wouldn't admit it to anyone he was too afraid to try. He could not get out of the park without getting involved again so he decided to stay where he was, in a tree surrounded by other frightened people.

On the platform the situation was deteriorating. A crowd of thirty or forty men had gained a foothold and were engaged in an all out fight to keep a similar number from climbing on.

Martin thought of the man and Doctor Porter still trapped under the platform. His conscience could not let him just sit there and watch. He had to do something.

Reluctantly he jumped down to earth and as he did so he noticed a group of soldiers pushing their way through to the centre and would soon be in a position to stop the fighting. He was glad he had been brave. He would be with the man when he was rescued.

He began to move slowly forward with the soldiers, pushing people aside.

Suddenly there was no need. His false bravery was meaningless. His cowardice, as it transpired, had been his saviour.

Without warning the air was rent by a mighty roar, a series of cracks and bangs mingled with the screams of the injured.

At first he thought and over-ladened tree branch had broken. Then he turned towards the platform and saw that it had disappeared in a thick cloud of dust.

It took a second or two for the implication to pierce his already befuddled brain. Then he realized exactly what had happened.

'Oh my God,' a voice shouted from somewhere. It was the cry of a young soldier trying to force his way into the rubble.

Fighting had stopped as though some powerful voice had shouted 'halt.' All eyes were now on the wrecked platform.

It was the most appalling sight Martin had ever seen. A gigantic pile of steel rods, broken planking, split ply-board and human bodies lay where the platform had been. The only sounds now were the cries and groans of those tangled in the wreckage.

Martin looked around hoping that, through a miracle, the man was safe. He was gripped by fear. He knew in his heart that non-one under the platform could have survived.

In a panic he screamed: 'The man ! He's under there !'

'Steady son,' said a calm voice behind him. It was a powerfully built, craggy army sergeant. his three stripes, two lines of medals and a lined face indicative of both age and experience.

'Let's do this slowly and bloody carefully,' he instructed those around him, including Innocent, who were moving quickly towards the wreckage.

Swiftly and efficiently he gave orders to the soldiers and other helpers, and there were now many of them. With what seemed to Martin like agonizing deliberation, they began moving bits of steel and wood, piling them away from the scene of the disaster.

'Come on lad,' the sergeant said to Martin. 'Pull yourself together and give us a hand. Watching won't help.' Martin joined Innocent who was still in a daze.

Gently they lifted away the injured. Some were only badly bruised and shocked, others had broken limbs. It was ten minutes before the first fatality was discovered. He was a good looking boy, probably still in his teens, with curly blonde hair. His multi coloured shirt and blue jeans were blood spattered and dirty. The blank steady stare from sightless eyes spoke of death.

Candice who had been standing near the platform protected by

Grimshaw and Gregg together with two soldiers, was shocked into silence, had not even screamed when the accident happened, seemed totally unaware of where she was, even of who she was. She looked at Martin as if he was a stranger.

Martin himself was near to tears. If this boy, near the top of the pile, was dead could those on the bottom still be living?

Martin's hopes rose as the rescuers dug deeper. A middle-aged black man with prominent streaks of grey in his tightly curled black hair, was brought from under a pile of steel rods and planks. Apart from cuts and bruises he was unhurt and still able to joke with those who pulled him clear.

Eventually the searchers came to the main floor of the platform, still held together in large sections. Most of those who had been fighting on and around the platform when it collapsed had now been carried away, only those who had sought safety under the structure were now left.

A hundred willing hands pulled and pushed the remaining wreckage, gently shifting it away. Apart from the clang and thud of metal and wood, the heavy breathing of the rescuers and an occasional order from the sergeant, a pall of silence hung over the scene that only minutes before had been a cacophony of riot and noise.

Griffith, the friendly ex-Welsh miner, was the first to be found, his grey hair matted with blood and dust, a huge gash in the back of his head. As the rescuers lifted him clear with gentle hands the way his head drooped as they lifted him showed clearly that his neck was broken. The man who had escaped death a mile below the earth's surface had met his end above it.

A shudder of fear ran through Martin's body as he realized that the force of the collapse, the weight of the platform and of the bodies that had been fighting on it, gave little chance for those beneath.

Martin began to pray aloud, little caring who was listening or watching him. He had prayed before like all people who are in fear or difficulty even though they would not admit God's existence when all was going well. Martin felt he was being hypocritcal but his prayer was fervent and he had no thought for himself.

A blue uniform appeared among the debris. It took the urgent efforts of the rescuers only a few minutes to pull out the body of one of the policemen. It was lifeless.

Then another body came into view. Martin recognized him as one of the man's followers he had met for the first time in the house. He thought his name was Fred Thomas, from somewhere in the Midlands.

The horrendous pile was now diminishing fast. An air of intense anticipation gripped the silent group still working. The tuneful warning bell of an ambulance which had forced its way slowly through the crowd and was now able to get close to the scene.

Another body appeared. It was a grey trouser leg that was first spotted by one of the searching soldiers. It was strangely twisted and brought a gasp from those watching. Carefully the perspiring rescuers, their faces pale and drawn in anguish, pulled away more steel and some splintered wood.

Tears welled up in Martin's eyes when he recognized the body as that of David Grant, the Express reporter who he had been met frequently and liked. They carried the body to one side and laid it with the others.

Martin's despair reached its nadir. There could be no other survivors. He stared with cold eyes at the ruins; his mind was blank unable to cope with the extent of the disaster. He looked again at Candice who was being ignored by all the working around. She seemed unaware of what was going on and did not even react when an excited voice shouted: 'This one is alive,' shouted an excited voice. The sound of the cry slowly infiltrated Martin's mind. He turned to see what was happening. Two policemen and a soldier were slowly lifting a body of a man on to a piece of planking,

He was tall, his face lean and not ashen like those of the victims found dead..

Martin looked closely and the body. He was dressed in a white shirt and blue suit, both now bloodstained and dirty, it was unmistakably the body of Dr Porter. As they moved the makeshift stretcher towards the waiting ambulance the body moved an arm, lifting a hand to his face. He was certainly alive, thought Martin. But I wonder for how long. Candice fell to her knees and bent forward to kiss the white face of her husband.

The pile of debris was now almost flat. A large section of the platform floor, lying slightly titled, was the only substantial piece remaining. It was heavy and a group of about a dozen men, Martin included, gathered round it and, under the sergeant's orders, lifted together and pulled it to one side.

Several women among the watching crowd screamed loudly and burst into tears. The men, now accustomed to death, gazed in disbelieving fascination, their eyes hypnotized by the scene before them.

The man was dead. There could be no doubt. No room for further hope.

But even in his grotesque death the message was there for all to see.

His strong brown face was unmarked, his eyes closed. A gentle smile had been frozen by death so that he still looked the kind, understanding man he had appeared to be.

His body lay flat and straight, his legs side by side close together. The sweater was stained by dust and blood. His arms lay straight out on either side, the palms turned upwards.

He looked, to those saddened, fascinated watchers, as if he had died on a cross.

★ ★ ★

# Part Six

## EPILOGUE

To Martin it was as if time had stopped. The clouds had blown away, a clear blue sky surveyed a totally silent scene. There was no sound of traffic, nothing moved, no excited chattering, shouting or cries and moans from the injured. It took him back to the hot summer days when he was a young boy. Made to go to bed early because in those days the only place for children was out of sight in their own bedroom, besides it was said, they need their sleep.. Of course it was still daylight so he would sit at his window looking over the gardens of the houses around, listening to the low hum of the warm atmosphere. There seemed to be no other noise, just the pleasant hum.

Ludicrously, Martin recalled a film he had seen about the life and death of Jesus. He remembered that when the crucifix had done its work, lightning seared across a sky which had suddenly darkened. Thunder smashed its angry way across the scene and rumbled discontentedly into the distance. Rain drops like heavy pearls of glycerine plopped sporadically on the parched ground. Suddenly it was as if a giant hand had pulled out a celestial plug and freed in one go rain that had been held back over the arid months. A vicious thunderstorm. John Wayne, as a Roman centurion became soaking wet while mouthing an idiotic script.

Nothing could be more contrasting.

After what seemed an age but could only have been seconds, the scene changed as cries of agony mingled with the buzz of traffic and the shouting of orders by police and army.

Eventually the last of the injured had been moved away in ambulances which scuttled away across the grass like giant white beetles. The six dead had been taken to park ranger's hut because it had proved impossible to immediately get ambulances through the crowds.

A posse of grim faced policemen had arrived quietly to begin their search for witnesses, reasons and explanations. They talked in low tones to small groups of people trying to sift the real from the imagined, the fact from the fiction.

A large proportion of the crowd had remained to stand silent and watch but there was little for them to see.

The area once dominated by the platform was now a scene of desolation. A pile of hastily stacked debris stood on one side where it had been thrown by the rescuers, a silent monument to effort.

Where the platform originally stood was a space, clear save for a few splinters of wood and odd nuts and bolts from the ill-fated scaffold. The spot where the man had died was free even of these relics and was surrounded by weeping women and silent men, their heads bowed in prayer. Miraculously someone had managed to find a bunch of flowers and placed it on the spot where the man had lain. The bouquet was now sodden, a bedraggled reminder of the tragedy.

Martin stared at the spot his mind a jumble of unrelated thoughts,. He watched sadly as a man he vaguely recognized walked up to the place where the tragedy had occurred and stuck a hastily constructed cross fashioned into the ground. His sobs were deep and heart rending.

* * *

Arnold Grimshaw could think of nothing else to do. He, like the others, just stood and stared at the spot where the man was found. He had to do something. He had to express his feelings in some way. He went to the wreckage of the platform, chose two pieces of wood, found a length of wire and made a rough cross. He walked over to the fatal spot and thrust it into the ground with an unspoken prayer.

He looked at the sad faces around him. He felt no sympathy for them. Half an hour ago they were probably yelling and shouting at the man and perhaps even fighting. A great wave of hatred for the human race swept over him. Damn them ! Damn them all!

He turned sharply to walk away when he had a feeling that he was being watched. He looked about him to see Liz. .

'Wasn't it awful,' Liz said, walking over to him and taking both his hands. Arnold nodded.

'What are you doing here?' he asked. He had left her in the hotel that morning after persuading her that he thought the crowds might be too much for her. Besides, he had wanted to see and, if possible, join the man on his own.

'I felt that I ought to be with you,' she said. 'But of course, it was impossible to find you. I was at the Serpentine end and I could only just see that something had happened and hear the noise. I couldn't get away but there wasn't much fighting where I was.' she looked at him sadly. Arnold found he could not speak.

Liz took his arm. 'Let's get out of here, go back to the hotel and change. We can talk later.' Arnold nodded.

'I'm sorry my darling,' she said suddenly. 'I have treated you awfully badly lately. I will try and change I promise.'

I hope so, thought Arnold. My God ! I really hope so.

* * *

Grace Golder stood some distance away from the scene of the tragedy. She was surrounded by those of the man's friends who had not been hurt when the platform collapsed.

It was a sombre picture. Miriam Cartwright, still tearful, was being held by her dark suited husband Charles whose face was tightly drawn as he looked over her head into the distance. Mary, who had been unhurt in the fighting around them thanks to the protective arms of Kenneth and his ability to move quickly whenever threatened, held hands and watched Grace closely as if waiting for a lead. They had spent some time helping to tend the injured before the ambulances arrived. Arnold Grimshaw, who had decided that they should not go straight back to the hotel but should wait to find out what was happening, stood alone. Liz was near him, a pace or two behind as if to indicate that she was with him but not part of this sphere of his life.

Harry Gregg positioned himself by Grace's side to be on hand if needed but kept his eye on the people around, ready to forestall any further trouble.

It was unnecessary for it was impossible that there were any potential trouble-makers left.

Edward Forbes was on the other side of Grace, a bewildered look on his face as if undecided as to whether he was really an active member of this group or just still an observer.

But Forbes' mind was really elsewhere. He felt desperately uncertain about his future not only with the man but within Parliament. He was still fearful of his ex-mistresses intentions. He had been on the periphery of the crowd watching in what was still a detached way

Fred Salmons was seated on a small pile of debris holding his head in his hands. He found it impossible to grasp that he had been involved in the recent scenes, had seen the man die and had lost his new friend Dai Griffiths.

'What are we going to do now?' asked Grimshaw, speaking to no-one in particular.

'We're going to keep together and carry on his work,' said a determined Grace Golder. 'We were brought together by various means for a purpose. I'm sure of that. We must make sure that that purpose is carried out. John Porter will lead us when he has recovered.' Harry Gregg looked at her questioningly.

'He will recover,' she said emphatically. 'I saw him in the ambulance. He was conscious and I don't think he was badly hurt. He was lucky...if luck is the right word.'

'But we don't know very much about his work,' said Kenneth Innocent. 'We only came to see him because we were sure that he had helped Mary.' Mary nodded.

'We can teach you if you are willing to go on,' Grace replied. 'But it will mean great strength and determination. It will not be easy...as you now know.' Those around her nodded.

Ruth Morton, thinking of the trouble she was already facing following her television statement about parents of ill-behaved children being detained, wondered whether they would really help her if she need it. She looked around at those still consumed with sorrow. There was, she realized, already signs of a unity of purpose. They would help, she thought, they would.

'I suggest we meet at Dai's....'she paused as she said the name of the dead miner...'in his auntie's house tomorrow to talk things over. This is no place to discuss the future.' The others signified their agreement and were preparing to leave when Grace was approached by two police inspectors who spoke to her briefly.

'I'm sorry but they want us all to go to the police station to make statements. There are several police cars ready to take us. We can dry off there and they will give refreshments, to those who need it.

The small party shuffled off to vehicles waiting at the edge of the park.

★ ★ ★

Martin was consumed by a wave of self pity. He had watched the group talking and knew that he was not part of it. He could not be. He could have saved the man, he thought illogically, or died with him. Instead he sat cringing on a tree branch. He was desperately ashamed.

He turned away from the scene and began walking across the park away from the crowd still standing round the debris of the platform and the out of the park into the Bayswater Road and through a maze of unknown streets. He saw no-one, he passed no-one. It was as if humanity was hiding its shameful face.

The brightness of the afternoon melted into night and the rain started again as a steady all enveloping drizzle. When Martin came to himself again and began to try and find out where he was, five hours had passed. He had wandered aimlessly around thinking about the future. He had heard the followers of the man who were present make arrangements to meet and discuss how they were going to continue the man's work. He determined that he would keep in touch with them. He would ask his Editor if could be assigned to reporting on their activities. In his mind he wished that he could join them but he reminded himself that he was a reporter. It was his job, his career, to report.

Dismissing his conjecturing as something for the future he found he was walking up Knightsbridge. He had walked in a giant circle and was being drawn back to the park as if it were a magnet.

He went into the park and towards the park ranger's hut where the bodies had been lain. Two young sentries were standing guard. They looked at him but did not know what to say. They had been told by their superiors to keep all sightseers away. For the first few hours this had been difficult as supporters of the man had filed past to pay their last respects to the body. But as the rain continued and day turned into night the procession had thinned and finally disappeared leaving the sentry lonely and a little frightened.

'Good evening,' said Martin. It seemed a ridiculous thing to say. It was certainly not a good evening.

'Hullo,' said one of the sentries simply.

They stood looking at Martin. Both of them glad to have found someone to talk to.

'Is that the casualty list?' Martin asked, looking at a typed list pinned to the door.

'Yes, we had to put it up so that the relatives of missing people could satisfy themselves they hadn't been killed.'

Martin walked over and examined it. There were five names, F.Thomas, D.Griffiths, PC Hilton, D.Grant, R. Hillier - and an 'unknown.'

What a way to describe the man, 'unknown.' But then, Martin thought, how else could they describe him. He never had a name, he had never given himself one. he had simply been known as 'the man' and he had seen this as a sort of symbolic title.

'I knew him,' said Martin, indicating Grant's name to the sentry. The soldier looked at Martin with interest but said nothing.

'Could I see him?' Martin asked. He was not sure why he wanted to see the dead body of Grant, they certainly weren't close. If he had been honest with himself he would have admitted he did not really want to see it. He simply wanted to be in the same room as the man for a few moments longer.

The senior sentry shook his head and was about to refuse when he seemed to have second thoughts. There were no officers around and unlikely to be in this weather. If he refused the chap might go away and they would be alone again. He nodded.

'You'll have to be quick,' he said.

He opened the door and they went in together. A small un-shaded electric bulb shone dimly from the ceiling giving the room an eerie and unreal atmosphere. The shrouded bodies, lying side by side, sent a shudder through Martin who half wanted to turn around and run out.

'You've no idea which one he is?' he asked.

'I wasn't here when they brought them in and I certainly haven't checked,' he replied in a low reverential voice.

Martin looked again at the bodies. There was no way of identifying them without removing the covers and he had no intention of doing that.

'I'll leave it then,' he said, half turning.

He suddenly stopped in his tracks. There was something wrong.

He turned and looked at the bodies again. He counted them. There were five. There should have been six. Martin looked at the sentry who had followed his gaze, and his train of thought.

'There were six when I came on duty,' he said in a trembling voice.

'And no-one has been in?' Martin asked.

'No.'

'Or out?'

The soldier shook his head.

Instinctively they both looked at the window but it was the type that did not open. It was a single pane of glass behind which were three iron bars.

They both stood, uncertain what to do.

Martin suddenly made up his mind. There was nothing else for it, he would have to look.

Mentally steeling himself for the task he stepped forward ignoring the sentry's restraining hand. He went to the end of the row and lifted the corner of the blanket. The dark uniform was sufficient to indicate it was the policeman. He dropped the blanket quickly.

The second body was small, too small to be anyone else but Dai Griffiths. It was.

The third body was that of the young blonde boy, the first to be found. The fourth was that of Fred Thomas, his face twisted in anger.

Martin lifted the last blanket. It was David Grant, looking more peaceful in death than he ever had in life.

Martin turned, pale and shaken, and looked at the sentry, Neither of them spoke as the significance of their discovery hit them.

'He's not here,' he said. 'The man has vanished!'

THE END

## *Michael Gunton*

Although he has written three books this is Michael Gunton's first novel, at the age of 80 years.

After serving in the Royal Navy during the Second World War Michael began a 40-odd year career in journalism which including working as a political and industrial correspondent for British and American newspapers and radio stations. He covered a wide range of stories including the Paris riots, the Northern Ireland troubles, the building and maiden voyage of the Queen Elizabeth II and the building of Concorde.

He then worked for 10 years as Chief Industrial Correspondent for the Government's Central Office of Information writing features about Britain for a large number of newspapers throughout the world. He then moved to Parliament as the Conservative Party's representative in the Parliamentary Press Gallery. During this period he worked for the Prime Ministers, Thatcher and Major and was. for three years, press officer to the Chancellor of the Exchequer, Nigel Lawson.

After the 1992 General Election he worked for three years in Eastern Europe, following the fall of the Iron Curtain, teaching parliamentarians and journalists how to operate in a democratic climate. He made 80 visits to the 13 former communist countries and advised several future Presidents and Prime Ministers. This was followed by a six month period as Press Adviser to Sir James Goldsmith and the Referendum Party during the 1997 general election campaign.

In the last few years he has written and published a small book 'Do you want Rendezvous?' describing his work in Eastern Europe..

He then researched, compiled and published 'A Hundred Years in the Life of Britain', a detailed chronicle of the period. It differs from the usual chronicle in that it details the passing years on a subject, rather than calendar basis. He then wrote 'Dive, Dive, Dive,' a history of Submarine Warfare' which was published by Constable and Robinson in 2003. It sold in both Britain and the United States.

He has another book 'A Fight to the Death' (as yet unpublished ) which tells the true story of an heroic Polish submarine during the first weeks of the Second World War. His most recent achievement was to reach 80-year-old in August of this year.

www.ingramcontent.com/pod-product-compliance
Ingram Content Group UK Ltd.
Pitfield, Milton Keynes, MK11 3LW, UK
UKHW040602210726
13854UKWH00008B/1837